# SEARCHER OF THE DEAD

ALSO AVAILABLE BY NANCY HERRIMAN

MYSTERY OF OLD SAN FRANCISCO

*No Pity for the Dead*

*No Comfort for the Lost*

ALSO AVAILABLE

*Josiah's Treasure*

*The Irish Healer*

# SEARCHER OF THE DEAD

## A BESS ELLYOTT MYSTERY

## Nancy Herriman

CROOKED
LANE

NEW YORK

Published in the United States by Crooked Lane Books, an imprint of The Quick Brown Fox & Company LLC.

Crooked Lane Books and its logo are trademarks of The Quick Brown Fox & Company LLC.

Library of Congress Catalog-in-Publication data available upon request.

ISBN (hardcover): 978-1-68331-538-4
ISBN (ePub): 978-1-68331-539-1
ISBN (ePDF): 978-1-68331-540-7

Cover design by Matthew Kalamidas/StoneHouse Creative
Book design by Jennifer Canzone

Printed in the United States.

www.crookedlanebooks.com

Crooked Lane Books
34 West 27th St., 10th Floor
New York, NY 10001

First edition: March 2018

10 9 8 7 6 5 4 3 2 1

*To Natasha, whose encouragement and support have never flagged, my eternal thanks.*

# PROLOGUE

*Michaelmas 1592*
*London*

"Tell me his name."

The crone had eyes as pale as chips of ice. So pale and clear that the irises nearly faded into the whites. Bess found she could not return the woman's gaze but instead searched for aught else to stare at. The rush mats upon the tiles of the hall floor. The orange depths of the hearth fire. The herbs Bess had strung to dry, her mortar and pestle at the ready upon the oak table yet forgotten in her distress. The tapestry of a hunting scene, the fleeing stag that always seemed to move when candlelight flickered across the surface. The steps adjacent to the hearth that led to the upstairs chambers, where silence hung as heavy as her thoughts.

However, she looked but briefly at the body stretched upon the settle where he had taken his final repose. A cushion had tumbled to the floor, and his arm dangled as if to reach for it. The cushion embroidered with birds he had so favored. *Because you stitched it, Bess, with those fine long fingers of yours . . .*

"Martin," she said, her voice breaking. But the crone would assume the break came of grief, which it did most certain, and not also of fear. "Martin Ellyott. My husband."

The woman scratched his name—when had someone of her impoverished circumstance learned the art of writing?—upon a scrap of paper. She had no penknife with her, and the nib of her quill was dull, leaving the markings blunt and large. Her knotted fingers struggled to hold the writing instrument, and as Bess had yet to light a lamp, she squinted in the dimness to see what she wrote. Their surname was misspelled; Bess did not correct her.

With a groan, the old woman rose from the stool Bess's servant had brought for her and went to the settle. Bess looked away as she examined him. Heard coals settle on the grate. She wanted to cry, but her eyes had ceased shedding tears and burned from dryness. More tears, she knew, would come later.

"No pustules upon him," the woman muttered.

"It was not plague," Bess replied. "He had pains in his stomach and nausea. Troubles of the bowels with great purging. Fever," she added, a hasty afterthought in her attempt to be convincing. "No pustules."

The crone nodded, and the edges of the kerchief she'd wrapped around her head slid across her furrowed cheeks. "The bloody flux, then."

Bess's pulse skipped. "Yes."

The old woman returned to her paper. Next to Martin's

name she inscribed "bloody flux." She blew upon the surface and, satisfied the ink had dried, rolled the sheet closed. She tucked the chronicle of deaths into a leather pouch suspended from her woven-tape girdle, alongside her quill and inkhorn. "God rest his soul."

"Indeed. God rest his soul."

Satisfied Martin's name would not be added to her count of plague victims and the house and its occupants would not need be boarded up, the old woman departed without further comment. It was done. The searcher of the dead had come and declared Martin—witty, sweet Martin—deceased from the bloody flux. Thus it would be recorded on the bill of mortality forever and ever. Leaving Bess alone to suspect the true cause of his death.

She stood in the street doorway and watched as the searcher hobbled across the uneven stones of the roadway. Slowly, the old woman progressed in and out of the shadows cast by the jettied floors of neighbors' houses, the red wand she carried extended to warn all of her passage. Warn all of the dreaded disease that might linger on her person. With a cry, the corner baker's girl sprang out of the old woman's path, almost dropping the basket of cheat bread she carried in her arms. The old woman paid her no heed. She skirted a fire burning to chase off plague, the sweet smell of pitch spreading with the smoke, as a mongrel ran alongside, snapping at her heels. Bess watched until the old woman was gone from sight and her heart had finally slowed its pounding and returned to normal.

Though normal would not ever be the same.

"Mistress?" Bess's servant, Joan, had crept up behind her to peer around the doorframe. "What do we now?"

"Flee."

She had no choice now but to bury her dearest Martin alongside their two sweet daughters, sell her goods, and leave London. Escape from the one who had brought death to her house and dread to her heart. Forget her life here, as good as it once had been. Start anew.

*God help me.*

# CHAPTER 1

*Wiltshire, 1 year later*

"The child will be well, aye?"

The woman, taller than Bess by a head, leaned over to observe as Bess tended her daughter's wounds. The girl, perhaps eight years of age, perhaps nine, had burned herself. According to her mother, the source had been the handle of a brass pot the child had pulled from the fire. Her wound was days old and had festered, forcing Bess to clean away the rot before she washed the burn and dressed it. The bruise upon her left cheek was far fresher.

She did not cry out as Bess rinsed her damaged hand with a clean linen cloth dipped in rosewater made from the last snow's melt. The cold to draw out the heat of the burn. Or so Bess prayed. There were moments—after failing to cure her own daughters when they had been stricken with a fatal catarrh, and after watching helplessly as Martin lay dying—that Bess doubted her abilities.

She pulled in a breath and willed away her uncertainty.

"What did you use upon the burns?" Bess asked Good-wife Anwicke.

She smiled at the woman's daughter, who had deep brown eyes and dirty, hollow cheeks. The girl did not return the smile. Her eyes were shadowed in a way that reminded Bess of her servant, Joan, when Bess had found her living in a London alley, hungry and desperate yet wary as an untamed cat.

"Sheep's dung. As my mother taught me."

Which explained the muddy color Bess's cloth was turning as well as the stink arising from the girl's hand. The child wiggled her bottom, which she had settled upon the three-legged stool her mother had placed by the open door. Aside from a low-burning fire in the hearth, its smoke limply rising up a smoke bay to a hole in the roof, the doorway was the only source of light in the thatched cottage. A rain shower had caused the woman to place shutters in the unglazed windows. Closing off the windows had trapped much of the smoke in the main room, which at least masked the smell of mold and rot, though it made Bess want to cough.

As it was, there was not much to see—a scattering of pallets and a lone chest, a few stools and a rickety bench thrust against a trestle table set by the hearth, an old spinning wheel. A wood tub, the offending brass pot, a solitary pewter mug resting upon the mantel, awaiting its owner. The plain walls were in need of fresh whitewash. The clay floor, mixed with ox blood and ashes and left to harden when the cottage had been built, was covered in rushes requiring replacement. Beyond the main hall, a cramped room contained farm supplies and a bedstead. Two rooms for this girl, her parents, and three other siblings. A common enough situation among the poorest cottagers of this town. Bess spared a moment's thought for the other children, questioning where they had gotten themselves to, as the only other one she could account for was a swaddled babe asleep in a cradle near the hearth.

The injured girl made a noise, a whimper like the sound of a wounded animal, and Bess cupped her hand. "Shh, shh. All will be well." Bess looked over at her mother. "Sheep's dung?"

Goodwife Anwicke harrumphed. " 'Twas good enough for my mother."

"And my grandmother may have done the same." Bess had no wish to chastise the woman, who had done the best she could.

"I knew her. A good woman, she was. A great healer."

"You knew my grandmother? I have nearly no memory of her. She died when I was young." All Bess could remember of the woman whose calling she had followed were her strong, chapped hands and the earthy scent that had clung to her clothing. "I pray I do her memory justice."

Goodwife Anwicke eyed her. "And now you are here."

"Indeed. All of her grandchildren have returned."

"Your mother married a fellow from someplace east." More scrutiny.

"Yes, she did. My father taught at Oxford." Bess's mother had missed the rolling hills of Wiltshire. Not enough, though, to come back home to this village partway between the valley where the River Avon flowed and the chalk downs where stood ancient henges of stone.

Bess finished cleaning the girl's burn and dropped the

filthy cloth in the wooden bowl she had brought. "But my brother and sister are here, and now I am here as well." Far from London. Hopefully far enough.

"Aye. You are."

The child stared down at her palm, the reddened blisters far more visible without an intervening layer of sheep's dung. Bess considered the girl, whose name she had not learned, and wondered if she was a mute. Wondered if the infirmity explained why Bess had been sent for and not the widow woman who lived near the market cross and also prepared simples. That herbalist might not wish to treat a child bearing such a defect, what many considered a mark of sin. Leaving Goodwife Anwicke to call upon the healer who had come to Wiltshire under a cloud of gossip.

*Ah, Martin, at least I am content here. And learning to find peace and a place within my brother's household.*

Bess patted the child's head, her hair covered in a linen biggin, its ties frayed along the edges. Beneath, she suspected, the girl's hair was likely no more clean than her hand had been. When next Bess returned, she would bring her salve of powdered stavesacre seeds and vinegar to treat the lice that may live there. "Not long now. I am near finished."

From a canvas satchel, Bess fetched out a pottery jar, unwrapping the cloth tied over it. Inside was a plaster she had prepared using the crushed leaves of water plantain and the green bark of an elder tree mixed with some oil and honey. If the child had sustained a cut rather than a burn, she would have chosen agrimony to mix with the honey.

"But the child . . . she will be well, aye?" Goodwife Anwicke repeated.

"Yes," Bess replied, without any of her earlier hesitation. Her patients' faith in her skills was as much a part of the healing as the plasters and powders she employed. "God willing."

Bess gently dressed the wound with a quantity of the plaster and wrapped a length of linen around the girl's hand, securing it with a knot. "Have you any black soap and honey to apply to her bruise?"

A sudden quiver convulsed the child. Who had struck her? Her mother? Her father?

Goodwife Anwicke's eyes darkened with hidden thoughts. "I can tend her bruise," she said. "What do I owe?"

The girl realized Bess had finished and hopped down from the stool. The sole of her right shoe flapping as she walked, she went to attend to the baby, who had begun to mewl in the cradle.

"You owe me nothing," Bess said, returning her supplies to her satchel. The goodwife could not afford the groat Bess was sometimes offered for her simples. The amount was a fraction of the sum exacted by the apothecary, who would expect at least five shillings for his remedies. The fee demanded by the local physician did not even bear mention.

The woman lifted her chin, her pride pricked. "I can pay—"

"I do not require payment," she said. "I shall return in two days to see how your daughter fares."

"Gramercy, then." She moved to follow Bess to the roadway.

"I will see myself off."

"God save you, Widow Ellyott."

Tossing her woolen cloak over her shoulders, Bess slipped her shoes into the wood-soled leather mules she had left near the threshold and hurried outside. By now, the rain was falling heavily. She dashed across the uneven surface of the highway, her satchel in one hand, her skirts and the black linen safeguard that covered them hoisted in the other. She glanced back at the cottage and caught sight of the silent girl standing at the door, a look of sorrow upon her pinched face.

★   ★   ★

The Anwickes' cottage was not far from town, but the slog in the rain seemed an eternity. Bess suspected she looked as mournful as a drenched rat. There were few to notice her misery as she entered the main part of town, she observed thankfully, despite it being market day. The trestle tables that had been placed in the square and before shop fronts had been cleared of their foodstuffs and wares and momentarily left, empty, to line the waterlogged street. Rainwater dripped from thatch and tile. All appeared to have hidden away behind stone and timber and whitewashed mud walls, and the town center was quiet save for splashing rain and the raucous laughter emanating from the Cross Keys, ale and beer ever a comfort on a damp day.

Hoofbeats sounded behind her, and a traveler trotted by on his way to the inn. He slouched beneath an oiled cloak and dripping hat, a tin spoon tucked into the band. He'd best have his passport; strangers were always viewed with suspicion, and vagrancy was a crime. She had not needed Martin's death to inform her how dangerously fearful the world had become.

As she passed the grammar school, the master locked the heavy oak door behind him and nodded at her before he hurried off home, dodging puddles. The schoolboys who normally played and tussled in the street after they had concluded their studies had vanished like the rest of the town, chased inside by the rain. Bess hastened across the market square and turned up the lane across from All Saints, the bells in its sturdy square tower tolling five times to mark the hour. A neighbor's swine had escaped its cote—the man would be fined for his carelessness—and contentedly snuffled in a midden pile. Another neighbor had left a broken-down cart awaiting repair outside his front door, forcing Bess to splash through the gutter.

Rounding another bend, she spied her brother's house— two comfortable stories of stone and timber framing plus a half-story—and increased her pace. Her stockings were soaked, chilling her to the bone. She expected a fire would be roaring in the hearth. In fact, the gleam of light that shone through the hall's street-facing oriel windows promised as much. Unlike the Anwickes, Bess would be warm and dry and well fed that night, and her slumbers would take place upon a feather mattress topped by a thick, soft blanket.

The outside chill and damp accompanied Bess past the house's heavy, oak front door. Inside the passageway, she removed her dripping cloak and hung it from a nearby hook. Likewise, she stepped out of her muddy mules, leaving them near the threshold alongside her satchel.

To her right, the door to the hall hung open, and she stepped through. Robert, his broad back to her, stood before the massive fireplace. Confusingly, the hall's large draw-leaf table was yet to be unfolded for supper. Mayhap she and Robert were to eat upstairs in the parlor that evening.

"I'faith, I am soaked to the bone," she announced, stripping off her safeguard and rolling it into a bundle. Her brother's brown-and-white water spaniel, Quail, leaped up from where he had been lounging by the hearth and bounded over to greet her.

Robert turned abruptly. The crackle of the fire had masked her footfalls upon the rush matting that covered the stone floor. "Bess."

The frown on his face halted any further pleasantries on her part. She liked to tease that the pointed beard he wore made him look somber, but at the moment, Robert had no need of a pointed beard to appear grave.

"What . . ." It was then she noticed their sister, Dorothie, seated nearby.

"She is back at last. Can we depart now?" asked Dorothie. Her eyes were red, and she wrung her hands as though she hoped to strangle her fingers.

"What is amiss, Dorothie?" Bess asked, offering Quail one final pat upon his head.

"'Tis Fulke." She sobbed the name of her husband.

Robert had drawn a stool over to the chimney, upon which Dorothie sat. The stays of her pair of bodies held her torso erect, though it seemed she would prefer to crumple. Her velvet-trimmed gown was dirty and damp. Strands of her golden-brown hair had escaped her coif. Proof she'd rushed there without care for her appearance, which normally consumed her.

She sobbed again.

"What of Fulke?" Bess asked. "Has he taken ill?"

"He has not returned," said Dorothie.

"Fulke left this morning, before sunrise, bound for Devizes on a matter of business," said Robert, looking over at Dorothie to confirm his account. "He was to return by supper this evening."

"But it is not yet too late for that." Setting down her safeguard for Joan to collect, Bess pulled off her shoes and padded across the hall to warm herself by the fire. Dorothie was ever prone to fussing and fretting. But as much as Bess wished to comfort her sister, she knew Dorothie would not welcome her affection. It had ever been thus between them.

"Fulke likely was delayed and will return anon," she added.

Joan entered through the opening that led to the service rooms, the household keys jangling from her girdle. She brought a pewter cup of malmsey, which she set upon a second stool Robert had dragged over to the chimney. Dorothie grabbed up the drink and gulped it down. Bess glanced at her brother, who gave a shrug.

"Wish you wine as well, Mistress?" asked Joan, whose light brown eyes conveyed a deeper concern than evidenced by her simple question. "You must be chilled."

"With supper, Joan."

With a nod, Joan collected Bess's mules and safeguard and withdrew to the kitchen.

"I want to find Fulke," Dorothie said, once she had finished her malmsey. "Now."

"We know not that he is lost." Bess stretched her palms toward the warmth of the fire. Quail came to lie at her feet.

"Besides, it is nigh on time for the sun to set, and the weather is too foul to go looking for him. We cannot search in the darkness."

"Bess is right, Dorothie," said Robert. "Let us wait another hour. You shall see—"

"'Bess is right,'" she mocked. "Elizabeth is always right, is she not? You have always sided with her, Robert. Ever since she was born. Well, I do not wish to wait another hour. It shall be too late by then."

"Too late for what?" Bess asked.

"I am not being foolish, Elizabeth, about my concerns," she answered crossly. "Fulke said he would return by now, and he has not. He is never late."

Bess did not correct that statement, counting in her head the many times a visit to a tavern or an inn had delayed her brother-in-law. But Dorothie's fear was palpable. Bess had a thought of Martin. *It cannot be. It cannot. Not again.*

"The rain has detained him," said Robert. "That is all. You know how the roads are in such weather."

"I do know how the roads are, Robert," she snapped. "Why will not either of you listen to me? Harm has befallen Fulke. I know it!"

Robert's frown deepened. "What was his business in Devizes, Dorothie?"

"He went to meet a solicitor. About a suit he planned to bring. I feared no good would come of his intentions, had a frightening dream . . ." Dorothie resumed strangling her fingers. "My mind did not calm when my servants remarked this morning upon Fulke's mistemper as he prepared to depart."

"Perhaps he decided to stay the night in Devizes," said Bess.

"He would have sent a message." Dorothie scrambled to her feet. "We must go to the constable and have him search for Fulke. We have to find him. For the sake of our boys! What will I tell our poor boys?"

That she did not fret for Margery, Dorothie's daughter from her brief first marriage, was sadly telling. Bess had never sensed deep affection in Margery, though, for the man who'd replaced her own father after his death in a horrible farming accident. Mayhap she would not be as distraught as the boys.

"The constable will not go," said Robert. "It has grown dark, and the rain is even heavier than it was before. Sit down and sup with us, Dorothie. By the time you have finished and returned home, you will find Fulke there with your daughter, missing you."

"Margery is with Fulke's sister, freshly delivered of a child, and will not return until the morrow. So do not think to cause me guilt over her feelings, Robert, in hopes of convincing me to meekly go home." Her cheeks flared red. "If neither of you will search with me, I will go on my own. To save Fulke before it is too late!"

She fled the hall, slamming the front door behind her. Bess made to follow.

"Bess, wait!" shouted Robert.

She paused in the passageway with her hand upon the latch. "But Dorothie—"

"Will not convince the constable to gather up men to

look for Fulke. Not in this weather. He will tell her to wait until the morrow."

Bess snatched her cloak from its hook. "Robert, you know her as well as I do. Once she gets an idea in her head, she persists. She will take to the highway on her own to look for Fulke." Dorothie had already lost one husband. How might she fare were she to lose another?

Robert strode across the room and took Bess's cloak from her hand. He replaced it on its hook. "I will go after her. Stay here. I will return with as much haste as I can."

"Joan," Bess called out. "Set a lantern outside."

Robert buttoned his doublet, and Bess offered him his broad-brimmed hat. "She will not have gotten far. It is too muddy to run fast in the cork-soled shoes she was wearing."

Robert kissed Bess hastily upon her cheek; his beard tickled. "I will knock her on the head if that is what is required to keep her from hying off to wherever Fulke has gone."

Bess smiled and let him out, a burst of rain wetting the patterned rush mat beneath her feet. Joan hurried out behind him and hung a lit lantern by the gateway to the rear courtyard. Its sputtering flare cast Robert in light before he disappeared down the street.

"What has happened to Master Crofton?" Joan asked.

"He is delayed on his return from Devizes," said Bess, wrapping her arms tight about her waist. "Mayhap my sister frets needlessly."

"Think you so, Mistress?"

Bess could not answer honestly.

Peace.

How short-lived it had been.

# CHAPTER 2

"You are joining us this fair evening, Constable Harwoode?" The alehouse keeper's wife greeted him at the door.

"Not so fair this evening, Mistress," Kit replied.

He slipped his hat from his head to shake off rainwater, which scattered across the rushes on the floor. The space, which had once been the house's hall, was more crowded than usual. Pipe smoke hung heavy in the air, and men clustered in groups, drinking their ale and laughing. A band of apprentices, freed from their labors for the day, stood near the hearth singing a ballad. The foul weather had encouraged the alehouse keeper to shutter the window through which he sometimes served drink, forcing customers inside.

"I've come for your freshest ale," said Kit, replacing his hat.

"Pardy, how you jest, Constable," she said. "'Tis certain you saw the ale-stake we set above the door. Our ale has been tasted by the aleconner and is most fresh."

Kit had the power to see them fined if the ale was not. And though the woman grinned, she did watch him warily.

"As it ever is, Mistress." Kit located the man he sought. A thick-chested husbandman, he hunched on a bench set far from the blazing fire and the light of a lantern suspended from a beam. "Serve up more for my friend there as well."

The woman eyed the fellow. "*He* is your friend?"

"He is for tonight."

Kit snaked his way between the stools and benches scattered about, greeting those who raised their eyes to watch him pass. Some of those gazes were friendly; others were not, as they hid the cards they'd been playing with before he had walked through the door. Not long ago, he had been one of them, at the alehouse for a night of drink and companionship. But then, as a jest, his cousin Wat had put forward Kit's name for constable, expecting him to refuse. Or to fail. But Kit was no longer an unruly lad in need of a lesson, time having worn away the sharpest of his rough edges, and he had not refused the appointment nor did he intend to fail. Leaving him, for now, more than just another alehouse customer.

"No gittern tonight, Constable?" a grizzled fellow wearing a red cap called out.

"When was the last time I brought it to play?" Months. No, a year. Before he'd accepted this role. "Besides, you have those fellows singing there for music."

The red-capped man smirked. "Aye. We do. What great fortune."

Kit reached the husbandman's bench and took a seat alongside him. Kit's booted foot encountered the alehouse's ratter. The cat hissed and scurried off. "Good even."

"Constable," the man grunted.

"You wished to speak with me."

"I've had a pig stolen." The man's eyes darted about, as if he thought the thief might be in the alehouse. "That animal is worth four shillings, Constable. Four shillings lost!"

A great deal of money for a man with patched tunic sleeves and bug-eaten hose.

"A goodly sum," said Kit.

The alehouse keeper's wife arrived with a large blackjack of ale and a tankard for Kit, who'd not brought his own drinking vessel. After she poured out the drink, Kit made payment and waited for her to depart.

"No need to skulk in a dark corner of this alehouse to report it, though," he said. "There is no shame in having a pig stolen."

"'Tis not all I need tell you." The husbandman's eyes darted about again, and he gulped down half his ale. "There be a curious fellow hiding in the ruins of the old priory."

"You suspect that some man taking cover in a pile of rubble has stolen your pig?" Kit asked. He sipped his ale; it was indeed fresh. He could enjoy it more if he and his companion were not being stared at by nearly everyone in the room. Kit glared at the inquisitive individuals until they determined the company of their mates was more interesting. "A man living among stones could not butcher and cook the creature without detection."

"He may have done!"

"There are others to more reasonably suspect." Such as the cordwainer's son. The lad was regularly accused of every petty crime committed in town, and on occasion, he'd even been guilty. Or the son of the cottager who lived hard by the priory ruins, almost as much a nuisance as the cord-wainer's boy.

"No one else." In one great swallow, the fellow finished off the ale and smacked his lips. Kit poured the remainder of the ale into the man's tankard. "It is the fellow hiding in those ruins. Mark my words. A vagrant, in violation of the law."

"I will search him out. Tomorrow, should the weather lift." If such a man existed. This sighting was the first Kit had heard.

"My thanks. And if he has my pig, hang him."

"Should I find him in possession of your pig, I shall leave the assessment of his guilt to the manor court."

"He is guilty. But you take care with him, Constable." The fellow leaned nearer. "He is a dangerous one."

"How do you know that?"

"He be one of them soldiers come back from the fighting in the Low Countries. The ones who cannot fight any longer because . . ." He tapped the side of his skull.

Kit cocked his head; the story was becoming intriguing. "You've seen him well enough to determine this?"

"Others have."

"No one has informed me," said Kit.

"They are afraid." He nodded, convinced of his story.

"If the vagrant is a soldier, he would have a pass and not need to lurk among the ruins," said Kit. "It surprises me that these 'others' who have seen him haven't claimed the fellow is a Jesuit come to kill the queen."

The man considered for a moment. "He may be." His thick eyebrows jigged up his forehead. "For there are men hiding in the shadows, Constable. And we're none of us safe."

★ ★ ★

"Did Master Crofton return from his journey, Mistress?"

In the light of a single beeswax candle, Joan eased an ivory comb through Bess's hair, the teeth encountering knots among the curls. Bess, seated upon a cushioned stool, stared out the window of her chamber, jettied above the kitchen and overlooking the dark street. The neighbors across the road had set a candle in their deep window, and it cast a pale light onto the rain-slicked gravel. A tiny four-legged creature snuffled in the shadows.

"No. He did not," Bess answered, wrapping her holland night rail close about her shift.

Joan noticed the motion. "Should I bring a chafing dish to heat the room?"

"The cold I feel has naught to do with any chill in this room, Joan."

Robert had located Dorothie and convinced her to return to her house, where they had been met with no further news of Fulke's whereabouts. Robert had stayed with her long past the ringing of the curfew bell before coming back home in low spirits. They could do nothing until morning. Meanwhile, sleep would prove elusive for all the family.

Joan set down the comb and began to braid Bess's hair. "The weather has delayed him."

"I have tried to persuade myself of that as well. I fear I do not succeed." She twisted upon the stool to look up at her servant. Joan's coif had slipped, and the scar that carved a path along her chin showed in the yellow flicker of candlelight. Bess had asked only once about the man who had inflicted it. "I cannot help but suspect the worst. Tell me I am not foolish."

Joan's fingers did not slow in their steady movement through Bess's hair. "You are never foolish." She completed the braid and tied the end off with a strip of lockram.

"Tell me also that I have not brought some sort of curse with me from London," said Bess. The curse that had struck down Martin.

"We know he has not followed us here, Mistress. He remains there yet."

Bess knew that to be true; they paid a London friend to keep an eye on the man who'd murdered Martin and alert them should he leave the city. Dangerous work. "I sometimes dream that his evil can spread like fingers of fog to touch us here."

"Laurence is but a man. Not a fiend of hell that can reach us in distant Wiltshire."

"You are right," said Bess. Laurence had been false, wicked, a traitor to the trust and affection Martin and Bess had bestowed upon him, but he *was* just a man. "I know you are right."

Joan closed the serge curtain at the window, its rings rattling across the iron rod, and withdrew. Bess stripped to her smock and climbed onto the bed, the linens cold against her legs. She huddled beneath them and stared at the shadows that danced with the movement of the candle's flame. She dreaded that morning would bring them no resolution, no peace. The shadows presented no answer to what had happened to Fulke, however, and no wisdom was to be found in the plop of rain dripping onto the muddy gravel beneath the bedchamber window.

She managed to doze off, a fitful sleep. Pounding on the house door roused her, followed by Quail's frantic barking. Bess sat bolt upright and hunted for her night rail and her slippers in the near darkness. The pounding continued, and she ventured out of her chamber and down the corner stairwell.

Robert had come down the stairs from his chamber and strode into the hall, Quail darting about his feet. "Joan, let them in," he called out, knowing she would have risen and run to the door.

Indeed, she had already gone to the door, for soon Bess heard Dorothie's panicked voice.

Bess hurried across the hall and into the passageway. Dorothie stood framed in the doorway, the sky beyond her purpling. The rain and clouds had lifted. From the court-yard behind the house came the crow of Robert's cockerel, and across the way, a neighbor's joined the chorus.

"Dorothie, what is the news?" Bess asked, dread pinching her stomach.

"Fulke's horse!" she cried, her face eerily pale. Robert reached for her, and she clutched his arm, support that kept her propped upon her feet. "His horse! It has returned without him. I came here as fast as I could."

"We must search," said Robert. "I shall have Humphrey ready my horse."

"I want to go with you, Robert," said Dorothie. There would be no dissuading her; she had dressed for a journey in her wool riding hood, low boots, and a fustian gown she wore while tending her knot garden.

"As you wish." He handed her off to lean upon Joan. "Take my sister into the lesser parlor and light the fire to warm her while I prepare to depart. I shall make haste."

"I shall come also," Bess announced.

Robert sighed. "Bess—"

"I insist." He had to know she would not back down.

"Then I shall have Humphrey go to the inn and rent a horse for you," he said and hurried off to prepare.

★ ★ ★

There were few roads in and out of town and only one that made the most sense to search if Fulke had gone to Devizes.

Dorothie rode out with Robert, seated behind him on his gelding and clinging to his waist. The sway-backed palfrey Robert had rented snorted, its breath clouding the air, as Bess hooked her knee around the saddle's pommel. She encouraged the animal to bob along at as rapid a clip as it could manage through the streets of an awakening town. The clang of the smith fashioning a harrow rang out, and the aroma of bread from the baker's shop drifted on the air. Servants and goodwives bustled along the streets, attending to their early morning chores.

Soon, the cobbled and graveled surface of the town lanes gave way to paths of clay and muck, bogging down their horses' hooves as they descended into the valley. The bar that blocked the roadway had been raised for the morning. After a short while, the road became a causeway above the damp fields, herds of sheep and cattle dotting the countryside. Several neighbors had agreed to scour the lanes and underbrush, and they spread out in sets of two or three. Their passage attracted the attention of a handful of cattle grazing near the roadway, the animals staring after them. The barley had long been harvested and the fields furrowed and ridged to await the sowing of the winter wheat, their emptiness providing broad vistas. It would be easy to search for any sign of a body.

They neared Goodwife Anwicke's cottage. The child Bess had treated yesterday had already arisen to sit upon the doorstep. She scrubbed soiled swaddling cloths in a wooden bucket of water. Her infant sibling rested atop a tattered square of canvas at the girl's side, restrained by its bindings. The bandage Bess had wrapped around the girl's burns was still in place, and the linen appeared, she noticed thankfully, clean enough. The washing was hard work, however, with only one good hand.

Bess nodded at her. The bruise upon her cheek had gone a dark purple. "Good morrow, child."

The girl blinked up at Bess as she slowly rode by. Her eyes were large, but the emotions and thoughts so easily read in other children's eyes remained as concealed as a gentlewoman's face behind a velvet traveling mask. The girl's demeanor was unsettling, and Bess urged the palfrey along.

They passed the grim remains of a cottage that had been burned in a zealous desire to thwart the plague when it had swept through these parts the previous year. Across the road stood the tumbled walls of a ruined priory. The structure was reduced to a handful of walls, some with the outlines of windows. Pointed arches graced empty doorways, and a

large portal marked what had once been the entry. Most of
the townsfolk avoided the ruin, thinking it was haunted
by the men who'd once lived there. Margery believed likewise. She never accompanied Bess when she came to collect
yarrow and wild carrot, which yet bloomed in the remnants
of the garden planted in the days before King Henry. Bess
had insisted there was naught to fear from piles of rocks.
Nonetheless, the rubble was a mournful reminder of death,
and Bess looked away.

Robert reined in his horse. "Bess, do you want us to
wait for you?" She had fallen behind.

"I am too slow." Bess kneed the palfrey, which stubbornly responded to her urging by easing up. "You go
ahead. At the crossroads, I will head in the other direction
for a short distance and catch you up later."

"Fulke was headed toward Devizes. He would not go
that way," insisted Dorothie.

"Indulge me, Dorothie. My search shall not take long.
Look, there are men checking rabbit traps." Bess pointed
up the lane. Three men moved among the furrows of a
dormant field, bending down every few yards to check the
snares placed along the rabbits' runs. They moved so confi-
dently that they had to be men of worth. Otherwise, they
would fear the game laws. "I will ask them if they saw Fulke
yesterday."

"Do not venture too far before you turn back. I do not
wish to have to search for you as well," said Robert. She
did not wish that either. "Let us continue on, Dorothie. We
will make greater progress if we go separate ways."

They trotted off, and Bess steered the palfrey along the

path as close to the verge as possible, where grass mingled with the mud and provided sturdier footing. Wisps of fog rose from a rivulet of water snaking alongside a stand of beech, the foliage already turning autumn's golden brown. A cascade of leaves blanketed the ground and covered the lane, knocked down by yesterday's heavy rain. The air was thick with the musky scent of decaying leaves, and Bess inhaled deeply. Some medical men warned that breathing in the smell of decay damaged a body's humors. She dismissed the idea that anything so pleasingly fragrant could be injurious.

The fellow nearest the road paused in his occupation when he saw she had reined in the horse.

"Good morrow, Mistress."

"Good morrow. I search for a man who is missing and may have come this way yesterday. I wondered if you had perchance noticed him."

Beneath his wide-brimmed hat, his pale eyes scanned her. "A runaway husband, mayhap?"

Bess blushed at his forwardness. "He is not my husband, sirrah. God called my husband to Him this past year."

"My apologies—"

"The man I seek is my brother-in-law, and his wife, my sister, is afraid for his life," she said.

"I see." He tilted back his head and considered her. "Do I know of you and this family of yours? Are you from this area?"

What gave him cause to ask such a question? "If you do not wish to help me, I shall speak to another of your companions."

She prodded the palfrey, and the fellow cried out for her to halt.

"Whoa, whoa, there," he said, clambering onto the causeway. They had drawn the attention of one of the other trappers, who was watching them from the field, a rabbit dangling from his hand. The third man had vanished. Perhaps to go make water in the copse of trees in the distance. "I will help you."

"He is a merchant named Fulke Crofton," Bess said. "When he travels, he wears a fox-furred green cloak and a tall hat. He is short in stature and would have been astride a fawn-colored Spanish horse."

"I know of Merchant Crofton," he said. "But I still do not recognize you."

"Does my name matter so greatly?"

"It does to me."

She eyed him. His padded doublet and trunk hose were of good material, but naught else marked him as a man of particular importance. "I am Mistress Ellyott. Some call me Widow Ellyott. My brother is Robert Marshall, with whom I live."

"Ah."

"Satisfied?"

He inclined his head. "My thanks, Mistress Ellyott. I must remark, however, that one attired in such fine clothing as your brother-in-law has likely been accosted by a highwayman."

A dispassionate assessment of Fulke's fate.

"He was bound for Devizes," Bess said. "You can see

the road from here. Did you notice him upon it yesterday? Were you and your fellows checking your snares?"

*In the heavy fog, Bess?* Not likely. She was on a fool's errand.

"We were here for a very short while yesterday. The weather did not favor us," he replied. "What time might Merchant Crofton have gone past?"

Bess thought back to what Dorothie had said. "Around sunrise."

"Hm." He buffed the backs of his fingers against the short dark beard growing along his chin. "Earlier than I was out here. And the fog was quite thick. His passage could have been unnoticed."

"Perhaps one of your friends . . . ?"

"Of course. Gibb," he called out to the fellow with the rabbit, which was now strung from his leather girdle. "Did you notice a man dressed like a merchant riding on the Devizes highway yester-morn? Headed away from town around sunrise?"

"No, Kit. I was still abed at sunrise."

*Kit.* She had a name for the stranger who, at that moment, rested his gloved hand upon the palfrey's flank.

"It appears we cannot help, Mistress," said Kit. "But why does your sister fret for her wool merchant husband?"

"He was to come home last evening and did not. Furthermore, his horse returned early this morning. Without him," she added unnecessarily.

"Good cause for concern, then."

Sudden shouts echoed across the field. The source of the

noise was crashing through the underbrush toward them, yelling as he worked on the laces that closed the front of his breeches. "Kit! Gibb!"

"Stop squealing," chided the fellow named Gibb.

"Come quick! Both of you. Now!" he said.

"Excuse me." With that, Kit sprinted away.

His friend gestured wildly at the trees behind him. Kit did not converse long with him before running for the copse. The urgency in their actions caused Bess to unhitch her knee and hop down from the horse. After tying the animal to a nearby hedge, she hoisted her skirts and chased after them, the stubble in the field crunching beneath her thick-soled shoes. The cut stalks snagged her petticoats, and she stumbled over soggy furrows, but she had to reach the trees. All she could think was that she simply had to reach the trees.

At the edge of the thicket, Bess stopped to catch her breath, her lungs laboring against the restriction imposed by her pair of bodies. Up ahead, the three men moved through the shadowed underbrush. She heard a cry—one of shock, it seemed—and hurried forward.

It was then she saw what she did not wish to see, dangling from a sturdy branch of a great oak just beyond the far edge of the woods.

She must have screamed, for the men turned as one.

Kit ran back to join her. "This is no place for you, Mistress Ellyott." He grabbed her arm and tugged her away.

"But it is Fulke! We must cut him down!"

"Gibb will attend to that. You should come away."

She was weeping now. *Dorothie. Poor Dorothie.*

"We must send for the constable. To fetch the coroner," Bess cried out, tripping over fallen branches as Kit pulled her along, tears clouding her vision. "To find the man who did this to Fulke. We must send for the constable now!"

"No need, Mistress," the man at her side said calmly. They broke into the sunlight at the other side of the stand of trees. "I am already here."

The pounding of approaching hoofbeats gave Bess no chance to respond. Her sister and brother had heard her and hastened back.

"She cannot see this." Bess struggled to release Kit's hold on her arm. Her feet slid beneath her, yesterday's rain making a mire of the fallen leaves and dirt. "She cannot!"

Dorothie's frightened gaze met hers, and she tumbled from the horse before Robert brought it to a halt. "Fulke!" she cried, ripping her skirts from the stirrup where they had tangled. "Fulke!"

She ran toward them and the copse of trees at their backs.

The constable comprehended who she was. "Stop her!"

His friends, though, were distracted by their efforts to cut down Fulke, and she evaded their belated attempts to prevent her from reaching the woods.

"Dorothie!" Bess shouted, at last wrenching free her arm and rushing to where her sister had gone. "No! Do not!"

Her warnings came too late, though.

For Dorothie could not hear over the sound of her own shrieking.

# CHAPTER 3

Dorothie had ventured as far as to where Fulke had been cut down before collapsing upon the ground at his side. She wept with no care for the mud caking her clothing.

"Dorothie, come now." Bess gently took her sister's arm. She was as limp as a child's poppet made of scraps of fustian, and her eyes were as empty and unseeing as those painted upon such a toy's face as well.

"Fulke. Fulke." Dorothie's wailing had turned her hoarse, and her voice grated. She reached for her husband's hand, slack against the trampled damp ground and tinged gray with death. A fallen leaf clung to his skin. Bess thought of another hand belonging to another man and felt sickness churn.

"Come now," Bess repeated. "Robert, prithee, help me lift her."

In one motion, her brother hoisted Dorothie to her feet. As he led her away, Bess glanced back at Fulke, his bare head face down in the dirt. The red line around his neck where the rope had bruised the flesh was visible above his sodden cloak's fur collar. She could not fathom it possible that Fulke, arrogant Fulke, had chosen such an end.

Their progress was a slow crawl to the roadside where the horses waited, their breath steaming in the damp morning air.

"This should not have happened," Dorothie muttered, her chin drooping over the embroidered edge of her cambric partlet. "I warned him . . . stupid man. Oh, Fulke."

"Do not blame yourself for what has happened, Dorothie," said Robert. "He would have thought your dream gave him no cause to cancel his plans."

"This time, he should have done."

The constable had sent the man named Gibb to town to fetch the coroner. His apparent haste through the streets had spread the news of Fulke's death faster than an announcement proclaimed in the market square. People scurried from the village to gather along the roadside. Plowmen abandoned their oxen. Farm laborers ceased their sowing. That they did not plunge across the field to gawp at Fulke's body was a surprise.

As Dorothie and Robert neared the roadway, those gathered upon it whispered behind their hands. In truth, some did not whisper but spoke aloud to one another. Bess wished not to hear them, imagining that if she pretended to be deaf, then Dorothie would not hear them as well. The unkind words spoken about a harsh and prideful man. That Fulke could no longer bear the burden of his sins, a comment that caused one fellow to howl with laughter.

"Stop!" Dorothie screamed, extinguishing the murmurs

and tittering as rapidly as two fingers closing about a flame. "Stop this now!"

"Dorothie," Robert soothed, "ignore them."

"No. They hated him." Her gaze swept over shocked faces. "You are happy he is dead. Are you not? All of you!"

Robert gave Dorothie a firm tug toward his gelding. "We must go. You benefit Fulke naught with this outburst."

The constable had followed them, and he overheard the exchange. When he met Bess's gaze, she could see speculation in his eyes.

"Should the coroner have need to speak with you, Mistress Crofton, where might you be found?" he asked.

"Why would he have need to speak with me?" she asked, trembling. "I am no witness to this crime!"

Her words encouraged a brisk wave of murmuring to fan out across the crowd.

Constable Harwoode's eyes narrowed. "Crime?"

"The coroner may find her at my house today, Constable," said Robert calmly, clasping Dorothie around the waist and hoisting her onto the saddle of his horse. "Please send news of the jury's finding to us there."

The constable nodded and proceeded to instruct the males of the assembled crowd to await the coroner. Once he arrived, fifteen would be selected from among their number to act as members of the coroner's jury. Given that none budged—for this was better entertainment than a traveling company of actors—the coroner would have sufficient jurors at hand once he arrived. They would examine the body for other wounds, search for footprints or hoof marks in the soft ground among the trees. Seek out witnesses and question them. Determine if it was suicide or murder.

Robert retrieved the rented palfrey and helped Bess onto the saddle. She glanced at her sister, softly crying, her tears dripping onto her gown. *This crime.*

Dorothie's words reflected a suspicion, a hopeful belief, perhaps, that Fulke's death was not suicide. The punishment for the unforgivable sin of self-murder was harsh. All of their movable goods would be forfeited to the Crown, every last coin, every last piece of linen, every last pot and spoon. As if the loss of husband and father was not punishment enough.

She noticed Bess watching. "Do not pity me, Elizabeth. Pity shall not return Fulke to the living."

"I well know that, Dorothie."

Wiping her eyes, she turned away. "I cry for our boys. Our dear, fatherless boys. They will have to be brought home from Cambridge. And Margery, bereft of a father again—" Her words were overwhelmed by a fresh wash of tears.

"Hush, now. The time to decide your sons' futures will come later. For now, let us speak no more of this matter," said Robert, climbing onto the gelding behind Dorothie and holding her close.

Robert clucked to his horse, and it trotted off. Bess made to follow them, but Constable Harwoode stopped her.

"Mistress." He cast a hasty glance toward the stand of trees. Leaves and branches obscured any view of Fulke's body. "You have my sympathy."

"I am not the one who suffers most here, Constable."

"Your sister, then." His gaze flicked to where Robert

and Dorothie slowly made their way along the road. "Your sister should realize that the coroner will not likely rule a death by hanging a homicide."

"Should I tell her so to comfort her?" Bess knew she sounded like a scold. She gripped the pommel of the saddle to steady herself. "A ruling of felo-de-se would destroy my sister's and her children's fortunes. Surely, you understand the consequences of deeming his death suicide."

His light eyes went hard as glass. "I will allow the coroner and his jury to make their ruling. They will be just."

His response angered her. "And you will not consider otherwise," she said. "My brother-in-law was not the sort to do this awful act. He was too proud."

Kit Harwoode's eyes went harder still. "The coroner rules, not I." He removed his hat and bowed over it. "I bid you good day, Mistress Ellyott."

Without returning the pleasantry, Bess yanked the palfrey's reins hard, turning the horse toward town. She left the constable to stand in the road among the curious townspeople, her shoulders held as motionless as possible despite their shaking from anger and grief.

And from fear.

★　★　★

Bess let the palfrey pick its way back to town. She had no heart for returning to the house to share in Dorothie's grief. Her sister's heartache would only make Bess relive the moments after Martin died. Feel afresh the distress upon realizing that she would never hear his voice again or enjoy the brush of his fingertips against her skin.

She glanced back over her shoulder to where the coroner and his jury were assembling. The coroner had passed her upon the road, his long black gown flapping about his legs as he strode toward the copse of trees. She could not see him or his jurors though; the intervening ruins of the priory obscured her line of sight even more than the distance. Bess squinted to search for what she could not discern. All that was visible were the rolling fields bathed in milky sunshine and the wisps of fog steaming above the nearby stream. How peaceful the setting was, as though another day like any other had risen with the sun. Appearances, though, could deceive. And she had been misled by outward prettiness before.

Subdued, miserable, she shifted on the saddle, facing straight ahead. The Anwickes' cottage stood just ahead on the side of the road. The road that Fulke had traveled upon. Someone at the cottage might have seen him pass. Witnessed if he had encountered anyone who might have caused him harm.

Bess reined in the horse, unhitched her knee, and hopped down. Her young patient no longer sat upon the doorstep, her bucket and infant sibling vanished with her. The door was closed firm, and the shutters were set in the lone window that faced the highway. No smoke curled from the hole in the roof. Bess rapped on the door nonetheless.

"Ho!" she called.

She heard a faint noise, like the scuttling of a mouse. Bess leaned nearer the door and rapped again. The response was silence.

Bess stepped back to scan the cottage as if another window or open door might appear. Of course, none did. Perhaps the news of Fulke's death had enticed the Anwickes to rush into town to collect the gossip like a windfall of acorns.

She remounted the palfrey and rode the rest of the way into town. Eyes followed her passage, as did whispers. The chandler's apprentice, who'd been hurrying across the market square before her arrival, came to an abrupt halt, his eyes wide.

"Good morrow," Bess said to him, since he was staring at her with obvious interest.

"Is it true? He's dead in the woods?" the teenage boy asked.

How abrupt boys could be. How very accurate as well. "Aye." Bess would not deny what everyone must already know.

"Zounds!" he replied. He turned on his heel and ran back to the chandler's. "It's true!" his voice echoed from the depths of the building. "It's true!"

"Mistress Ellyott!" cried a female voice.

"Mistress Stamford," she said to the woman hailing her. Amice Stamford stood before the windows of her husband's shop. The red kirtle showing through the opening of her flaxen-yellow gown's skirt was as vivid as a blot of blood against a scrap of parchment, drawing the eye. A morbid comparison. At Amice Stamford's back, her eldest daughter leaned across a stack of scarlets and broadcloths to peer through the window. She nearly knocked over the woolens in her eagerness to spy.

"Is it true?" Mistress Stamford asked. She must not have heard Bess's exchange with the chandler's apprentice; Bess could not fathom how the woman had not.

"Do you mean Fulke?"

"Yes." She stepped into the road and walked up to the palfrey. It was brave of her to wish to speak to a member of Fulke's family when, if he had indeed hanged himself, they were all disgraced.

"Has the coroner made his ruling?" asked Mistress Stamford. Her actions had brought them the attention of everyone nearby. A goodwife exiting the neighboring poulterer's, a plucked chicken in her hand, stopped to openly gawk.

So it was fresh gossip Mistress Stamford sought. "Not as yet. And I would be with my sister when she receives the news. So if you permit—"

"Arthur will want Mistress Crofton to know he wishes her God's peace in this painful time."

Not gossip, then. A desire to assuage Stamford guilt. Arthur Stamford no more wished a Crofton well than he wished to have a plague of moths eat through his stock of worsteds. In recent months he had feuded with Fulke, though the details of their quarrel were unknown to Bess.

"Your husband may tell her so, when next he sees her," Bess responded. "Should propriety allow him to say as much to Dorothie. I fear others will not be so kind."

Mistress Stamford pressed her lips together into a thin pink line. "No one blames her."

"For what? Forgive me if I do not follow, Mistress Stamford. For what would any blame my sister?"

Amice Stamford abruptly retreated to the security of the shop's doorway. "I will pray for God's mercy upon your family, Mistress Ellyott."

"And I will pray that it is proved my family is in no

more need of God's mercy than any other. Good day to you."

Bess jabbed her heels into the palfrey's flanks and urged the horse to trot across the square, his hooves clattering against the cobbles.

★ ★ ★

"What say you, one and all?" The coroner tilted his head to scan the assembled men.

A better sort had been chosen, their hair and beards trimmed, their breeches and jerkins in good repair. Kit recognized most of them, familiar faces on the lanes around town. They had dutifully attended to the coroner's facts as he presented them—the lack of a weapon or other wounds besides the mark around Master Crofton's throat, the absence of any sign of a struggle, the extreme difficulty of getting a victim to willingly put his neck in a noose to be hoisted to hang. The jurors indulged the coroner and his crude jest with a smattering of uncomfortable laughter. So far as Kit knew, though, they were good and honest men. But to expect them to be able to correctly determine how a man had died . . . He may as well expect them to discourse in Latin upon the movement of the heavens.

"Gibb," he said, as he and his cousin waited for the inevitable, "have you heard rumors of a vagrant in the area?"

Gibb, the rabbits they'd snared still strung from his belt, looked over at him. "The other day I was told about some stranger seen near the mill. I presumed the fellow had confused the stranger for one of the soldiers returning from the war."

"If this stranger has a right to passage, he need not lurk," Kit pointed out, as he had also explained to the husbandman missing a pig. "See what else you can learn. If anyone else has seen such a person."

"But 'tis just past Michaelmas." His frown shifted the faint scar that cut across his upper lip. A scar Kit had given him with the edge of a hornbook when they were both rough boys at petty school. *Those Harwoodes.* Kit could still hear the scorn in their schoolmaster's voice. "My father requires my help with this quarter's accounts."

"See what you can learn between adding and subtracting, then."

The jurors finished their deliberation, and silence fell over the gathering of men.

"Felo-de-se," the loudest among the coroner's jury proclaimed. Kit did not like that he seemed to relish the pronouncement. "Self-murder."

"Aye!" one among the assembled shouted.

"Aye!" another joined him.

*Aye.* A single word strong enough to fell Dorothie Crofton's future. And the outcome Kit had expected.

The coroner's gaze passed over the men again. "And no cause to believe he was non compos mentis?" Of unsound mind.

"Besides his vile temper?" a bold fellow asked, drawing more chuckles. "Nay."

"Constable Harwoode, you hear the jury's decision," boomed the coroner. His voice always had been thunderous. He'd missed his calling in the church.

"I do," Kit responded, dropping his hand to the hilt of

his dagger, its sheath tucked into his belt. Gibb muttered under his breath.

The coroner inclined his head. "Then, this even, his body shall be taken to the nearest crossroads under the cover of darkness, where it will be buried with a stake through the chest so that he may not haunt the good citizens of our town. And let all who pass think on their own sinfulness."

Aye, he'd missed his calling.

"The crossroads?" Gibb searched the faces of the jurors, looking for sympathizers and finding none. "Have pity!"

Kit grabbed his arm and dragged him backward, silencing him. "The coroner follows the law. You know that as well as I."

"We should speak to Wat," he grumbled. "He could see it undone."

Their cousin, the lord of the manor. He may be able to overrule the coroner's decision to have Crofton buried at the crossroads, but would he?

The coroner selected a handful of men to inter Fulke Crofton that evening after the sun had set. From among their number, he chose one to stand guard over the body in the meantime.

"More property for Wat, however," said Gibb, watching the rest of the jurors disperse along the road back to town. The coroner, rather than following the men, turned south. Toward Wat's manor, perhaps.

"Our cousin does not need the goods of a dead man." Though, as the holder of a royal patent that gave him the right, Fulke Crofton's movable property was now Sir Walter Howe's. "He has more than enough."

"Wat never has enough!"

True. Much would have more.

"I have another task for you, Gibb." Kit looked toward the body. Someone had covered Crofton's face with his sodden cloak, its brilliant green a slash of color in the shadows. "I need you to go to Master Marshall's house and inform Mistress Crofton of the coroner's ruling. But I warn you, she will be distressed. She appears to think her husband did not die by his own hand and will not welcome this finding."

"I have to tell her?" Frowning, Gibb tossed the end of his short cloak over his opposite shoulder. "There are times I wish you'd not convinced me to help you with this work of yours, coz."

"Go to. You've told me often how working on your father's accounts bores you."

"I might not mind the boredom, given what has happened here today." He gestured at the rabbits strung from his belt. "Shall I go with these jangling about my hips?"

"I will take them to Wat," said Kit. Gibb handed over the rabbits. "I hope I can also convince him to allow Mistress Crofton a week among her goods. She's become a widow in a humiliating fashion; she does not need the additional pain of having her belongings hastily snatched away."

"And will you try to convince Wat to have Master Crofton more respectably interred? The crossroads. With a stake!" Gibb shuddered.

"Aye, Gibb." Kit exhaled as he wrapped the strings holding the rabbits around his fist. "I shall see what I can do."

# CHAPTER 4

"The coroner's jury will call it suicide, Bess," Robert whispered.

There was no need for whispers; Dorothie was fast asleep in the chamber above the hall, her daughter at her side. Margery had returned to town but an hour earlier to the news of Fulke's death. Upon her arrival at Robert's house, she had gone straight to Dorothie.

"The Crown will even take the property her first husband left to her," he added. "Barbarous."

He stood in the doorway to Bess's still room, where she prepared her physic. Her precious dried herbs and spices, stored in sealed stone pots, were lined up in tidy rows on wooden shelves. A round brick furnace occupied one corner, and upon the table at its side stood her supply of conical copper alembics for condensing the waters that would be boiled off. Her many vessels in which to collect the liquids also waited there. Drying flowers hung from the rafters overhead, adding their scent—sweet, spicy, earthy—to the air. The still room was more than the place where Bess prepared her physic; it was her refuge.

"They will not remove her plate. Fulke dowered that to her." Bess brought over a stool to where dried lavender dangled in bunches. "The law cannot take it."

"Small comfort." Robert rubbed the back of his neck. "Her boys will have to be fetched back from Cambridge to live in that empty house with her and Margery. And her plate."

His words sank like weights in Bess's uneasy stomach. Joan had tried to feed them when they had returned with Dorothie, but all Bess had been able to manage was a bite of cold mutton pie. It sat like a stone alongside Robert's words.

More than his words and Joan's mutton pie pained her stomach though. Something was amiss about Fulke, more than the incredible manner in which he had died. But she could not recall what it was.

Bess bent to pin her petticoats out of the way. "And what shall happen to us, Robert?"

"None will condemn us for Fulke's death," he replied.

"Believe you that? In truth?" Grabbing up her scissors, she stepped onto the stool and snipped at the twine suspending the lavender. Robert fetched the broad wicker basket from her bench and brought it over. "Amice Stamford stopped me when I rode through town. She wished me to believe the same as well."

"Stamford's wife wished to comfort you?" he asked, scoffing.

Bess laid the lavender into the basket. "She must be feeling guilty. Nonetheless, you know many of the townsfolk will condemn us, Robin," she said, using her pet name for him. "They will believe Fulke's sin reflects on us all. A stain upon the reputation of our family."

"Come now. You're near as bad as Dorothie to fret over gossips."

"But gossip can scar and burn far more than truth." More lavender went into the basket. Though she worked to keep her thoughts from wandering in directions she did not wish, one thought would not obey. "Arthur Stamford would not have harmed Fulke, would he?"

"What mean you by such a question? Fulke took his own life."

"But why? What reason had he?"

"Dorothie told me not the other day that some of the clothiers in the area are balking at buying Fulke's wool, thinking it of lesser quality," said Robert. "She believes Stamford the source of their misgiving. Fulke was concerned the rumors might damage his business and was distressed."

"So you have confirmed my suspicion," said Bess. "Arthur Stamford did wish to harm Fulke."

"Stamford is a petty man, but slander is the extent of his criminality, Bess," he said. "Cease thinking he meant worse for our brother-in-law. Such thoughts will give you unease."

"Too late, Robin."

He took her elbow to help her as she stepped down to the flag flooring in order to move the stool. "And we will aid Dorothie. Should she ask," Robert added. "She and her children could live here. There is enough room."

"I thought you planned to wed again, and soon," said Bess, climbing back onto the stool to cut down the remainder of the lavender. "The addition of a bride would result in far too many women in this household to please any of us, should Dorothie and Margery also move here. Besides, Dorothie will not wish to share a roof with me again."

Robert's face set into hard lines. At that moment, he looked so much like their father that Bess's heart contracted. So many people to miss and to mourn. Their parents. Martin. Robert's wife, gone to her reward in Heaven not long before Martin died. Bess's two sweet children, buried in a cold London churchyard. She would dream of the girls tonight, kiss their soft cheeks once more, the joy of reunion as ever turned to bittersweet sorrow upon the morn.

And now Fulke—pompous, sanctimonious, ill-tempered, yet unexpectedly witty Fulke—to add to their number.

"You and Dorothie should love each other better," her brother chided.

"I would, if she would let me." The crack in their relationship was too old to mend.

"Perhaps after this she will. We must be prepared for the coroner's ruling," he said. "We are the strong ones, Bess, you and I. We must be strong now."

The last of the lavender collected, she returned the stool to its proper place and unpinned her petticoats. Joan would set the dried flower bunches among their linens and place them under pillows to help give restful sleep. Sleep they all needed.

"It is not strength to concede that Fulke killed himself." Bess strode from the still room through the lobby connecting it to the rest of the service rooms. She turned into the hall, where Quail lounged in a spray of sunshine streaming through the room's many windowpanes of leaded glass.

"Bess, he was a man of strong and unruly passions."

"And none that would lead him to this. Not even some concern over his business. He would not. He was too proud," she said, repeating what she'd told the constable. Who had appeared no more convinced than her brother did at that moment.

"Hush now, Bess. Your distress is causing you to have fancies. We must accept—"

"If the coroner rules felo-de-se, I shall not accept such a conclusion. Not when the result is the ruin of Dorothie and her children!"

He shut the door behind him. "There is no need to shout. Dorothie and Margery will hear."

"I am not shouting!" she insisted, her voice echoing off the decorated plaster walls and wainscot. Quail awakened with a yelp. The dog got to his feet and plodded off. "So I am. I am sorry. But Fulke had enemies. You know he did. Even Dorothie said as much this morning. 'They hated him.' Who, Robert? Who?"

"She imagines slights where there are none," he said. "And Mistress Langham has forgiven Fulke."

Another enemy, which made at least two.

"I would I could be as certain as you that she has forgiven Fulke for what he did. Her husband died in Fleet Prison."

Master Langham had perished from a fever, though his family had paid for a cell in the best part of the prison and for food and a bed. He had languished in the Fleet because Fulke had informed the authorities that he believed the Langhams hid Jesuit priests in their rambling house. The queen's men, looking to crush every last Catholic who might assist in plots to end the reign of a Protestant monarch, had been quick to investigate. They had found a hidden chamber. Its emptiness had not saved Master Langham from his fate.

"She is a good woman, despite what they claim about her and her family." A muscle twitched in Robert's jaw. Discussion of Mistress Langham discomfited his conscience. And Bess's as well. "I would not see her accused in your desire to preserve Dorothie's fortune."

"I do not attempt to accuse her. I merely attempt to point out that Fulke had enemies."

"Bess, rule your thoughts." He took her hands in his. They were warm and strong, as strong as he was. "And promise me that you will submit to the coroner's judgment. If you do not, I shall not leave for London on the morrow but will remain here to govern you."

"But you must go," she said. "Your business requires your presence in the city. And your potential bride awaits your arrival as well. She might think you have changed your mind about asking her to wed."

"Then promise me."

Slowly, she inclined her head. She did not, however, speak the words aloud.

"Be steadfast for the both of us in my absence, Bess. Your sister will need you."

"Dorothie has never needed me."

"That is not so. She is merely too proud to admit as much."

Fingers tapped upon the hall door, and Joan entered when bid.

She offered a curtsy. "The constable's man is at the door, requesting an audience, Master Marshall."

Robert released Bess's hands. The news had come. "Send him in, Joan."

★ ★ ★

"Kit! What brings you here?" His cousin Sir Walter Howe strode across the paneled hall, his boot heels rapping against the tile floor. The spangles decorating his rose-red jerkin and trunk hose reflected the light streaming through the diamond-shaped panes of window glass. "You should have told me of your visit. We could have shared dinner."

Kit stood in the opening of the screens passage, which spanned the gap between the kitchen and the hall and led to the front entrance. "I left the rabbits we captured with your kitchen maid. However, I cannot stay for dinner."

Wat—taller than Kit by a head and two hands wider—clapped him on the shoulder. He had a broad face and big features to go with his height and breadth; he looked nothing like a Harwoode. Of which he was proud.

"You can always stay for dinner. I shall tell Cecily you are here. She would wish to see you."

"Do not disturb your wife." A frail young woman, she was heavy with child. Her fourth attempt to bear Wat an heir. "Truly, I do not plan to stay long. I do, though, wish to discuss a matter with you."

"So you can spare a moment."

He grabbed Kit's upper arm and pulled him into the hall. The size and the opulence of the room was meant to dwarf those who passed beneath the plaster ceiling covered in geometric moldings. Rich tapestries hung above the linen-fold paneling. Armor and weaponry were displayed upon the far wall. A massive table covered with a Turkey carpet managed to look dwarfed as well. Wat, however, was undaunted by the magnificence he'd inherited. In fact, he seemed to swell in confidence to fill the expanse.

"Come and sit and tell me about this matter of yours."

Kit accepted a seat before the immense carved fireplace while Wat took the matching chair set at an angle to him. Though it was yet morning, a fire burned upon the hearth, beating back the October chill.

"It concerns Fulke Crofton," said Kit. "The coroner has made his ruling."

Wat nodded. "Felo-de-se. I heard."

The coroner *had* run here in order to deliver the news. "The Croftons will be ruined. Allow Mistress Crofton at least a week with her grief before taking all her goods, Wat."

"'Tis the churchwarden's decision on when he and his men will remove what the Croftons now owe the Crown."

"And you can tell the churchwarden a week, no sooner. Be generous."

"As you wish, Kit," he said. "A pity for Mistress Crofton and her children though."

"They are to bury Fulke Crofton at the crossroads." Kit leaned forward. Now to get Wat to commit to another task. "If you would truly prove your generosity, do what you can to have the fellow buried near the church."

Wat scowled. "Cousin, do not ask me to defy the law. 'Tis one matter to ask the churchwarden to delay, quite another to request that the vicar permit a man who has committed suicide to have his bones rest within the churchyard."

"Crofton was a gentleman and does not deserve such barbaric cruelty. Make it happen, Wat."

"You make too much of my authority," Wat replied. "And I would not be so certain Master Crofton does not deserve such cruelty. I am only surprised he died by his own hand and not another's. He owned more enemies than you have fingers on one hand."

Mayhap Mistress Crofton's belief about what had actually happened was not without merit. *And I should apologize to Mistress Ellyott, whose misgivings I so readily dismissed.* "Who are these enemies?"

"Anyone he ever had dealings with." Wat considered Kit. "Why do you ask? The coroner has made his ruling. Fulke Crofton killed himself. 'Tis sad indeed but the truth."

"What if it is not the truth?"

"Mean you to investigate a murder that has not occurred?" Wat shook his head. "Tend to your other duties, Kit. I hear the baker upon the high street has been adding bean flour to his wheaten bread again. He needs must be fined. *That* is your responsibility."

Kit bristled. "I am aware of my responsibilities."

"Good. Then I need say naught else." Wat stood. "Good day to you. I've my own business to attend."

He marched off across the checkered tile.

Kit rose. "Wat," he called out to his kinsman, "see that Master Crofton is not buried at the crossroads. Do what is charitable. Not merely what the law insists upon."

His cousin hesitated at the doorway leading to his privy

rooms beyond. But he made no promise and swept from the hall.

★   ★   ★

"Tell me again what the constable's man said, Elizabeth." Dorothie sank into the goose-down pillows at her back, her face hidden in the shadows of the tester bed. At Bess's request, Joan had shut the window curtains, leaving the bedchamber dark save for the thinnest sliver of early afternoon light.

Seated upon the bed at Dorothie's side, the feather mattress sagging beneath her weight, Bess reached for her sister's hand. It was cold.

"Did you not hear me the first time?" Bess asked gently, unhappy to repeat Gibb Harwoode's words. At least he had been kind and respectful as he had relayed his horrid news.

"I would hear again."

Bess glanced over at Margery, who stood in the corner of the chamber, her tawny gown blending into the paneling behind her. Bess had not seen her shed a tear over her stepfather's death as she moved around the house like a cipher, a shadow. Far more subdued than her usual self, her eyes bright with wit when she came to learn about physic at Bess's side or simply to visit.

"Margery, fetch a bite of dinner for your mother," said Bess. "Joan will assist you."

With a nod, her niece left the room, quietly closing the thick oak door behind her.

"I am glad Margery has returned so she can be here with you," said Bess.

"She dared, though, to tell me she was certain Bennett Langham would send his condolences upon hearing the news," said Dorothie. "What does she mean, to mention his name at such a time?"

"Margery is but seventeen years of age, Dorothie, and believes herself in love with him. She simply wishes you to regard him kindly."

"The Langhams are papists," said Dorothie. "And they hated Fulke just like everyone else in this town."

*The Langhams had more reason than most*, Bess did not add.

"And she should have nothing to do with them," said Dorothie. "I have told her so, but she will not listen."

"Beneath all, she is a Marshall, and very much like you and me and Robert. Stubborn."

"I am *not* like you and Robert, Elizabeth."

*Love each other better.* An impossibility.

Dorothie, her dismay over Bennett Langham spent, slumped farther into the pillows. She looked drained and hollow. *I must have looked the same after losing Martin.* She should ask Joan what she remembered of Bess's actions after his death, for Bess could not recall. One day, they were in London, packing to leave. The next, it seemed, in a foreign town in Wiltshire, a chill rain upon Bess's face.

"Might I light a candle, Dorothie? It is near black as night in here."

"Tell me again what the constable's man said."

Bess gripped her sister's hand more firmly. "Come next Tuesday, the churchwarden and his men shall begin to remove all of your goods and take possession of the contents of Fulke's warehouse as well as any leasehold property—"

"But not my house. And not my plate."

"Not your plate." Merely all else that could be transferred. Perhaps she had misjudged Dorothie's affection for Fulke, after all; perhaps she had been mourning the potential loss of her silver salt cellars and spoons. "Robert has gone to speak to the men who will take the inventory of your belongings. He has promised to secure whatever clothing of yours they will allow you to keep."

Dorothie's eyes widened. "The queen's men are at my house now?"

"To ensure you do not attempt to hide any of your goods from them before they begin the inventory on the morrow. Robert claims they are most generous to allow you a week to adjust to your circumstances before removing everything."

"'Tis not so generous seeming to me. The thieves." Beneath Bess's hands, Dorothie's fingers bunched into folds the blanket draped over her legs. "Roland will not let them into the house. Robert need not have gone. Roland will not let them into the house."

"Your manservant cannot keep out men performing a duty for the Crown."

Chin drooping, Dorothie lifted a hand to her bare throat, her fingers splaying.

Bess stared at her sister, the image of Fulke's throat suddenly coming to mind. His throat. That was what had been wrong. What had been bothering her. "Dorothie."

"I am tired and would like to rest, Elizabeth, before I return to my house. The one being pawed over by the churchwarden's villains," said Dorothie. "I am done speaking."

"No, Dorothie, wait and hear me out. Fulke's throat."

"How can you mention that?"

"The line around his throat. It was where your fingers were just resting against your skin. Right above his collar."

Dorothie looked down at her hand as if it were a poisonous creature about to strike. "My fingers?"

"Yes. Yes. There." With her forefinger, Bess traced a line across her sister's neck about halfway down its length. "If Fulke had died from hanging, the rope would have left a mark beneath his jaw, not here, so much lower."

"What are you saying?"

Bess said what was obvious and what the coroner should have noted yet had not. "Fulke was strangled, Dorothie. And not by his own hand."

Dorothie sat upright and grabbed Bess's wrist. Her grip was tight and made Bess's fingers tingle. "We must tell the constable. And the coroner. Tell Robert and get those awful men out of my house."

"'Tis possible I recall falsely."

"Why have you told me if you are not certain? You vex me, Elizabeth. You always have." Dorothie groaned and flopped against the pillows, sending a puff of feathers flying.

"Then I must *be* certain," Bess said, though the dangers of obtaining sureness did not bear thought.

"Yes. Yes!" Dorothie sat upright again. She threw off the blanket and swung her legs over the edge of the mattress. "Let us go and see Fulke now. Confirm what you believe."

"A man is guarding him. He will not allow us near Fulke. They expect we would wish to spirit him away so they cannot desecrate him by burying him at the crossroads."

Dorothie lay back down. "Then we shall wait until they

do bury him and dig him up and see. I know where Humphrey keeps the garden shovels."

"Dorothie, consider what you say." A widow should not examine her husband's corpse; she would faint dead away.

She paled. "No. You are right." She clutched the blanket to her chin. "You can tend to this matter. You have the taste for such unhealthy things. But you will be prevented. Since none of us are to be allowed near to him, you will not be permitted to examine his body. Perhaps you could ask the coroner—"

"He would not aid my efforts," said Bess. "No. I must examine Fulke under the cover of dark."

"But what of the curfew?"

"The constable's men have not been enforcing it strictly of late. They make their rounds but rarely." Unlike London. "Should I be stopped, I could claim I am on my way to attend to an ill person."

She had done so before, but not because she meant to sneak out of town and dig up a body.

"When shall you go? Tonight?" Dorothie asked.

"Tomorrow, for I do not know precisely when they intend to bury him tonight, and I would not risk encountering them."

"Do not tell Robert," said Dorothie. "He would lock you in your chamber if he knew."

"He leaves for London in the morning." An even better reason to wait.

"Well, make certain Humphrey does not learn of your plans either. He would send the news by fastest courier to Robert and have him back here in a trice to punish you.

Tush, knowing Humphrey, he might even alert the constable himself!"

Bess leveled her gaze at her sister, whose cheeks were now spotted with color, visible even in the dim light of the room. "I'faith, Dorothie, I have no intention whatsoever of letting either Humphrey or Robert learn of my plans."

# CHAPTER 5

Undoing the latch of her chamber's mullioned window, Bess swung open the casement and leaned through the narrow opening to stare at the street below. The air outside was fresh and cool, and birds sang in the apple trees behind the cottage across the way. Afternoon was fading into evening, and the townsfolk either gathered for their suppers or were completing all the tasks that must be finished before they went to their beds. Peace would soon settle upon the town. But Bess feared peace would not settle upon her heart.

Beneath her, a servant hauled buckets of water taken from the town well to her master's house. Two men, one a fop with a towering feather tucked into his hatband and his doublet pinked in so many places it threatened to fall from his body in tatters, ambled by, chortling over the new serving girl at the corner tavern. At the end of the lane, they encountered Kit Harwoode, whose sudden appearance caused them to straighten and march on. She thought to call out to the constable, but he moved out of her sight before she did so. What a curious man. She did not understand why, instead of delivering the news himself, he had sent his cousin Gibb to tell them the outcome of the coroner's inquest. Perhaps he had not the stomach for upsetting widows. He had not seemed weak though. Merely inscrutable. And unwilling to listen.

Joan stepped into the road to toss a kitchen scrap to the neighbor's cat. The animal streaked, a blur of orange and white, to retrieve the food and hare off with it to a secret spot. Smiling, she wiped her hands on her apron and returned to the house. Bess little understood Joan's affection for the creature, which spit and snarled at everyone else. Mayhap she felt a kinship with the animal, its ill-tempered manners disguising fear and mistrust. Joan had been as ready to strike out when Bess had taken her in. However, months of kind treatment had worn down the young woman's defenses.

Laurence, though . . . forsooth, he had been altogether another animal.

Joan had understood who he was, *what* he was at first blush. It was because of her success with Joan that Bess had taken to him though. Because Bess had thought, in her naiveté, that she could save another urchin. Rescue him from a destiny that could lead only to Newgate or death in an alleyway. What did she, the cosseted youngest child of an Oxford academic, know of such folk though? What did she know of those who scraped and begged in the streets, whose sole friend was their own cunning? Bess had seen them as she made her way from the house she shared with Martin, slinking through the shadows that filled every lane of the city. Or in the market, ragged creatures that darted among the vendors' tables and carts, their fingers fast and their feet faster. Bess had thought herself so wise that she noticed them when others of her station paid them no more heed than the rats that scuttled among rubbish piles or the curs that snapped and growled over butchers' scraps at the Leadenhall Market.

Joan, though, had tried to warn her about Laurence. That he sought the companionship of dangerous fellows. Bess had—so very, very foolishly—presumed her complaints came from jealousy. That she feared her mistress was to replace the affection she felt for Joan with affection for a new pet. Bess had told her not to have concern. Had told her that Laurence, whose curling hair and shining eyes had charmed her, would make them proud. Joan had ceased arguing, but she had watched him carefully, each time he came to sup or sit at Martin's side, learning his trade and Bess's as well. Soon, Martin treated Laurence as he might a son, a son Bess would never give him. Loved him as one as well.

By the time Bess's eyes were opened and she came to agree with Joan's opinion, it was too late to change the onward rush of events that would sweep away her husband and her pleasant life. Too late to escape the entangling schemes of Laurence's dangerous fellows, men who plotted against the monarchy. For the serpent had lived alongside Martin and Bess, its fangs already drawn.

Bess latched the window and turned to lean back against the cold panes of leaded glass. She prayed she was not being blind again. That it would not again be too late before she learned whom to trust, what to believe at all.

★ ★ ★

"I did not have to speak to Mistress Crofton," said Gibb, quaffing a mouthful of beer and looking content. At the beer and at having succeeded in dodging a difficult situation. "Her brother, Master Marshall, heard what I had to convey. Along with Mistress Ellyott."

Kit sat across the table from him, his stool teetering upon the uneven stone floor of the Cross Keys. The tavern consisted of the large front room of a timber-frame building set upon the town square, the tavern keeper and his family having their private chambers on the floor above. It was far more spacious and comfortable than the cramped room of the alehouse. The drink, however, was proportionately more expensive.

"How did they take the news?" he asked. The hum of conversation from their fellow patrons masked their own conversation. Which was why he often chose to meet Gibb here to talk—though they were surrounded by others, they were not so easy to hear.

"Well enough, though they were most displeased with what is to take place tonight." Gibb looked toward the tavern's windows, out at the darkening sky. "Not long from now, if you could not persuade Wat . . ."

"I could not."

" 'Tis cruel."

" 'Tis the law, Gibb."

"Fie on the law."

The tavern keeper's daughter Marcye sidled over. She had a winning smile and lively eyes, which were focused upon Kit as though she were a cat and he a spot of cream. "Need you more drink, Masters Harwoode?"

Behind his tankard, Gibb snickered. He regularly teased that she meant to snare Kit as a husband. In turn, Kit would regularly remind his cousin that he'd grown skilled at evading the most cunning female's snares. He'd seen what an ill match had done to his parents, turning them bitter and hard, ever wounding each other with their words and their slights. He would not make the same mistake.

"My cousin might," said Kit, winking at Gibb.

"Ah," she answered, crestfallen. "Then I shall fetch more."

"Me?" hissed Gibb, once she had left them. "I've no interest in Marcye Johnes."

"Neither do I."

Gibb sipped at his beer, looking thoughtful. "However, that Mistress Ellyott . . . She is a fair one. Think you not, coz? Fine brown eyes."

"'Od's blood, Gibb. I did not send you to Master Marshall's to become tender-eyed over Mistress Ellyott," he said. "I thought you pursued the apothecary's youngest daughter."

"I merely make an observation."

"While you were observing Mistress Ellyott, what did you make of the rest of the family?" asked Kit.

"You know Robert Marshall."

"I know him," said Kit. But he'd not ever noticed Mistress Ellyott before. She did not try to draw attention to herself with loud laughter or coy glances, unlike other townswomen he knew. Simple of dress and measured of voice, she was an unshowy bird among pheasants. But he suspected that, like the feather of a raven, which revealed secret colors when turned into the light, she had a hidden side as well. "Not the rest though."

"They seem refined and respectable people, though there are rumors that the Crofton daughter forms unwise liaisons."

"And what of Mistress Ellyott, besides her fine brown eyes?"

Gibb swallowed more of the beer and swiped the back of his hand across his mouth. "A mystery. She arrived in town last year with only the thinnest of stories as to why she departed London. Some mistrust her, and I've heard that often the only patients who search out her physic are the ones no other healers will attend. A few weeks past, she treated the boy with the birthmark." Gibb gestured at his cheek; Kit knew the lad he meant. "The one whose family lives on the lane behind the churchyard."

"How much gossip *do* you listen to, Gibb?"

His cousin chuckled and finished his beer. "Did you not ask me to listen?" he asked. "Because gossip has told me that there *is* a vagrant. The wheelwright off Church Lane says he's seen this fellow. Not far from the priory ruins. Tried to chase him down, but the man escaped him."

"The priory ruins are where the husbandman who first mentioned him to me claims the fellow is hiding."

"Do you want me to search them?"

"Aye. In the morning," said Kit. "If your father, my good uncle, frees you from scratching in your account books."

Gibb scowled, then suddenly leaned across the table.

"You said Mistress Crofton thought her husband was murdered. Think you this vagrant could be responsible?"

"The coroner has ruled felo-de-se," Kit felt required to say. "Wat did mention, though, that Crofton had many enemies."

"An enemy that might want the man's hat?" asked Gibb. "It was not near his body, which I thought odd. I looked around for it, after you'd gone to visit Wat, but did not find it."

*Damn . . . how did I not notice that Crofton's hat was missing?* Mayhap *he* had been distracted by the mysterious Mistress Ellyott's fine brown eyes. "But no coins were gone from his purse. Does one murder a man for his hat but leave his purse dangling from his belt, then go to the extravagance of stringing him from a tree? I think not, Gibb."

His cousin sat back, disappointed.

"I will set the watch upon the town," said Kit. "To either catch the vagrant or prevent him from causing mischief. We will find him."

"The wheelwright wanted to know if I thought the vagrant was one of those Jesuits sneaking into the country from France."

Kit's finger, which had been tapping against his tankard, stilled. He had only been jesting when he had mentioned the possibility to the husbandman who'd had his pig stolen. 'Twere dangerous times indeed if assassins had come to this quiet part of Wiltshire.

"I must speak to the Langhams about this vagrant." The father of the family had perished in Fleet Prison for supporting Jesuits; they might continue his treason.

"Think you they would be so unwise again, Kit?" asked Gibb. "After losing Master Langham?"

"The Fleet has not taught the families of other traitors wisdom," said Kit. "Although if this vagrant *is* a Jesuit, and has taken to hiding among the priory ruins, the Langhams have at least learned the danger of concealing such a fellow within their house."

"They will not answer you true about him and chance a second offense. The entire household would be sent to the Tower." Gibb leaned across the table again. "I know Bennett Langham. He is a good man. He is no traitor."

"If they intend to harm the queen, then we must do our duty," said Kit. "No matter our personal feelings about the Langhams."

★ ★ ★

"I am not pleased to leave you and Dorothie at such a time," said Robert the next morning. "Or Margery either."

They stood in the courtyard under a cloud-filled sky. Several of their neighbors had begged him to take gifts to family and friends in London. Bess watched as he loaded items they had pressed upon him—a small wheel of cheese, a length of broadcloth—into the leather sumpter slung over his horse. If he had not refused, he would have been laden with chickens and fresh eggs as well. Goods would return with her brother, likely more than he now departed with. He also carried a letter from Joan to a friend. Unbeknownst to Robert, this friend tracked Laurence's movements in London. She took great risks to do so.

"We shall be well," said Bess. She would not see him again before a week was out. If he rode hard and the weather held, he might make it to the city in two days. "Joan has already been to Dorothie's house this morning to inquire after her, at my request, and Joan reports that she appeared calm."

"There is disbelief at first, then she will come to realize he is truly gone, and . . . well, I need not tell you how these matters proceed."

No. He did not.

Robert finished loading the sumpter and tied it closed. "The churchwarden's men come to make their inventory today. Their presence will distract her. I am surprised, though, she does not wish Margery to be with her as a comfort."

"She thinks it best Margery stay here, where there is some measure of quiet and no rooms filled with strange men searching every chest and counting every last item," answered Bess. "Dorothie mistrusts the men the churchwarden has sent to her house. She thinks they mean to pocket some of her goods."

"Ah, Dorothie, ever suspicious. I am ready, Humphrey," he said to his manservant, who had been helping him pack. The fellow, thickset and strong, held the horse steady as Robert hoisted himself onto the saddle.

"Safe travels, Master Marshall," said Humphrey.

"Mistress Ellyott is your mistress in my absence. See that you attend to her."

Humphrey cast a baleful glance at her from beneath the

brim of his woolen cap, tugged low to hide the smallpox scars upon his forehead. Reluctantly, he bowed in compliance before slouching off.

"I know not why he mislikes me so," she murmured to Robert.

"He mislikes everyone," he said.

"Then why keep him on?"

His expression turned grim. "He tended to my wife and her maidservant when they lay dying, when I was too ill and no one else would help. I value such loyalty."

"Of course."

"Take good care. I have heard that the constable has had a watch set. Apparently, a stranger has been seen in the area. And Bess, I see the look in your eyes. This fellow's presence has naught to do with Fulke's death. Do not torment yourself or your sister with any such ideas."

"Yes, Robert."

He glanced up at the house. "Do give my love to Margery."

Their niece was not fond of farewells; Bess suspected Margery peered at them now from behind a curtain.

"Be assured I will."

"Here. Kiss me goodbye." He leaned down from the saddle, and she raised up on her toes to peck him upon his cheek.

"Safe travels," she said. "And if you make time to enjoy a play, do not tell me when you return, for I shall be most jealous. Before I left the city, I heard of a new playwright, a fellow named Shakespeare. I had so wanted to see one of his plays."

"Plague continues apace in London, Bess. The theaters have been closed most of the year, from what I understand. The people should not gather in such tight quarters."

Bess grabbed his hand. "I'd not have you stricken with plague." She could not lose him, her dear brother, as well.

"I have accommodations at the edge of town, away from the pestilential air. Besides, I am not in London long enough for entertainments or for mingling."

"Yet you mingle with Mistress Tanner to woo her, do you not?"

"That is not the mingling I meant," he said. "You shall like her, I promise."

"What shall you say to her of Fulke's death?" she asked.

"Naught for now." Robert kissed her fingers, and she released her grip. "Keep away from trouble while I am gone."

"When do I ever cause trouble, Robin?"

"When you become overcurious, Bess. Which occurs too frequently for my comfort."

He tipped his hat and spurred his horse through the gate adjacent to the house, which led from the courtyard onto the road. Humphrey swung the broad door closed behind him. The resounding clang of the iron latch as it dropped into place was mournful, final.

★　★　★

"When will Uncle Marshall return?" asked Margery.

"No sooner than a week," said Bess. "You know how long his visits to London take."

Margery trailed after Bess as she moved through her

still room, collecting what she needed for her visit to the Anwickes' daughter—fresh linen bandaging, more of the plaster for her burn, the salve of powdered stavesacre seeds and vinegar for the girl's lice. Her niece's stony silence had lifted, but her spirits had not risen with them. Perhaps she had cared more for Fulke than Bess had suspected.

"Will Mother and I come here to live when he returns?" asked Margery. "Even if he brings a wife?"

"He would like you to. Even if he brings a wife. I cannot say, though, what your mother wishes to do." Bess reached for her niece's hand. The bones of Margery's fingers were delicate and her skin soft, and her hand fit easily within Bess's too large one. "I am sorry for your loss, Margery. Fulke—"

"My thanks, Aunt Bess," she said, her gaze steady but her hand trembling.

"Know that you may stay here with us as long as you desire. You can help me in the garden and the still room, if that would please you."

"I would welcome that," she replied. "There will come a time when my mother shall realize she wants me with her though, think you not?"

The pain in her words struck Bess deeply, and she placed a kiss upon her niece's head, the scent of lavender rising from the caul she wore over her dark hair. "My sister would be a great fool to not realize the value of your companionship."

Bess finished gathering her supplies and placed them carefully in her satchel. She bid her niece a fond farewell and departed for the Anwickes'. Rather than meet Mistress Stamford again, Bess chose the path that skirted town and followed the bend of the river. Once she was beyond the last houses, she could rejoin the highway.

The uneven, rocky surface of the track kept Bess from hurrying. A girl, carrying a basket of eggs in one hand and a squawking goose under the other arm, greeted her as they passed each other. Bess paused to watch the girl, wrestling with her goose to keep it from flapping free, as she walked toward town. There were always people, much like her, out and about. It seemed impossible that someone had not noticed an attack upon Fulke, if that was what had truly happened. Unless that was *not* what had truly happened, and she simply hoped for a different reason for his death than the one the coroner had proclaimed.

Bess resumed walking. The houses that stretched along the highway thinned, and she neared the large dairy that stood at a curve in the road. A servant, turning the cheese wheels resting upon the shelves of the dairy, watched Bess through the building's open door. Eyes everywhere.

She reached the road. Up ahead lay the Anwickes' cottage. A tendril of smoke rose from the opening where the smoke bay pierced the roof's ridge. Good news.

In front of the open door, Goodwife Anwicke had set out a stool and was busy hand-spinning thread in the sunshine. Her swaddled babe slept at her feet. A wiry lad with shocks of red hair sticking out below his cap mended a break in their woven wattle fencing, meant to keep rabbits from their garden and foxes from a handful of scrawny chickens. He had to be one of her other children. The lad looked over but decided Bess did not warrant his attention and resumed his chore.

The woman spotted Bess's approach, set down her spindle and distaff, and stood. "Widow Ellyott."

"How is your daughter's hand today? I came by yesterday, in the morning, but you were not at home."

"Ah, that. Well. I was in town." She cleared her throat. "And she is much better. She's gone with her father and brother to help the widow over the hill glean her field, else I'd have you see for yourself." She gestured toward the shadows that shrouded the interior of her cottage. "Would you come in?"

"My thanks, but no." She would not force this woman to extend hospitality when the Anwickes had none to spare. "I have brought more physic for her burn and a salve to keep the scalp clear of unwanted things."

She handed the items to the goodwife.

"Gramercy," she said. "I have heard the news about Master Crofton. He was your sister's husband, no?"

"Yes. He was."

The goodwife tutted. "Sad, that. Most sad. But only God can understand the workings of our hearts," she said. "And to think I saw him the morn of the day he died. Gives a person pause."

"You *did* see him," said Bess, her heart beginning to beat more rapidly. "I wondered if you had."

"I'd come to the window to take down the shutters and saw him on his horse. There." She pointed toward the roadway about one hundred feet distant. "Even with the fog, I could tell it was him, what with his bright green cloak. Always have admired that long cloak and his tall-crowned hat. Aye. Most handsome."

"Did you notice him with anyone? Did he appear upset?" The words tumbled from Bess's mouth, chasing one another in their haste to unearth answers.

"Upset because of what he planned to do?" she asked. "Did not seem so. Either then or when I noticed him in the afternoon. Of course, he was too far away to say for certain."

"You saw him in the afternoon as well?"

"Aye. Before you came to tend to my girl. He rode along the highway, hunched under his collar and hat because of the rain that had begun."

But he had never completed his journey home, and Bess had been near enough to where he had died to perchance have witnessed the crime. Gooseflesh prickled.

"It does amaze me, it does," Goodwife Anwicke was saying. "A man like that. With all the world in his hands. Now my husband, he's a one with troubles. Not a man like Master Crofton though. Well, except for that bother with them papists. And the arguments he has had with Master Stamford. Ugly, those."

"Who told you of arguments between them?"

Goodwife Anwicke eyed Bess warily. "My husband saw it for himself at the Cross Keys, but I've said enough. I know my place." Her swaddled babe let out a timely wail. "I've my baby to tend to. Good day to you, Widow Ellyott."

The woman returned to her child and her spinning. Feeling Goodwife Anwicke's gaze on her back, Bess returned to the road. She now had greater reason to expect that tonight she would confirm that there were two lines around Fulke's throat. Put there by Arthur Stamford, perhaps, who had argued with Fulke. Or the Langhams, who might wish to avenge the death of a husband and father.

*Margery, for your sake I pray I am wrong. But what if I am not?*

She looked south. In the distance stood the copse of trees where Fulke had been found. And beyond it, Sir Walter Howe's manor house, which commanded a sweeping view that encompassed fields, pasture, woods, and town. The Langhams' house was erected on an opposing rise. The building was less grand than the Howes' manor of brick and stone but impressive nonetheless, with its multiple stories of elaborate timber construction and whey-colored daub infill. Where it was rumored that Jesuits plotting the overthrow of the queen had hidden behind walls, the openings to their priest holes cleverly concealed. From all except Fulke, who had somehow learned of their location and played informant.

And who now was dead.

# CHAPTER 6

Bess climbed the staircase and strode into the upstairs parlor. Through the half-open door in the far wall, Bess could see Joan in Robert's chamber, leaning across his dressing table to peer into his looking glass. She had pulled the flap of her coif away from her cheek to reveal her scar. Frowning at the image reflected back at her, she brushed a fingertip across its ugly faded-red line.

On soft feet, Bess crossed to the doorway. "Joan?"

With a start, her servant looked over. "Mistress, you gave me a fright."

"You should not fret over your face." She had said as much many times. *I may as well tell myself to stop mourning my children and Martin.*

"Have you not anything to remove it?"

Bess ached for her servant who was more her friend, or the sister she wished she had. "That scar is too old for any of my physic to remedy. I am sorry."

With a parting glance at the looking glass, Joan let the flap of her coif fall into place against her cheek. "They may be old upon my skin, but they are fresh born every day upon my heart."

"You are fair and kind and honest, and that is all that should matter to anyone of worth."

One corner of her mouth lifted with a wry smile. "As soon as you find a man of such worth, prithee do let me know."

There had only ever been one such man, and Bess had married him.

"I came looking for you because I could use your help in the garden, Joan. I need to take slips of the marjoram." Tasks to keep her mind and hands busy until night fell.

"I would finish in here, Mistress, if you do not mind." She retied the strings of her coif. "I had come to turn Master Marshall's mattress and let myself become distracted by my vanity. Here I am, fretting over my face when the family is sorrowing. I am most pitiful."

"I would never think you pitiful, Joan. You have been stronger than I in so many ways," said Bess. "I need your strength and courage again. For I have another favor to beg of you."

"A favor?"

"I require your assistance in a delicate matter, and I would not have Mistress Margery learn of what I intend to do, for she would become alarmed," she said. "I would not have Humphrey learn of my plans either."

"A delicate matter you do not wish Humphrey to learn of?" asked Joan, a sly smile twitching the corner of her mouth. "Aye, Mistress, I shall gladly help."

* ★ *

"You are here because of Fulke Crofton, are you not, Constable?"

Bennett Langham stared Kit full in the face. They stood in the hall of his family's house, facing each other like combatants upon a field of war. Around five-and-twenty years of age, he was a handsome fellow, in the way of people who had long enjoyed the comforts of wealth. Proud in his purplish-red, padded silk doublet and matching paned trunk hose, a fine ruff at his neck, a beard trimmed in the latest fashion. His family may have suffered materially since the death of the patriarch four months past, but it seemed the young Master Langham intended to not allow their decline or their disgrace to show.

"I am here to ask if you are aware of the presence of a stranger in this area, Master Langham," Kit said. "He has been spotted near the priory ruins."

If he looked out the windows of this very room, he could spy the tumbled stones of the building, its remnants across the highway from the narrow lane that led to Langham Hall.

"I have seen no such fellow," said Bennett Langham, not a single twitch revealing if he lied or spoke truth. "I have been back home for only a week though. To tend to the Michaelmas rents due to us from our few tenants."

"Where is it you have come from?"

"From Bristol. My family has a minor shipping concern there."

"More than five miles." The queen had enacted a law forbidding Catholics to travel more than that distance without permission, which was difficult to obtain. "Do you have a pass allowing you to travel?"

"I do. I attend church in Bristol and am not deemed a Catholic there," he said. "Does that surprise you?"

"Yes, it does," Kit answered honestly.

"Well, if you have asked all your questions, I must get back to my rent books."

Bold and direct. He might like this fellow under other circumstances. "I am not finished, Master Langham. You say you've not seen this stranger, but I must ask if your family is aiding him."

"I know what it is you look for." The other man lifted his chin. "Search the house. My mother is at the market with a servant. You will not disturb her."

"I will send my cousin Gibb to do so." Kit inclined his head. "Many thanks."

Langham twitched at that; he'd not expected Kit to act upon the invitation. "If that is all—"

"You mentioned Fulke Crofton earlier," interrupted Kit. "Why did you think my visit has anything to do with him?"

"You are aware of the connection between him and my family. 'Tis the reason you send Gibb to search my house."

"I expect his death does not grieve you, Master Langham." He would be a far more forgiving man than most if it did.

"He was the stepfather of someone I am fond of. Further, I would never rejoice at any man's death," he answered directly. "To be found upon Sir Walter's land seems a fitting location for Master Crofton to make his end, though. A final insult to a man he despised."

*Oh?* "Do you know his reason?"

"Sir Walter and Fulke Crofton had a long-standing feud, Constable, which I am surprised you do not know about. I am not privy to the details. I am familiar only with the magnitude of their enmity." He considered for a moment. "If Master Crofton had become distraught enough to take his own life, where better to commit the act than upon grounds owned by a foe?"

★   ★   ★

Clouds covered the sun as it lowered to the horizon, dousing Bess's bedchamber in darkness. She lit her oil lamp with a rushlight brought from the kitchen and prayed it would not rain that night. The task before her would become more difficult if it did. For her to succeed, so much must fall properly into place, like the interlocking wheels of a clock mechanism.

She loosened the back ties of her gown with a long-handled hook and pulled the garment off over her head, stripping down to the dark kirtle beneath. She would wear it and her black cloak for her sole disguise, hoping she would blend in with the night. Now that the constable had set a regular watch, she would have to wait to depart until the watchman passed the house. He would do so about an hour after the curfew bell had been rung, which had occurred a few moments ago.

Bess had just finished strapping on her thick-soled mules when Margery abruptly stepped into the room.

"Aunt Bess, I was hoping to speak with you about the aqua vitae we plan to distill tomorrow . . ." Her gaze took in Bess's attire, pausing at the mules upon her feet. "What are you doing?"

"It is unwise for you to know my plans, Margery."

"Forgive me, but if it is unwise for me to know them, it is likely unwise for you to pursue them."

"Well said," said Bess. "However, if I tell you what I mean to do, you must promise to never inform Uncle Marshall or Humphrey."

"What would you not have them know?"

Bess collected her cloak from where it lay upon her mattress. "I suspect that your stepfather may not have died by his own hand, and I intend to prove so."

"You mean . . ." She stared at Bess. "Murder?"

Bess swung the cloak over her shoulders, clasping it about her neck, the wool scraping across her bare skin. No ruffs or partlets this even.

"All this may be a fancy of mine, Margery, but I believe I saw strange marks upon his throat and would confirm my memory."

"But you shall have to look at his body again in order to do so." She reached for Bess's elbow to clutch it. "The watch will stop you. You will be punished for breaking curfew. No, Aunt Bess."

"How can I not try?" Bess asked. "You stand to lose everything, save for the few items you inherited from your father. If the coroner has made an error in his ruling, it must be overturned."

There came a knock upon the door, and Joan entered. "Ah, Mistress Margery," she said cautiously.

"She knows," said Bess. "But why are you here now? 'Tis too early."

"The spare key to the garden gate, Mistress. I cannot find it," she whispered.

Because the watchman prowled the town streets, Bess had reasoned it safest for her to exit through the garden gate, away from sight. They needed that spare key to the gate, though, in order to let Bess out. Once the sun set, Humphrey secured all the exterior entrances.

"It is not on the hook by the entrance to the service rooms where it always hangs," said Joan. "Every day save this day, it seems."

"Jesu!" Bess cursed.

"Mistress." Joan held up her hand to quiet her. "Humphrey has just returned from the Cross Keys and sits below us in the hall, lingering over his supper. You do not wish him to hear."

"What does it matter if he hears? Without that key, my imprudent idea is doomed to failure."

"Aunt Bess," Margery interrupted. "I may know where to find the key to the gate lock."

★ ★ ★

"I care for none of this," said Joan.

"You shall not lose heart, shall you?" Bess squeezed her servant's hand.

"Mistress, your fingers are cold."

Because she was frightened. "I have never sought to dig up a person before." Or sought to examine a corpse. She dealt only with those who were unwell, not those who had passed away.

Yet now *she* had become a searcher of the dead.

The chamber door opened, and Margery hastened inside. "I have what I promised." She reached into the pocket hanging from her girdle and held aloft an iron key. "I remembered noticing earlier today that Humphrey had left his keys outside the still room door when he replenished your stock of firewood, Aunt Bess. He must have forgotten where he had left them, which is why he must have borrowed the spare set to lock the doors. These were still there when I went looking."

Bess reached for her and pulled her near, kissing her upon the cheek. "Bless you. But does he remain inside the house?"

"He was gone when I finished tidying the hall and seeing to the fire, Mistress," said Joan. "Just before I came back up here."

Humphrey would have retreated to his room above the stables. "Where is Quail? If he barks at me, Humphrey might hear and come to see what is amiss."

Margery handed the keys to Joan. "I shall find Quail and take him into my chamber and keep him quiet."

"Now we wait for the sound of the watchman," said Bess. And there it was at that moment, the steady rapping of his staff upon the street and the tang of his bell to mark his presence. Bess's heart raced, and she considered the women watching her. "Shall we proceed?"

Margery nodded and left to find Quail.

"Come." Bess signaled to Joan to follow. They departed the bedchamber and felt their way through the heavy darkness of the winding stairwell. The steps creaked more loudly than Bess ever recalled them doing, and the thick soles of her mules made her falter in her attempts to find the edges of the treads. "I would we could light a candle."

"Humphrey would come nosing about to see why a light shone in the hall at this hour," said Joan. "He'd hope to catch me wasting good candles when I was not to."

They reached the ground floor. Outside, the clouds had parted, and moonlight spilled through the hall's bay windows, easing their passage.

"Here, Mistress." Joan went ahead, into the alcove that led onto the rear door, to open it. Bess could smell the cool night air through the gap.

"Where can I find the spade I need?" she asked, walking outside. As she crossed the threshold, Bess knew there would be no turning back. She must go forward and pray none stopped her.

The outbuildings, which housed the garden implements, Robert's chickens, and Humphrey himself, stretched directly back from the right side of the main building. Joan pointed toward the last door in the line of doors. "The spade is there. Just inside the opening. Let me fetch the lantern."

Joan hurried off to the kitchen and returned with a lit horn-pane lantern she had draped with a kerchief to dim its glow. Bess would keep it covered until well free of town and prying eyes.

"'Tis the stable lantern, Mistress, and the best one for your purposes."

They proceeded, the gravel of the courtyard crunching beneath their feet. All of a sudden, barking sounded from within the house. Bess ducked behind a barrel. Glancing over her shoulder, she saw that Joan had frozen in place behind her. Bess's pulse thudded as she waited for Humphrey to lumber from his room, but he did not appear, and the barking halted.

"My thanks to you, Margery, for your help," Bess murmured, and Joan rushed to join her. "Hurry. We must hurry."

Joan opened the far door and fetched around for the spade. She handed it to Bess, who slid it upside down into her girdle, its point jabbing her in the ribs.

Joan undid the lock holding the latch in place and pushed the garden gate open. "Godspeed."

Tugging the cloak's hood about her cheeks, Bess passed through and out into the night.

★  ★  ★

Since Robert's house stood at the edge of town, Bess had not far to travel before she was beyond sight of most of the townsfolk. Curtains were drawn over windows, and in those without glass, the shutters had been put in place for the night. The good folk trusted the watchman to defend them against intruders and to alert Constable Harwoode and his men.

She left the houses behind her and chose a path hugging the stream that flowed from the river. Fulke had been buried not far from where his body had been found. The path, trodden into the grass and mud by countless feet that had gone that way to fish along the banks or swim in the waters on a hot summer's day, allowed her to avoid the long pole that barred entry into town on the southern road. She could also avoid the ruins of the plague house and the priory, which loomed ahead. She cared not to pass those stones in the daytime. She cared less to pass them in the gloom of night.

The water shimmered back the glow of the moon, which ducked beneath scattering clouds, forcing Bess to pause until it reappeared. Her slow progress exasperated her, but she would not speed along and risk injury or detection. Nor would she hurry so near to the stream. Water frightened her, and Bess believed she could drown in a puddle. Robert, in a moment of sport, had once teasingly threatened to toss her into the millpond, only to have her slip from his grasp and fall in. As she had plunged beneath the surface, the shock of the cold water had been enough to make her heart clench. She had churned the pond into a murky brown in her frantic attempts to gain purchase on the muddy bottom. And how she had gasped for air, only to draw in water. Robert had reached in to drag her onto the bank, his apologies desperately sincere while she retched onto the grass.

After which, there was no more teasing.

An owl hooted from a tree looming over the riverbank, and creatures scuttled among the sticks and fallen leaves. So long as one of those creatures was not a rat, she did not mind their company. Bess passed the location of the bar and scrambled up the incline toward the road, happy to be away from the water. Her feet slipped on the damp grass, and the spade repeatedly stabbed into her side. In the morning, Bess suspected, she would find a bruise.

Out here, beyond the outermost limits of the town, the whitewashed stones that lined the road grew sparse and came to an end. She did not require their assistance to help her find the way; she removed the kerchief she'd thrown over the lantern and cast its light upon the lane. Up ahead rose the dead tree beyond the crossroads, its trunk charred and split by a lightning strike, its branches twisted arms reaching into the night sky. Coming nearer, Bess could see the mound of freshly tilled dirt that covered Fulke's body.

She placed the lantern upon the ground near his grave and took out the spade. Kneeling, she started to dig. The soil was soft and the work quick; the men had done a poor job and had not buried him deeply. Good fortune was with her, for she had chosen the proper end to start with and soon located the sheet wound about her brother-in-law's torso and head.

"Oh, Fulke. God rest you." She pressed a hand to the cloth and felt the outlines of his face beneath. Her gorge rose, and she swallowed hard. "And God help me."

Lacking a knife—too late to wish she had been wiser and thought to bring one—she used the point of the spade to tear a hole in the winding sheet. Grabbing the opening, Bess split the material away. Fulke's face was taking on a sickly greenish hue, and his mouth hung open, the rigors of death stiffening his body. Hastily, she concealed his head with the torn edge of the sheet.

Careful to avoid touching his cold skin with her bare fingertips, Bess peeled back the material to reveal his throat. She raised the lantern to examine it. There were two red lines gone purple, one much darker than the other and slicing across the midline of his neck. Just as she had recalled. A thin, deep line that had not been left by the thick rope used to suspend his body from a tree. Rather, the sort of line that would result from a length of twine wrapped around his neck and pulled tightly, choking off his air.

Bess rocked back on her heels. Here was the proof she had sought. A heinous crime had been committed, and the man who had killed Fulke was out there, somewhere.

She scooped dirt back onto his body, returning the mound to its prior condition as best she could.

Restoring the spade to her girdle, she retraced her steps along the path. Her thoughts were sour. First Martin killed, and now Fulke.

She could not say when she finally realized that the night sounds along the stream did not now belong only to creatures. She increased her pace. Were the noises the footfalls of a person? They could be. Extinguishing the lantern flame, she scurried for the road and began to run. She panted for breath and could not hear if the footsteps pursued her. Stumbling upon a hole in the highway, she fell to her knees, the lantern flying from her grasp.

*Dear God. Dear God!*

She scrambled to her feet, her ankle protesting. Wincing, she hobbled forward. She would not retrieve the lantern. She had to get away.

Bess arrived at the untended bar and scrabbled underneath it. Taking possibly misguided comfort from the barrier between her and her pursuer, she dared look back. But all she saw were the shadow-deep stones of the priory, the haunted remains of the burned plague house, and the far-off glow of a torch burning at the gates of Highcombe Manor.

She released a breath. She would have to concoct a clever story about what had happened to that lantern, should Humphrey ask after it.

With a relieved laugh, Bess turned just as a light was thrust into her face, blinding her.

# CHAPTER 7

Kit lifted the lantern. The woman's hood was pulled taut about her face. If it *was* a woman beneath the enveloping clothing.

He withdrew his dagger, the blade gleaming in the light. "What do you here?"

"Do not stab me," the person croaked, the hood falling away. "I can explain."

*Bloody* . . . Kit lowered the lantern. "I would take great pleasure in hearing your explanation, Mistress Ellyott."

"It is *you* who has been following me."

"Following you?" he asked. "I would have been, had I known you were out here, skulking around after curfew."

"I am not skulking."

"Then tell me what it is you *are* doing."

She lifted her chin, but her eyes—those brown eyes Gibb so admired—had difficulty meeting his. "I went to visit my brother-in-law's grave. To mourn over him."

He did not believe her story for a moment.

"A vagrant has been spotted near here," he said, sheathing

his dagger. Unfortunately, Gibb had not located the fellow's hiding place, and the watch had, so far, also not uncovered the man. "You risk your life by walking about at night." He cocked his head and considered her. "Unless you intend to discover this fellow's whereabouts yourself in order to obtain reward from the Crown."

As Fulke Crofton had done when he had informed upon the Langhams. It would be difficult this time to link the vagrant's presence to the Langhams, however; Gibb had not found a fresh priest hole at Langham Hall either.

"How might I gain reward by discovering the whereabouts of some vagabond, Constable?" she asked.

"He is rumored to be a Jesuit. Need I say more?"

His reply startled her into silence. But silence, for Mistress Ellyott, did not appear to ever last long.

"No," she replied. "Nonetheless, the vagabond's identity is not my concern. As I said, Constable, I went to visit Fulke's grave. I risked being prevented from my task should I venture there during the day."

So she intended to continue with her tale. Which made him question all the more what it was she sought to hide. "I am curious how the spade you have tucked at your waist assisted your visit."

A blush stole across her cheeks, and she pressed her lips together.

"The law does not look kindly upon attempts to unearth the body of a criminal," he said.

She wrapped her cloak tightly about her. "You will find Fulke where the churchwarden and his men left him, Constable. For how would I, a lone woman, be able to haul him away?" she asked bitterly. "Go see for yourself, if you do not believe me."

"If I were a superstitious fellow, I would think you plotted some unholy scheme. Mistress Ellyott, you must admit your actions are strange."

"I am an herbalist, not a witch, Constable Harwoode. I plot no unholy scheme."

"Then be truthful about the reason you went to his grave," he said, shifting to a more comfortable stance. "I can stand here however long is required."

She returned his stare. He would add fearless to the attributes he had ascribed to her. And her eyes were fine, even in dim lantern light.

"Meet me at his grave in the morning," she said. "Two hours past sunrise, and I will show you my response."

"A prospect I am looking forward to. Come." He took her elbow. "Let me guide you home. I'd not wish you to become lost upon the way and wander off again."

"You will not arrest me for breaking curfew?"

"I find myself astonishingly generous this night."

She accompanied him without protest. When they arrived, he was not at all surprised that the servant who opened the door was fully dressed.

"I will speak with you and Master Marshall on the morrow," he said to Mistress Ellyott.

"My brother has gone to London."

Leaving her free to ramble as she pleased. "Do not break curfew again, Mistress. I will not be so gracious a second time. And you," he said to her servant, "keep her here lest I lock you both in the stocks."

★　★　★

*"Bess . . ."*

*His voice was a raspy whisper, like the rustle of dry leaves, as the sound fought to leave his throat.*

*"Bess."*

*"Hush, my darling."* *She sat upon the floor by the settle and gripped his hand. It was clammy, and her heart seized with the knowledge he was dying.*

*He tried to reach up to dry her tears, but he could not lift his hand. The poison, the purging, had weakened him. Nothing she had given him had healed the ill Laurence had wrought.*

*"Do not,"* *he croaked.* *"Do not blame . . ."*

*"Hush."*

*"Bess . . . Laurence . . ."*

*His life left his body on a breath of air. He was gone.*

*She heard Joan wail into her apron. Her own sobs joined her servant's, her tears streaming as she raised her eyes to look upon him. But his face. His face had changed, twisted, turned into Fulke's face.*

*She recoiled, a cry of alarm sticking in her throat.*

Bess woke with a start, her heart pounding, and sat upright. The nub of a candle burned at her bedside. Its dim light showed the clothes she had hastily discarded after returning from Fulke's grave and telling Joan and Margery the grim news. As though doffing her kirtle and cloak could rid her of the reality of Fulke's death.

"Dearest Lord. Blessed Jesus. What have I done?"

She snuffed the flame and dropped back against her pillows, dragging the sheets and the blanket up about her body. The image of the deep bruising line around Fulke's throat filled her mind. She had searched the dead and had discovered the ugly truth. *That* was what she had done. Learned afresh the evils of the world.

On the morrow, she would have to persuade the constable to believe her conclusions. And that she intended no "unholy schemes" but sought only the truth. And justice.

★　★　★

"Mistress, have you taken the lantern that usually hangs by the stable door?" Humphrey, his head slightly bowed, peered up at Bess. "It is gone and that . . . and Joan says she does not know what has happened to it."

Bess stood in the passageway, readying herself to visit Dorothie and deliver her news. Out of the corner of her eye, she noticed Joan in the parlor to her left, eavesdropping.

No clever explanation came to her mind. "I am in a hurry, Humphrey. If you cannot locate this missing lantern, I will have my brother replace it when he returns."

"Aye, Mistress." Frowning, he bowed and shuffled off through the hall.

Joan rushed into the passageway to help fasten Bess's hat upon her coif. Her cloak hung near the door. Joan had cleaned the dirt from it before the sun had risen that morn, wiping away the evidence of Bess's late-night excursion.

"Take care, Mistress."

"Do not fret over the constable's threats to place us in the stocks. The dog that barks does not bite."

"I am not so troubled by him." Her world-weary eyes reflected that they had entered upon a freshly dark world. "Take care."

"And *you* do not permit Humphrey to bully you."

Joan allowed herself a smile. "Have I ever?"

The walk to Dorothie's house required passing through town and taking the eastern road. Bess felt eyes upon her as she strode briskly across the market square. Mistress Stamford stared from her shop window. The baker from whom they bought their bread returned her greeting with a blank look.

So this was how matters would be.

She arrived at Dorothie's house, a modest but comfortable manor built of stone and timber-framing, and rapped hard upon the portal. Her pounding was answered by a man Bess did not recognize, who squared his shoulders beneath his quilted jacket and glared.

"I must speak with Mistress Crofton. I am her sister."

He had narrow-set eyes and weather-worn skin. "I have been told to allow none to enter while the queen's work is under way."

"I beg you, sir, let me in," she said. "My errand is most urgent."

He grunted and moved aside. "She is in her hall, weeping and cursing."

Bess heard Dorothie then, shouting at someone to put down an item.

Thanking the fellow, Bess hurried through the vestibule and into the hall to her left. Her sister was no longer weeping but pounding fists against a bandy-legged man who held a stack of table linens in his arms.

"Put those back in the trunk now!" she demanded. "I have told you over and over that I own but four cloths plus ten linen napkins. You need not count them!"

"Dorothie!" Bess rushed to her side and took hold of her arm. "My apologies, she is distressed."

The man glowered and marched the linens over to the massive hall table, where every object once contained within chests and trunks was spread across its surface.

"Come away," said Bess, putting her arm around Dorothie's waist. "Have your servant bring you some malmsey to restore your strength, and we shall sit in your parlor until you are recovered."

"There are men in my parlor, too," she said, sniffling. She pulled a handkerchief from her pocket. "And I shall not ever recover." She blew her nose and looked at Bess above its square of linen. "You are here with news. Tell me what you found."

"Let us go to the parlor and sit. Perhaps we can convince the fellow within to leave us in peace."

Dorothie's manservant, Roland, stood by the set of parlor windows that overlooked the side garden, the green outside broken into diamond shapes by the panes of glass. He was tall and sober, with a jutting chin and intense clear eyes, which broke off from watching another of the Crown's men paw through Dorothie's cupboard to observe their arrival.

"Roland, have Lucy bring a glass of malmsey for your mistress," said Bess.

Owning excellent manners, far better than most servants one might employ in this area of the country, he gave a polite bow and glided out of the room.

"Sir, if you could but leave us for a short while," Bess said to the man who'd not paused in his inspection of the cupboard. "Out of respect for the widow."

"Don't take nothin'," he grumbled and departed. Bess followed him to make certain he did not linger outside the parlor and shut the door.

Dorothie dropped onto the crimson-painted chair by the window and looked out it. From here, if she craned her neck, she could see the dead tree that spread its deformed branches above Fulke's grave. Bess crossed to the curtains and drew them closed; her sister did not need to look upon such a sight.

"What did you discover?" she asked.

"It is as I thought," said Bess. She straightened her sister's coif, which she had knocked awry, and tucked a loose strand of hair beneath its edge. "There are two lines upon his neck."

Dorothie gasped. "Oh, why, Elizabeth, did this ever have to happen? Does Margery know?"

"Aye. She took the news passing well."

Fingertips tapped upon the door, and Lucy entered with two glasses of malmsey, the wine a deep tawny hue in the parlor's gloom. "They'd not let me bring a tray to serve you with, Mistress. They say I shall steal it away!"

Bess took a glass from her.

"'Tis dreadful," the girl sniveled. "They be in the buttery now, drinking the cider you just put up."

Dorothie snatched the other glass, sloshing wine to the rim, and took a long drink. "See, Elizabeth? See? They mean to rob me before that villain Wat Howe takes all that remains!"

"Where am I to go?" asked Lucy. "Roland has a place. He's told me, he has. A house he has inherited in distant Suffolk. And proud he is of it. But what am I to do? None will have me as a servant after this, and I've no family to take me in."

"Go to, Lucy." Dorothie swatted at the air. "I care not for your concerns when I and my children will be in the gutter as well."

Sobbing into her apron, Lucy dashed from the room.

"You need not be so harsh," said Bess. "She has every reason to fear for a position when you cannot provide her a reference, should your situation stand."

Abruptly, Dorothie set down her glass and stood. She contemplated the room. "What shall I do without my things, Elizabeth?"

Wandering about the space, she ran a hand down her velvet curtain, drew fingers across the trestle table set against the wall. She opened the carved oak box that sat upon its surface. The box served no function but to be admired, which was, for Dorothie, the greatest purpose of all. Next, she rubbed at a dull spot on a brass candlestick and fluffed the goose-feather cushions that lined the settle.

Bess and Dorothie and Robert had come far from the life they had all led in Oxford, the children of a scholar who had spent his earnings upon books and manuscripts. Leaving Mother to replace worn hems and collars and cuffs rather than purchase new clothing with money she did not have.

Dorothie looked at Bess. "How did you leave so much behind in London without a care?"

"I have never claimed I did not care, Dorothie."

Bess had winnowed the contents of her house to what could be contained within a few compact trunks on the back of a wagon. It had been hired with the proceeds from selling all the rest. A speedy flight had been her goal. Certes, there were moments she missed her embroidered linens and carpets, pewter tableware, and imported glasses. Not as much as Dorothie would miss her possessions, however.

Suddenly, her sister's eyes brightened. "But now, after what you have discovered, now I may be able to keep all my goods. Might I not?"

"Only should I convince the constable of what I believe, and then *he* must convince the coroner to reverse his ruling. No easy task."

"But you shall try."

She could not guess what he might think when she showed him Fulke's body. "I will do what I can."

Dorothie took the untouched glass of malmsey from Bess's hand. "'Tis Arthur Stamford. I know. They fought at the Cross Keys the night before Fulke died."

"I have heard about their arguments."

"They had taken to quarrels of late. Over the wool Fulke had sold him. Claiming it was inferior. Master Stamford only said that to defend why he'd not repaid the credit Fulke had extended to him. Fulke warned him that he would bring a suit to see that debt repaid. 'Twas what Fulke planned that . . . that awful day. To go to Devizes to bring a suit against Arthur Stamford." Dorothie exhaled a sob. "Wool! For that, I have lost a husband! The more I think upon it, the more I know Arthur Stamford killed Fulke. And you must get that constable to believe so, Elizabeth."

"I will tell him what you have said and show him what I have seen. That is all I can promise." Bess leaned down to kiss her sister upon her forehead. "I shall visit again soon."

She left the parlor. In the hall beyond, Roland snapped

to attention, rotating sharply upon his heel to march ahead of her to the front door, which he opened for her.

Outside, Bess consulted the sun, which peeked between clouds. It was time for her meeting with the constable.

★ ★ ★

He was waiting for her at the crossroads, his face stern beneath the hat he wore.

When she reached him, he briefly lifted it in greeting. "You have no spade with you this morn."

"It appears I have forgotten." She nodded at the scabbard holding his dagger. "Perhaps you will sacrifice your blade for what I have to show you. The digging is not difficult. Most could be accomplished with your hands."

He nodded and extended his arm toward the base of the tree. "After you."

By the head of Fulke's gave, she lowered to her knees. Off to her left, a cow stood at the edge of a field and languidly watched them.

"Here, Constable Harwoode. Dig here, if you will."

Kneeling across from her, Kit Harwoode removed his dagger and thrust it into the loose dirt. Soon, he set it down and used his gloved hands instead to pile dirt to one side, making a hole. The winding cloth, beginning to stain with the body's secretions, quickly came into view.

"Allow me," she said, leaning over to unwind the strip of cloth that would reveal Fulke's throat. It had started to bloat. "Note the two lines that cross his skin. Two lines of differing thickness, and one, the lower one, deeper and darker. To me, that suggests it is the mark of the rope or twine that choked my brother-in-law to death."

He examined the lines, his brow furrowing. "A line not caused by a thick hanging rope," he said. "I owe you an apology, Mistress. For doubting your sister's belief that a crime might have been committed."

Bess nodded her thanks. "I came here last night to confirm what I had observed when we found him," she said. "Not to practice unholy schemes."

"Another apology for thinking I might need to accuse you of witchcraft." The constable sat back upon his heels. "The coroner had to have seen these lines."

She re-covered Fulke's neck with the cloth. "If he made note of them, why did he not conclude as we have done?"

Constable Harwoode exhaled and returned his dagger to its sheath. "I will not share my opinion of his skills with you."

He pushed the pile of dirt onto the hole he had opened and patted it down. He rose, and so did she.

"Prithee, persuade the coroner to reverse his finding," she said. "There is this proof upon Fulke's neck, and also I have learned that the night before he died, Fulke argued with Arthur Stamford. He is the draper whose shop is near to the market cross. They argued at the Cross Keys. I suspect the fight was due to my brother-in-law's plans to go to Devizes to employ a solicitor over a debt Master Stamford owed him."

The constable brushed his hands together, swiping dirt from his gloves. "Leave this matter to me."

Not the reassurance she sought. "Tell me I have convinced you, Constable."

"You have given me much to think on," he answered.

"And I *will* think upon it, Mistress. You can rely on that. But this task is mine to undertake. Not yours."

His gaze slid to Fulke's grave, taking in the mound of dirt that once again concealed the sorry visage of her brother-in-law.

*Searcher of the dead.* Fulke had not died by his own hand. And Martin had not perished from the plague.

"When my husband died, an old woman came to look upon his body for pustules. In the city—London, that is— these poor women are employed to make a count of the plague victims. Only the most desperate embark upon such a deadly task. These women are called 'searchers of the dead.'" She did not know why she wished to tell him this, but she continued anyway. "I have come to understand a little of how they must feel at the execution of their task. To look upon the dead with such unconcern for the person who once gave breath and warmth to a gone-cold shell—"

She shuddered. The constable placed an arm about her shoulders and drew her away from Fulke's grave. She welcomed the comfort of his touch.

"Come, Mistress Ellyott. Do not compare yourself to that old woman. You are not at all like her."

"Am I not, Constable?"

His eyes were kind as they studied her. "I see no such woman here."

A flush spread in response to his words, alarming her. She jerked free from his embrace. "I must hasten home, Constable. They will be missing me."

Hiking her skirts, she scrambled over to the road and broke into a run.

# CHAPTER 8

Bess leaned against the far garden wall and stretched her feet, revealing her stocking-covered ankles beyond the hem of her petticoat. She sat in a flat area of the tended garden bed, where in the summer gillyflowers and Madonna lilies bloomed, in order to think. Or not to think, but rather to drift. Church bells tolled the hour. The neighbor's infant daughter cried over some hurt, speedily attended to. Across the courtyard, Humphrey perched upon a stool in the courtyard, scrubbing feed buckets clean, occasionally pausing to tut at one of the chickens. When he appeared so affectionate toward the birds, she felt a trifle sorry that one or more of them would become meals during the winter ahead. In any other household, tending to the chickens would be Joan's task. But Robert's manservant guarded those birds as attentively as the queen's Master of the Jewel House guarded its contents. A streak of sentimentality in a fellow who could be so surprisingly angry about the lantern she'd been forced to discard.

With a sigh, Bess tilted her head back to watch a hawk circle in the cloud-filled sky. To listen to the clatter of wheels out on the roadway beyond the courtyard gate. She should be at her work, as she had much to do. She had shown the constable the lines upon Fulke's throat and told him about the argument between Fulke and Master Stamford. He had said he would attend to what he had learned.

Truth be told, however, she had her doubts about the constable's willingness to be thorough. After all, his cousin stood to gain from Fulke's suicide. Sir Walter Howe may be displeased to have those goods—which included a warehouse filled with surpassingly fine wool, despite Arthur Stamford's claims otherwise—snatched away by something so inconvenient as the truth. So, what would Kit Harwoode do—choose family obligations or the proper execution of justice?

*And what, Bess, will* you *do with what you felt when his arm encircled you?*

Forget. No doubt at all. Forget.

The back door opened, and Margery stepped through. Humphrey lifted his cap as she passed.

"My first thought should have been that I would find you out here, Aunt Bess." She went to the far corner of the garden to collect another stool, which she placed alongside Bess's. "How fares my mother?"

Her niece possessed a proper amount of decorum and kept her feet tucked beneath her skirts. *Mayhap I remain a trifle difficult to govern.* Certes, Robert would say as much.

"Better than I expected." Bess sat up straight and slid her feet toward the stool, flicking the hem of her petticoat over her ankles. "She holds great faith that I . . . that the constable will prove the manner of your stepfather's death and your family will not lose all you own."

"Has the constable promised to investigate?"

'Twas the question of the moment. "I would that I knew for certain."

The back door opened again, and Joan hurried across the courtyard to Bess and Margery.

"Mistress," she bobbed a hasty curtsy. "Bennett Langham has come. To speak with Mistress Margery."

Standing, Bess glanced at her niece, whose cheeks had gone pink.

"I pray you do not mind that I speak with him, Aunt Bess," said Margery, the set of her face indicating she was willing to defy Bess should her aunt refuse the meeting.

Only because Robert was not at home would Bennett Langham dare come there. Robert supported Dorothie's plans to wed Margery elsewhere. The most recent candidate was a distant cousin of theirs, a curate in need of a new wife to mind his four young children. He had visited once to meet Margery. Bess appreciated the practicality of the potential union, but she could not help feeling that Margery had been put on display like a ewe or a filly on market day. Margery had felt likewise.

However, an entanglement between Margery and a Langham would never do.

"Your mother would not be pleased with me if I permit this visit, Margery," Bess said.

Margery clung to Bess's arm. "*I* will not tell her. And Joan will not tell her either. Will you, Joan?"

Joan shook her head. Her scars, her past miseries had not stopped her from being tender-hearted when it came to love. "I will not speak, Mistress Margery, but what of . . . ?" She twitched her head to indicate Humphrey.

"He will tell my brother, who will in turn inform your mother," Bess said to Margery.

"I am willing to chance that," she said. "Prithee, Aunt Bess. For a brief few minutes only."

Bess relented. Her niece's pleadings ever weakened her defenses as surely as a battering ram, and she knew it. "Under my supervision."

Margery dashed off, and Bess rushed after her.

As she entered the parlor, Bennett Langham made a leg. "Mistress Ellyott."

She could not fault his manners or his appearance. He was a tall and handsome fellow. She also thought him sensible and genuinely affectionate toward her niece. Which softened Bess's heart as much as Margery's pleadings had done.

"Good day to you, Master Langham. What brings you here?" Bess asked.

"I would offer you condolences on the loss of your brother-in-law." He spoke the words to her, but his gaze did not leave Margery's face. "And to Mistress Margery on the loss of her stepfather. My mother extends her good wishes as well."

'Twas generous, indeed, for the woman who must condemn Fulke for the death of her husband to extend good wishes.

"My thanks," said Bess. "You are both most kind."

"I would be less than honest to pretend I feel grief over Master Crofton's death," he said. "But, upon my honor, I did not wish harm to befall him."

"I am glad to hear you say so."

"Condolences are not the sole reason I have come," he

said. "The constable and his cousin visited us at Langham Hall yesterday."

"Why?" asked Margery fretfully.

"A vagrant has been seen in the area," he answered.

"Ah." Bess regarded Bennett Langham. She saw resolve in his bearing. And secrecy. "Does the constable suspect you of hiding this fellow? He has told me the vagrant is rumored to be a Jesuit."

"You understand." He smiled softly at Margery. "It is unwise for you to be seen in my company. At such a time."

"No, Bennett." She made to grasp his hand but quickly thought better of the impulse. "Did they find anything? No, for you would not be free to walk about if they had."

"I will see that my niece heeds your advice, Master Langham. Fare you well."

He bowed and departed. Bess grabbed Margery's hand to keep her from following.

"I thought you liked him," said her niece.

"My question had naught to do with whether or not I like him," Bess said. "And Bennett was not angered by it."

"He should have been, since you want to discover if he had a reason to fear my stepfather. Because of some vagrant who might be a priest," she said. "And now that you have tried to convince the constable that my stepfather was murdered, he will suspect Bennett."

Bess eyed her. "Do *you* fear that Bennett could be responsible?"

With a jerk of her chin, Margery marched from the room. Answer enough.

★  ★  ★

"I and my jury have made our ruling. You were there, Constable," said the coroner. "I must presume Mistress Crofton has come to you, begging pity for her situation."

The fellow, whom Kit had found in the man's privy office, wrapped his long black robe tighter about his bones to ward off the room's chill. *If he would bring a chafing dish set with hot coals into the room, he might not be so cold.* Kit suspected the coroner did not lack the funds to warm the space; he merely preferred the moral comforts of being a miser.

"Mistress Crofton has not come to me," said Kit. "I act on information I have learned from Mistress Ellyott."

"Ah, her." The coroner lifted an eyebrow. "The herbalist."

Kit was thankful he did not call her a witch.

"How well did you examine Fulke Crofton's neck?" he asked.

The coroner frowned. "I saw that it had been bruised from the rope. No one had slit it."

*Droll.* "I have learned that Master Crofton had numerous enemies. Yet you did not demand that those assembled reveal the name of any who might wish to kill him."

"Why might I do so when it was clear the man had killed himself?"

"There were two lines, Crowner. Two distinct lines about his throat made from two very different cords," said Kit. "I have seen them myself this morning," he added before the man could interrupt.

The coroner looked appalled. "You dug up the fellow to look upon his neck?"

"Did you notice the two lines?"

"This is impertinent. I always did doubt your cousin's idea to recommend you for the post of constable, Master Harwoode, as did several of the other burgesses. They consented only because Sir Walter insisted." His frown became a deep scowl that creased his face. "'Tis a blessing you serve for only two years."

Wat might agree. "And what of Master Crofton's hat?"

"There was no hat."

"Precisely so, yet he left the house that morning with one upon his head. My men have searched for it and not found it."

The coroner dismissed Kit's remark with a wave of his hand. "Someone came along and found it near the body. A valuable item like a fine hat could be worth fifteen, twenty shillings."

"So this person stole the hat but did not pause to take anything else from the body."

"They had not the stomach for it. They grabbed up the hat and ran." The coroner smirked, pleased to have an answer. "'Tis simple enough to reason out, Constable."

Kit scowled. It was clear he would have to identify the killer before he could convince the coroner to overturn his ruling. The man would never admit to a mistake unless forced to.

★   ★   ★

An hour after Bennett's visit, Margery remained closeted in the chamber she borrowed. She had not responded to Bess's pleas to come out.

*She is young and longs to follow her heart. As I once did.*

"Ah, Margery. I pray Bennett is worthy of your love."

Bess opened the door to the still room. The various aromas she could always conjure whenever she thought of them—those of fennel and marjoram, wormwood and lavender, licorice and aniseed, and so many others—greeted her. Bess had been instructing Margery on the secrets of distillation, a woman's work should she be able to afford such fine equipment as filled this room. They had planned to make aqua vitae today, the most important of waters. Perhaps if Margery heard Bess working in the still room, she might repent of her upset and join Bess.

Bess slid wide the shutters covering the unglazed windows, letting in the light. Tying on a heavy holland apron, she proceeded to select the ingredients she required. The "water of life" was meant to ease aches in the bones and calm the symptoms of cold sickness. Bess had once cured a neighbor's child of the colic with aqua vitae. It had done nothing to ease the catarrh when Bess's daughters had first taken ill, however. Nor had the powders of peppers and caraway seeds healed their coughs as they had worsened. She had failed them, and now she fought her self-doubt. Yet she would not abandon the work that gave her life meaning and solace.

"Mistress."

Bess had not heard Joan's tap upon the doorframe.

"You are called to Langham Hall," said Joan. "One of Mistress Langham's kitchen servants has cut her hand and craves your skills."

"Why does she not send for the surgeon?"

"I asked the same of the man who brought the message,"

she said. "He says the girl is afraid of the surgeon. She blames him for killing her mother when he tried to remove a great stone in the woman's bladder and she bled to death."

Bess gazed longingly at her still. The preparation of the aqua vitae would have to wait.

"Joan, help me gather my salve of turpentine and cloves. And I shall have need of my flaxen thread and a set of clean stitching quills."

Bess stripped off her apron and folded it aside. How peculiar the timing of this request, when Bennett had been to their house just an hour earlier. But to presume a servant had intentionally cut herself so that Bess could be summoned to Langham Hall was preposterous.

Nonetheless, as she collected her squares of linen bandaging, she found herself intrigued. Most intrigued.

★ ★ ★

"The tavern is not open yet, Constable Harwoode," said the owner, standing inside the doorway. "Or are you here to see our Marcye?"

Master Johnes had a lean face and eyes as sharp as his daughter's, making him look more the part of a schoolmaster than a tavern keeper. He glanced over his shoulder at Marcye, who scrubbed tables and pretended to not be looking their way.

"She is a fair girl," said Kit. "As fair as Marcye is, though, I am here to speak with you, Master Johnes."

"Well, you know you'd be welcome to share a meal with us any a night, Constable, should you desire to," he said.

"Marcye, fetch some of the boiled hare for the constable. And a spoon. The constable has not brought his own."

Blushing, she hurried off for the tavern's kitchen. Kit and her father crossed the empty room to a table by the window.

With a groan, Master Johnes lowered himself to the table's bench. He bent down to rub his knees. He noticed Kit looking. "These old bones." He lifted an eyebrow. "Which is why I need a son to take over this place."

*A son like me.* "Your other daughters' husbands have no interest?"

"Not the ones they've married." He sighed. "You know Marcye lost her husband in the Low Countries. I had hopes for that one. Ah, well."

His daughter returned with two pottery bowls of food, one for each of them, dipped a curtsy, and walked off. But not too far.

"Feel free to speak," said the tavern keeper. "You've no need to mind her. She works in a tavern. She knows how to keep secrets."

Kit took a bite of the hare, swimming in a broth flavored with herbs and onions and currants. "Very good," he said to Master Johnes. Far better than the typical fare.

The man smiled. "From our own dinner, Constable. Not what I'd serve the usual sort who come in here and get too drunk to enjoy my wife's cooking."

After several bites—he'd not eaten more than a meager hunk of cheat bread to break his fast that morning, and he was hungry—Kit set down the spoon. "I would ask you about Master Crofton."

"Ah." Master Johnes finished chewing. "But I do not understand how his death is a matter for you to be concerned with."

"Let us just say I am curious about a matter."

The tavern keeper waved his spoon to encourage Kit to continue and then bent to scooping up his meal.

"I have heard that he had an argument with a fellow the night before he died," said Kit. "Here at the Cross Keys."

"Aye, *that* night. What a great fight there was." Master Johnes squinted at Kit. "'Tis lucky for me you did not hear of it, for I'd have had to pay a terrible fine!"

"We shall let that pass."

The other man tipped his cap at Kit. "Well, as to Crofton, he was drinking more than he ought. My wife told me to not refill his tankard, but a sale is a sale. I should have listened." He nibbled more of the hare, looking reflective as he chewed. "'Twas about halfway through his third . . . mayhap fourth tankard that all that talk of going to Devizes for an 'important' meeting started. That fluffed some fur."

"What did he say about this meeting?"

"He need not say much. Everyone knew he was going there to meet with a solicitor about his complaint against Stamford."

As Mistress Ellyott had said. "Details?"

"He and Stamford have been battling, they have, ever since Crofton became the largest wool merchant in this area. Jealous, Stamford was. Aye." Master Johnes nodded sagely.

"Tell me about this complaint," Kit prodded.

"Well, Stamford owed Crofton money. He'd been crediting Stamford for the wool the fellow was buying to supply his weavers in Chippenham. I heard, though, that Stamford had fallen behind on his payments. An investment had failed and left him short of funds. Rather than entreat Crofton for new terms, Stamford accused him of selling inferior wool not worth the price charged. Worse still, he was trying to convince other clothiers and weavers to not buy from Crofton, too," he said, shaking his head over the schemes of men. "That is what I've heard, Constable. Though there may have been some merit to Stamford's claims. Crofton never accused him of slander, now, did he? I was never much fond of Crofton, 'tis certain, for he had a foul temper. Could start a fight with a painted image of a saint."

"So Crofton's meeting in Devizes was a threat to Stamford." Stamford's standing as a merchant in this town would be damaged if such a suit came to pass and Stamford faulted. If he stood accused of not paying his debts, only a fool would wish to work with him. But was that sufficient reason to kill?

Master Johnes wiped food residue from his mouth with the backs of his fingers. "Stamford was furious that night. Threw his tankard, he did! A bad aim, luckily for Crofton's skull," he said. "Stamford's not free of those debts, though, as your good cousin Sir Walter has taken them over along with the rest of Crofton's goods. Though Sir Walter might be forgiving, as he and Stamford are mates."

"Master Johnes, as you have mentioned Sir Walter, what do you know of a dispute between him and Fulke Crofton?"

"Oh, that! Sir Walter desired a slice of land that Crofton owned. Hard by the river. But Crofton would not sell it. Would not even lease it to him. I'd heard there had been threats leveled," he said. "But you did not hear about those threats from me, Kit Harwoode. I'd not have your cousin call me a gossip and have you slap me in the stocks. Or worse."

"I shall say naught to him." Wat would not get that land though. The law left it and Crofton's empty house in his wife's hands. Frustrating Wat, no doubt.

"Wonder if Mistress Crofton will be prepared to deal, as she will be in need of money now," the tavern keeper mused.

*Kit, you are stupid.* Certes, she would deal, and Wat would win again.

"So to be clear," said Kit, "the night before Fulke Crofton died, Stamford was in this tavern and heard Crofton boast of his plan to go to Devizes the next morning." The journey a possible opportunity for Stamford to accost Crofton at a distance from town.

Master Johnes narrowed his gaze. "Why ask you all these questions, Constable? You make me think Crofton's death . . . God 'a mercy!"

"Stamford was in here and had learned of Crofton's pending travel," Kit repeated.

"He was not the only fellow who might have been interested in Fulke Crofton's plan to travel, Constable," the tavern keeper said, his brows lifting. "Sir Walter was here that night, too."

"My cousin was here?" A man who'd once before proved to be dangerous.

"Indeed so, Constable," said Master Johnes. "Indeed so."

# CHAPTER 9

A young female servant showed Bess into the entryway of Langham Hall.

"Through here," the girl said, leading Bess through the screens passage.

Through the break in the passage's partition, she could see the hall. It was a room possessed of fringed silk cushions, a long table covered in a patterned carpet, and oak paneling upon the wall. Above the paneling, there were empty expanses, the outlines of tapestries and painted cloths that had once hung upon the plaster, now ghostly reminders. The valuable items had been sold to pay Mistress Langham's debts to the Crown, Bess supposed, for daring to defiantly cling to the religion she so loved yet that had caused her husband's death.

"Mistress," the servant nudged.

They went into the service rooms. A parlor of sorts, where the staff might take their meals rather than in the hall as Joan and Humphrey did, occupied the space between the pantry and the kitchen.

Another servant girl, who looked to be about Margery's

age, clutched her right hand in her lap. The cloth wrapped around her fingers was red from blood.

"What have we?" Bess asked, setting her satchel upon the trestle table in the center of the room.

The girl would be pretty were it not for the pain creasing her face. "I've cut my finger."

"Come by the window here so I might see better."

The girl drew the stool she sat upon over to the light of the unglazed window and held out her hand. Bess slowly unwrapped the cloth. It had stuck to the wound, which took to bleeding afresh. She had more than a simple cut; she had nearly sliced off her finger, and bone showed between sinew and flesh.

The other servant, the one who'd shown Bess into the room, clapped her hand to her mouth.

"Fetch me the freshest water available and some clean cloths," Bess said to the girl before she could faint. She happily scurried off.

Bess dropped the soiled cloth to the ground and drew the satchel near, taking out the jar of salve and squares of linen. Placing another stool across from her patient, Bess sat and pressed a wad of linen to the wound to stem the bleeding.

"I'm clumsy, I am," said the girl, her face averted.

"I shall try to save your finger."

Horror made her blanch. "I might lose it?"

"Not if I can prevent it."

Hearing footsteps on the flags outside the room, Bess turned, expecting to see the servant returning with the water. Instead, a woman in a silver-gray taffeta gown banded with black velvet stood in the doorway. She was tall, with a sweep of auburn hair held in place beneath her coif by pearl-encrusted pins. As she moved, the scent of rosemary lifted from her clothes.

Bess made to stand.

"Do not rise, Mistress. And many good thanks for getting here so quickly," she said, though she'd no need to thank a woman of Bess's standing for answering the summons of a woman of hers.

"I would not delay attending to a patient, madam."

The other girl returned with a basin of water and a stack of cloths, which she set next to Bess's satchel, then once again fled.

Bess dipped a cloth into the water and daubed the servant girl's cut. Blood dripped onto the tiled floor.

"You are good to have come nonetheless, Mistress Ellyott," said Mistress Langham. "And at such a sorrowful time for your family."

"What better way is there to mend any sorrow than by striving to heal the living?"

"That may be so, but I remain astonished you did not refuse a summons that came from Langham Hall."

She looked over at Mistress Langham. *Why send for me, if you thought I would refuse?* Bess had forgotten her Christian name—Ellynor? Helen?—and at that moment it seemed important to remember. "I regret any past ill will between our families, madam."

"What of any current ill will?" the woman asked.

The servant girl whimpered; Bess must have pressed

upon her wound with too great of a force. Abashed, she lowered her gaze and collected her stitching quill and thread.

"I know naught of any current ill will," said Bess. From beneath her lowered eyelids, she noticed Mistress Langham twisting the emerald ring she wore. She was no more comfortable with this encounter than Bess. "I do fret, though, for my niece Margery's contentment."

Bess suspected, though, that dismay over the affection between Margery and Bennett was not the ill will Mistress Langham referred to.

"Squeeze your eyes shut," Bess said to the servant. "I shall be quick."

She thrust the threaded quill through the cut, and the girl cried out. Bess sewed rapidly, a few loose stitches to bind the wound closed but not tightly so. If she sealed the cut completely, it might fester, and she did not wish to return to remove a gangrenous finger from the girl's hand.

"There. The worst is over," Bess said, cutting the thread with a knife retrieved from her satchel and tying a knot.

The servant girl hiccuped a sob as Bess dressed her cut with the salve, her touch light in order to lessen any further pain.

"You are gentle, Mistress Ellyott," said Mistress Langham.

"My brother would be astonished to hear someone say that of me. He thinks me unruly."

Mistress Langham smiled, a dimple forming in her cheek. Bess had only ever seen her from afar. From the distance of a few hand-widths, she was not the severe woman Bess had imagined her to be.

"Does he, now?" the woman asked. "I would not imagine any would say that of you."

Bess set aside her pot of salve and collected a square of linen to loosely wrap over the girl's cut. "You do not listen to the gossips, then."

"Sadly, I do," she murmured, the smile fading.

Bess's treatment finished, Mistress Langham bid her servant leave. The girl departed, her damaged hand braced by her good one.

"You must wonder why I sent for you, Mistress Ellyott."

Resealing the pot of salve, Bess placed it, her clean squares of linen, and her stitching quill within the satchel. They had arrived at the topic they had been avoiding all this time. "Was it not to tend to your servant's wound?"

"Not solely, as I believe you realize." She pressed her hands to her waist, the emerald upon her finger winking in the light. "I took advantage of my servant's mishap to send for you in particular. I would ask you directly if it was you or your family who set the constable upon us."

"I would not dare hurt Margery, which is what would happen if I had." It was an honest admission that Bess would protect her niece's heart over following some obligation to the law.

"Yet you sought to question Bennett about some strange fellow seen hereabouts."

"Mistress Langham, I have *many* questions," said Bess. "For I have reason to believe Fulke did not kill himself."

Mistress Langham went ashen. "No," she breathed. Her gaze was steady, though, as she stared at Bess. "Do you blame us, then, for his death?"

"Ought I?"

"Bennett was here with me. All that day. The weather was foul, and we did not leave the warmth of the hall," she said, her voice strong. The accusations against her family and her husband's death had not weakened Mistress Langham. "*All* of us were at home that day."

An alibi for Bennett. Though Bess could not conceive how anyone could be certain of another's movement within a house this large. 'Twould be easy to slip out one of the many doors and then return, unobserved.

"It is time I go," said Bess, lifting her satchel. "By your leave, madam."

"You have not answered me."

Bess looked into the other woman's eyes. She searched for guilt but could find none. "I do not blame you."

Mistress Langham exhaled. She reached into the embroidered purse hung from her girdle and held out a shilling. "Your pay, Mistress Ellyott."

"I do not need your coin, madam."

Bess left the shilling in the woman's outstretched hand and hastened for the front entrance. She was but halfway through the screens passage when she heard rustling near the large staircase in the hall's corner. A man in plain brown robes sped up the steps. Based upon his thin, almost scrawny, frame and how swiftly he ascended the stairs, he was a young man. A young man who acted eager to not be seen.

Before Bess could act on her impulse to follow him, Mistress Langham stepped into the passageway. She shot a glance at the stairwell, then at her servant, who had scurried across the hall from a far portal.

She gestured to the girl to see to the front door. "Good day to you, Mistress Ellyott."

Feeling the woman's gaze on her, Bess left and headed for the road. She did not look back to see if she was being watched.

However, no amount of scrutiny from the occupants of Langham Hall could stop the fresh questions arising in her mind.

★ ★ ★

Kit strode into the draper's shop. Amice Stamford looked up from her conversation with a customer and frowned. She returned to the woman at her side, who was fingering a length of blood-red wool.

A young woman hastened over instead. She was lithe, dressed as brightly as Mistress Stamford, and handsome. He recognized her as one of the Stamford children, but he did not know her name.

"Good sir, how may I help?" She inspected his attire subtly and critically. As her mother might do.

"I am not here to purchase cloth," he said. This shop was a woman's place, among the rolls of material, the lengths of ribbon and lace in colors and textures that drew the eye. The space was scrupulously clean and tidy. Kit wondered if its appearance reflected Mistress Stamford's character or her husband's. "I am here to speak with your father."

"He readies for a visit to his weavers in Chippenham," she said.

"I insist."

She dipped a hasty curtsy and consulted with her mother

before scurrying up the stairs visible just beyond the shop's rear door.

Mistress Stamford watched him out of the corner of her eye but did not cease attending to her customer, who had moved on to another length of material of a finer weave. And no doubt more expensive.

Footsteps sounded upon the stairs, and Arthur Stamford entered the shop. He was a tall man, thin to the point of being composed of angles and lines, and had to duck to enter the room. Stamford often dressed to conceal his thinness, and today was no exception. The fellow's velvet doublet was padded more than was warranted for the needs of warmth.

"Constable Harwoode?"

"I would speak to you in private, Master Stamford," said Kit, nodding toward the man's wife and daughter. And the customer, whose interest in the shop's woolens had noticeably waned.

"I am a busy man. I leave within the hour and need make ready."

"Then I shall keep my queries about Fulke Crofton brief."

Glowering, Stamford strode out of the shop. He stopped several feet distant from the door. "What of Master Crofton?"

"I have learned of your dispute with him."

"Of what import is our disagreement?"

"You had learned the night before his death that he intended to go Devizes to go to suit against you," said Kit. "Witnesses have said you were . . . irate."

He flushed. "As you have spoken with people who are willing to gossip, you must also be aware of Master Crofton's attempt to cheat me. I was angry that he wished others to believe me at fault. That is all."

"The day he died, where were you?" asked Kit.

"Am I to also be faulted for his desire to take his own life?" asked Stamford. "Preposterous."

The customer bustled out of the Stamford's shop with a paper-wrapped roll of cloth and a pinched look upon her face, as though she might burst if she did not disgorge the tittle-tattle she had collected while buying wool. Beyond the windows, not as hidden in shadows as she believed herself to be, Mistress Stamford spied upon Kit and her husband. Across the way, Marcye at the Cross Keys repeatedly whisked a broom across the threshold stones while she stole glances at them.

"I have asked a simple question, Master Stamford, and I am certain you have an excellent answer."

"It was market day. I was at my shop. Many people saw me there," he said. "Though I suppose you have heard from the Croftons' servants that I came to inspect the wool at his warehouse that day."

This was news. "You knew he had gone to Devizes. Why would you go to inspect his warehouse at such a time?"

"To avoid Fulke," he said. "My weavers complain that the quality has been inferior of late. I will not sell poor cloth in my shop. I would see for myself."

"You did not attempt to stop him upon the road, keep him from his mission?" asked Kit. "Perhaps allow a quarrel to get out of hand?"

"What mean you by such a suggestion? This is absurd! Fulke Crofton killed himself."

Kit leaned toward him. "But what if he did not?"

Stamford blanched. "I will speak to the other burgesses about these questions, Constable. And see you dismissed."

He turned on his heel, nearly colliding with the coster-monger's daughter who had wandered too near, and stormed into his shop.

Kit nodded at the wide-eyed girl and took off for a copse of trees south of town. If the constable had overlooked two lines upon Fulke Crofton's throat, what else might the fellow have missed?

★　★　★

There was one possible answer to the question of the identity of the man at Langham Hall. An answer that greatly unsettled Bess.

She trudged homeward, scarcely heeding the dairyman's boy moving cattle from one meadow to another. Or the farmer and his family spread out across a hedged-in field in the distance. They slowly moved across the furrowed dirt, dipping their hands into sacks slung across their bodies, then casting the seeds of winter wheat upon the ground.

Certes, she could be wrong about the man she had seen. Bess did not know how many servants the Langhams employed or who might be visiting them. She was permitting Constable Harwoode's suspicions to taint her judgment.

But what if the brown-robed fellow *was* a Jesuit? And what if Fulke had learned of his presence and come to once again believe the worst of the Langhams? Perhaps his journey to Devizes had been not to attend to his lawsuit against Arthur Stamford but to inform the Crown of the Langhams' new crime, which would have presented a grave danger to them.

She should also consider the possibility that Fulke had encountered the vagrant, flushing him from wherever he was hiding like a bird in the brambles. He might have killed Fulke in desperation. But she had not noticed bruises upon her brother-in-law other than those around his neck. And why such an elaborate ruse as to counterfeit a suicide, rather than merely leaving Fulke in the nearest ditch?

*Jesu. I know not what to think.*

Bess noticed one of the nearby husbandmen's daughters, a willow basket in one hand, hurrying along the high road. Aside from the sound of a plowman coaxing his oxen forward to plow over stubble and the chirrup of a swallow, the fields were quiet. Soon the snows would arrive, muffling all in a blanket of white. Bess hoped she would have the answers to her questions by then. If she did not, she might never.

The girl turned off onto a path between a break in the hedge, leaving Bess to survey the gentle straw-colored swells of the harvested fields, the trees releasing their golden leaves and baring their branches. Her eyes were drawn to the copse where Fulke had been found, as she feared they always would.

Upon the rise beyond that place stood Highcombe Manor. From here, Bess could not see the narrow lane that led to the front door, concealed as it was by intervening undergrowth. She knew, though, that Sir Walter's house stood hard by the far edge of the trees. The home of the man who had gained from Fulke's death so near to the place where that death had occurred.

A blur of brown caught her eye, moving quickly from the copse to another stand of trees to its west. Before good sense forestalled her, Bess secured her satchel firmly over her shoulder and took off running in the fellow's direction.

"You there!" Bess cried out, crashing through the stubble, which poked and jabbed her exposed ankles, tearing at her stockings. She gave a brief thought to Joan's unhappiness that she would need to mend them again. "Halt!"

He did not slow but continued to rush along, shoving branches out of his way.

At the field's edge, Bess leaped across the shallow ditch that separated it from the roadbed and shouted again, "Halt!"

This time, the fellow paused and looked over his shoulder. Bess could see by the bend of his shoulders he intended to take off running again.

"Halt! I would speak to you!" she cried.

To her surprise, he did halt and turned to face her. Bess cautiously approached across the field. She doubted he was the fellow she had just seen at Langham Hall, for he would have had to pass her upon the road in order to arrive at the trees before she did. He also did not appear as tall as that man, and the color of the hair that poked from beneath his cap was redder than that fellow's.

"What d'you want?" the fellow . . . the *boy* asked, his chin going up.

When she drew nearer, Bess saw that his was a familiar face. "You are Goodwife Anwicke's son, are you not?"

"Who is it wants to know?"

"I am Widow Ellyott." She stopped well short of the shadowed thicket where he stood. "I treated your sister's burn the other day. Do you remember me?"

He nodded, and his eyes slanted toward the trees behind him. *How curious.*

"Do you come to this place often?" she asked, gesturing at the field and the woods, so near the copse.

"My mother does not mind," he answered defensively. "I've done my work for the day. She's happy to see me away."

"And your father? Is he happy to have you gone from the cottage?" She was curious about the treatment this wandering lad—with his greasy red hair and worn frieze coat, which was too narrow for his shoulders and held closed at his waist with a scrap of thick cord—received. If she searched, might she find burns or bruises upon his body, as she had upon his sister's?

He made no reply to her question.

"I would ask you something. Did you come here the day I treated your sister for the burn she had upon her palm?"

The boy blinked, once, twice, and shrugged. "May have done. Cannot say for certain."

"You must remember the day, though. It cannot be often that a stranger, such as myself, comes to your house," she said, keen to uncover another witness.

"I said I cannot remember."

"For if you were near these woods that day, you may have seen the fellow who murdered a man. The victim was a merchant in a fine, fur-trimmed green cloak and wearing a tall, be-feathered hat. He was astride a fawn-colored Spanish horse."

"I do not know!" he snapped, and ran off.

Bess was yet staring after the boy, who had turned up the highway and was halfway to his home, when she heard the sound of sticks breaking beneath the weight of heavy feet. The noise was headed in her direction. Alarmed, she turned and scrambled backward, her pulse slowing only when the fellow cleared the shadows and broke into the sunlight.

"Constable, you frightened me."

Doffing his cap, Kit Harwoode glanced after the boy, no longer visible. "Well, did you learn anything?"

He did not sound pleased with her. "He is the brother of a patient. That is all," she dissembled.

"You dashed across a field to speak to a boy who merely happens to be the brother of a patient?" he asked. "Mistress, honesty is advisable when speaking with a constable."

"As you wish. I was curious what he had been doing in the woods," Bess said. "So near to the copse where Fulke died."

"I have already told you this matter is my responsibility, have I not?"

She lifted her chin. "Do you think me incapable of useful assistance?"

He cocked an eyebrow. "Ah, Mistress, you do test me."

"My sister says 'vex.' "

"She may be more accurate than I. Come." He looked over at the trees. "I would have you help me search."

He turned away, expecting her to follow. Which she did.

"For what do we search?" she asked.

"I am not certain. But whatever it is, it occupied Rodge

Anwicke so intently that he did not notice I was watching him."

"You know his name."

"I do," he said. "The boy is often suspected of petty robberies. He has not ever been convicted though, else he might be missing an ear or two as punishment."

*To have gone from minor thievery to murder . . .*

They entered the trees, where the branches overhead cast shadows upon the ground and the musty aroma of damp earth and rotting leaves filled the air. The constable strode in the direction of a fallen tree. It had toppled so long ago that saplings now grew up around the log, which was thicker than the torso of a stout man.

"The boy was nosing about in this area," said the constable, stopping to look around. The collapse of the tree had created a narrow clearing among the others still standing.

"The leaves are trampled into the dirt here." Bess pointed to a spot near the end of the log. "I would guess the boy . . . or at least someone comes here frequently."

"Agreed." Kit Harwoode bent to more closely examine the ground.

She scanned the earth as well. The soil and leaves were most definitely crushed by the regular stamp of feet. Perhaps Rodge Anwicke came here to hide from his family. It was quiet, removed from the view of the road and the fields. Most importantly, his cottage could not be seen from here.

"When I was young," Bess said, her memories prompted by her surroundings, "my siblings and I would play all-hid among a stand of trees near our house in Oxford."

"You grew up in Oxford?" the constable asked. He did

not lift his attention from his examination of the area, but he did prove he was listening.

"Yes." Bess nudged aside leaves and sticks with the toe of her shoe. "One time, my sister lost interest in the game and neglected to try to find me. I stayed in my hiding spot behind a spiny thicket of gooseberries for so long I began to cry. And then Robert finally came . . ."

Her brother. Ever her savior. Before Martin.

"Hiding . . . ah!" Partway along the length of the log, he had come to a stop. He dragged away branches that leaned against it. "Ah!" he repeated

"What?" Stepping over the log, Bess hurried to his side. "What is it?"

"The log is hollow. Rotted out." Kneeling down, he reached into the cavity and started pulling out detritus.

"It is but filled with the leavings of woodland creatures that likely have used the hollowed log for warmth," she said. "What has this to do with the Anwicke lad?"

"When *I* was young, Mistress Ellyott, I engaged in hiding things from my cousin. Items Gibb valued. In order to torment him." As proof, from within the depths of the log, he pulled out a small woven bag. Bess peered over the constable's shoulder as he undid the ties that bound it shut and spilled out the contents—a silver aglet once attached to the end of a lace, a carved clay pipe with a broken stem, a substantial length of fine violet silk ribbon, a pair of oft-handled bone dice.

"The boy has been hiding his trinkets here. They do not look like items taken from his siblings, however," said Bess. More likely they were items he had found or, perhaps, stolen. She peered at the ribbon. "I believe I have seen that very ribbon in Arthur Stamford's shop. What a curious connection, think you not, Constable?"

"Aye, most interesting, Mistress," said the constable. "As is this."

The final item tumbled from the bag onto the dirt. One silver sixpence, imprinted with the image of Queen Elizabeth. An amount the boy might earn for a day's labor, and too important to the needs of his family to be tucked away.

"His mother could use that coin for food for her children," said Bess.

"She could. The question is from whence it came. But these items are not all."

He stretched his hand deeper into the cavity and, with a grim twist of his lips, withdrew a crushed hat. The constable shook it to restore its original shape. It was a most distinctive hat, with a tall crown and a feather, and covered in mud.

Fulke's hat.

# CHAPTER 10

"Where do you think the boy found Fulke's hat?" Bess asked. Battered and dirty, it was still recognizable.

Constable Harwoode looked up at her. "He took it from the body of a dead man, Mistress."

"Does this mean Rodge is the murderer?" Relief swept over her. If the boy had killed Fulke, she need no longer suspect the Langhams or Master Stamford. Or the vagrant. "Although Fulke's hat could have fallen to the ground and he merely picked it up."

The constable gathered the coin and the trinkets he had spilled out and returned them to the bag. "We shall know where he obtained it once I ask him."

Hat and bag in hand, the constable stood.

"Why might the boy be honest?" Rodge would fear a charge of murder or a charge of theft. And either would be a hanging offense.

"Perhaps he will surprise the both of us, Mistress," he said. "Accompany me to the boy's house. I would not have you accuse me of putting false words in the lad's mouth."

He did not wait for Bess's agreement and charged ahead. Encumbered by trailing skirts and a satchel that banged against her hip, she hurdled branches and muddy patches of dirt, which he easily strode over.

"Constable, I must ask if you have ever searched for a murderer before."

"Thankfully not. Although I have served for only a year so far." He looked over at her. "Do you question my competence?"

She supposed that she did. "How did you come to be constable?" she asked when they reached the road. Such a role was given only to men of substance, a burgess of the town.

"My cousin Sir Walter put my name forward."

"He trusted your integrity and intelligence."

He released a self-mocking laugh. "Quite the opposite, Mistress. Wat thinks me an undisciplined churl. As most Harwoodes are, in his estimation."

"Yet if he put your name forward, he had to have faith in you."

"A bit of fun at my expense, Mistress," he said, a wry smile on his lips. "I came here to live with my cousin Gibb's family when I was no longer welcome in the town of my birth. Because of them, I was provided opportunities that enabled me to become a man of property. Wat still held the opinion I'd not learned proper manners, however. He had not forgotten the wild boy he'd known in his youth." The constable paused, perhaps to recall that wild boy and his reproving cousin.

"And yet . . ."

"He thought it a great witticism and a lesson to recommend me for the position of constable," he continued. "Somehow, he managed to convince the other burgesses that I was the best candidate and that my brawling days were past. As none of them wanted to be constable, they were not so difficult to convince."

"Has being constable taught you proper manners?" she asked.

He stopped and gazed down at her. "What think you, Mistress?"

"I know you not well enough to say."

He chuckled, and soon they neared the Anwickes'. A wisp of smoke rose from the smoke bay, and the shutters were down from the windows, permitting a burst of afternoon sunlight to enter. Bess's patient leaned against the whitewashed mud wall, the toes of her bare feet curling in the dirt, her face uplifted to the sunshine. The bruise on her left cheek had begun to turn from purple to green, a sign that it was healing. She twirled a drop spindle, spinning yarn from a teased mass of wool she had draped over her shoulder. Bess did not see her brother. 'Twas possible he had not returned to the cottage and their visit here was wasted.

Upon hearing footfalls upon the road, the girl's eyes went wide. She pushed away from the wall and rushed with her bundle of wool and drop spindle into the cottage. The chickens that had been pecking near the wattle fence startled and fluttered off.

"That was the Anwickes' daughter, whom I treated for a burn," said Bess, an event that seemed as though it had occurred months ago, rather than only a few days earlier. "I think she is unable to speak. Poor child."

"She did not appear happy to see us," said the man at her side.

"You have said Rodge has been accused of multiple crimes. I expect none of the Anwickes would be happy to see you heading for their house."

Goodwife Anwicke stepped through the open door, her infant cradled in her arms. The baby, removed from its swaddling cloth, squirmed. Bess's patient peeked around the doorway.

"Good day, Widow Ellyott," she said, eyeing the constable. "Might I ask what brings you here today, Constable?"

"I would speak to your son," he answered.

"What is he blamed for now?"

He held up Fulke's hat and the bag. "Is he fond of collecting items and hiding them in a log in the woods?"

"There is no crime in doing so," she said. "Rodge be a magpie, liking his shiny things. Fetch your brother, Maud."

*Maud.* At last Bess had a name for the girl who did not speak, and whose name she had not thought to ask.

She ran inside. Shortly thereafter, Bess heard the raised voice of an angry boy.

"Pardon me." Goodwife Anwicke, whose babe had begun to whimper, its tiny face pinching in readiness to howl, retreated into the house. She returned without her infant, shoving her son before her.

"The constable begs to speak with you," she said. She cuffed the boy on the ear, which caused Bess to wince far more than he did. "I do not want to learn that you've gone and taken something valuable."

"I've not done!" he cried, his face pinking with humiliation and rage.

"And remove your cap when speaking to your betters, boy!" his mother demanded.

Rodge grabbed his cap from his head, his cheeks turning redder.

"Among the items in this bag is a sixpence," said the constable. "Where did you get the coin and this hat?"

"A sixpence?" Goodwife Anwicke glared at her son. "Money? What else have you been hiding, Rodge?"

The constable waited out the tirade. "Boy, I would have you tell me where you got that coin and this hat."

When Rodge hesitated, his mother roughly prodded his shoulder with her elbow. From inside the cottage came the howl of her baby. "Tell the constable, Rodge," she said. "Else your father will learn of this."

"I shall not see you charged with theft this time," Constable Harwoode added. "If you help me."

The lad peered at him. He had sharp, intelligent eyes, watchful as a hawk's and as calculating as those of a cutpurse taking the measure of his next victim.

"I get paid. For work," he said.

"What sort of work?" asked the constable.

Rodge's focus did not waver from the constable's face. "You know, this and that."

Goodwife Anwicke prodded him again. "Be plain, Rodge."

He dodged her elbow. "This and that!"

"And the hat?" Bess asked. "Where did it come from?"

"I found it. In a ditch near the woods."

"Near the body of a dead man hanging from a tree?" asked Constable Harwoode.

His words were blunt, meant to startle the lad into an admission. He had not anticipated the nauseating effect they might have upon Bess, still reeling from the manner of Fulke's death.

Goodwife Anwicke gaped at Bess. "Rodge had naught to do with your brother-in-law's suicide, Widow Ellyott. How could he?"

"I saw no dead man," her son said, his chin high. "I found the hat in a ditch hard by the road near the trees. There." He pointed to the south of where they stood. "'Twas there."

"And when did you make this discovery?" asked the constable.

"A few days past."

"Which day?" Bess asked. "At what time?"

"Tuesday," he answered quickly. The day that Fulke had met his end. "Late it was, once I had finished helping my father clear stones from our neighbor's field."

The constable buffed the backs of his fingers against his beard. "Late. Did it not rain heavily late that day?"

"What care I for rain?" Rodge responded.

"So you vow, Rodge Anwicke, that you have no knowledge about the death of Master Fulke Crofton, though you came to possess his hat," said the constable.

"I do not," said the boy. "I do not!"

Abruptly, Constable Harwoode thanked them both and

strode toward the road. Bess offered her goodbyes and rushed after him.

"He could be telling the truth, Constable."

"I do not care for Rodge Anwicke and his supposed 'truth,' if you would know my mind," he answered.

"Then why did you not arrest the boy, if you are so certain he lied to you?"

"I shall set Gibb to watching the lad. Rodge Anwicke knows something or saw something that he wishes to keep quiet. Short of torture . . ." A muscle in his jaw twitched. "I fear I cannot get the boy to tell me what that *something* is. I must wait to have him reveal his knowledge in some other fashion. Perhaps we might also learn where he obtained that coin."

"Did Rodge perchance witness the crime and then was paid to hold his tongue?" she asked. "Or mayhap he was paid to assist."

"Either is possible," said the constable. "And if so, I am most interested to discover who it was did the paying."

★ ★ ★

"Two lines across Fulke Crofton's neck have convinced you that he was murdered." Wat pushed aside the papers he had been reading and leaned back in his privy office chair. He folded his hands across the carnation silk of his doublet, its dozens of silver buttons winking in the gleam of a lantern he'd lit against the gloom.

Kit had come to the manor immediately after accompanying the inquisitive Mistress Ellyott home and finding Wat's summons waiting at his house.

"They have," said Kit.

"Our crowner has been at his work for many years. I believe he knows what he is about. And he is not happy with your disputing his ruling."

"He came to you to complain. That is why you sent for me."

Wat did not answer. Wat did not need to answer.

"Our coroner's vanity will not allow him to admit any error," said Kit.

"And neither will your pride allow you to admit you might be mistaken in this regard, coz."

Kit tamped down a sharp-tongued retort. "The fellow had gone to Devizes that morning to level a complaint against Arthur Stamford. For monies owed to him," he said. "Such plans do not sound like the actions of a man who intended to kill himself that same day."

His cousin tapped fingers against the table. "What is it you want to prove, Kit?"

*Your guilt? My worth?*

His cousin had always been taller, stronger, cocksure. The man who stood to inherit position and wealth while Kit stood to inherit only his father's debts. *Be thankful, Kit, for any good your aunt's family bestows upon you*, his father had said a few months before he'd died. What good had thankfulness to the Howes done for his father though? It had required years of hard work for Kit to pay off those debts. To become a freeholder with sufficient property to no longer need to bow and scrape before the Howes.

"What of the land that Crofton owned along the river?" asked Kit. "You wanted it, but he would not sell."

Wat drew in a lengthy breath, exhaling it with a lift of his fingers. "I desire to open a mill. The sole one we have is inadequate for the needs of this area. In order to do so, however, I require that land. The location would be perfect. Crofton had no particular use for it, aside from grazing some sheep, yet he would not sell it to me."

"His wife might though. Now that she has nothing but a house and a bit of ground by the river."

"Do you suggest I am responsible for those lines around Crofton's neck?"

Kit shrugged. "You knew he was bound for Devizes that morning—"

Wat stood, the suddenness of his movement knocking over his chair. "You push the bonds of kinship too far, Kit Harwoode. I owe you no loyalty."

Did he not? Did he not owe Kit years of loyalty in exchange for Kit's silence over what had occurred one summer's day so long ago? A bit of rough play had gotten out of hand, and the injured fellow had slunk away from the village. So Wat claimed. Kit, though, did not believe his cousin's story. And he'd not forgotten what he had seen.

He stared at his cousin until Wat was forced to remember as well. "Tell me you had naught to do with his death, and I will be satisfied," said Kit.

"I vow to you I had naught to do with Crofton's death," he replied. But that was not the question Kit had asked. "The man killed himself."

"I have another question." Kit eyed his cousin. "Do you happen to know a lad named Rodge Anwicke?"

Wat looked genuinely confused. "Who?"

"A boy. Red-haired. A cottager's son."

"Why might I know a cottager's son?"

Could he trust Wat? "I wish I could say."

★  ★  ★

Bess sat by the hall's hearth after supper, tucked onto the settle, which trapped the fire's warmth with its high back. Logs popped and spit sparks upon the hearth. Joan came and set a blanket upon Bess's knees.

"Do you require aught else, Mistress?" she asked.

"No. But I find I am exhausted. These past few days have been terrible," she said. "Though it seems we are near to understanding who is responsible."

"You believe the constable will act upon what you have shown him?"

Bess looked over at Joan. She did not trust officers of the law. Life in London alleys had taught her that too often watchmen and petty constables cared only for the complaints of the wealthy, who deemed it of primary importance that their skirts and robes not brush against the poor of the streets, vermin to be eradicated.

"I have no choice but to believe," she said. "He *must* act."

"Aye, Mistress."

Joan departed, and Quail loped into the room. With a hearty sigh, the dog sank upon the flags near the hearth.

"Aunt Bess?" Margery called from the doorway that led to the stairs by the service rooms. Barefoot, she hugged her night rail about her shift. "Might I speak with you?"

"Of course." Bess beckoned Margery to join her. "Why are you not asleep, though?"

Margery took Robert's chair, drawing her knees to her chest. "I would apologize for being angry that you questioned Bennett. I've come to realize you merely wish to absolve him of any guilt."

In the soft firelight, with her braided hair hanging past her shoulders, she looked like a young girl instead of a young woman in love with the wrong man.

"Margery, have you noticed a man in brown robes at Langham Hall recently?"

"Are you asking if I have seen a priest there?" She scowled. "You still mistrust them."

"That is no proper response," said Bess. "Have you?"

"There are always servants about. I pay them no heed."

Mayhap that fellow simply was a servant, and Bess had no cause to wonder otherwise.

She contemplated her niece. "Bennett's mother has provided an alibi for him."

Margery looked appalled. "You asked her?"

"She offered when I told her I've come to believe your stepfather was murdered."

"Well, I am glad he cannot be blamed."

"As am I," said Bess, though Mistress Langham's word would not be enough to save her son if the constable doubted Bennett's innocence. "By the by, Constable Harwoode has found your stepfather's hat, which had been missing, and the boy who had hidden it. A possible link to Fulke's death."

"Does Mother know of this news?"

"I sent Joan to tell her this afternoon. Before supper." The oak draw-leaf table sat folded moved aside by the wall.

Margery had not joined Bess for the meal, and it was lonely to eat there by oneself.

"I wish I knew who would harm my stepfather. 'Tis true he argued and fought with many people—surely you recall my mother's complaint that none would share a bowl with us at the revels this summer—but to go this far?" Margery hugged her bent knees closer. "Did you think my stepfather was a bad person, Aunt Bess?"

"I thought Fulke had a great temper. But bad? No."

"When I was younger, he used to scare me so. Other times, he could be witty and kind. He gave me a poppet for my tenth Christmas, and I thought it meant he cared as much for me as he did for his sons . . ." She shook her head. "I cannot believe this has happened. Such a bad dream I want to awaken from. A horrid nightmare."

Bess leaned over and touched her arm. "I pray we find resolution soon."

"I merely want life to return to normal. Will that ever be possible?"

Bess thought of London and the visit by the searcher of the dead and Martin's cold body. She had longed for normal then. It was not to be had.

"Go to bed, sweeting. And rest well."

Margery rose, kissed her upon the cheek, and retired upstairs to her chamber. Quail lifted his head to watch her go, then dropped it to his paws again.

Bess tucked the blanket about her waist and closed her eyes. Joan would leave her thus until the fire dwindled and the room turned cold.

She had to have dozed, for she was awakened by the sound of Quail barking. Throwing off the blanket, she got to her feet.

In the entry passage, Joan was chiding the dog to be quiet.

"Joan, what is it?" Bess called, treading across the room and opening the door to the passageway. "Quail, hush now."

Joan had grabbed the scruff of Quail's neck to pull him away from the door. "First he started at the kitchen window, scaring me so that I dropped the pot I was cleaning. And now this."

Bess stepped forward to unlatch the door.

"Mistress, stop!" Joan cried, her terror clearly seen even in the shadows of the passageway.

"Do you think we are in danger from what is beyond that door?" Bess asked.

"Quail does not bark without cause," she said.

Bess retreated to the hall doorway.

"Ensure all the doors are barred, Joan." She stared at the thick door and was glad for its solidness. "And the windows latched tight."

# Chapter 11

"See that you keep the door locked while I am at the baker's, Mistress," said Joan, securing her blue fustian cloak tight about her. Bess had given it to her out of Martin's belongings, and it brushed Joan's shoe tops. She had need of the cloak that morning, for the day had dawned with the sky spitting a fine drizzle, cold and ugly.

"'Tis daybreak, Joan. None will disturb us now. Further, I have the brave Quail to keep me safe." She patted the dog's head as he sat at her side.

Joan looked dubious. "If an intruder be a waterfowl, then Quail will be most fierce indeed."

"Fret not."

Tossing the cloak's hood over her head and gathering the basket that waited by the door, Joan departed and picked a path down the road, the compacted gravel shiny from rain. Bess was about to close the door when she spotted the robust shape of the churchwarden, his rabbit-fur-lined black robe swirling about his legs, headed in the direction of Robert's house.

"Widow Ellyott," said Master Enderby upon arriving at the front threshold. The weight of his role had carved sternness across his heavy features, outlined by a rounded beard. Or perhaps the sternness had existed before he'd been made churchwarden, his character a perfect match to the flinty nature of his occupation.

"Welcome." Bess ushered him inside. The smell of camphor and pennyroyal clung to his black robe, black doublet, and black hose. A cloud of scent, stingingly sharp in the damp morning air. "My maid has gone to the baker's, else I would offer you food. We have malmsey in the buttery, if you would care for some wine this morning."

"No need." He shook droplets of rain from his robe and onto the woven rush matting beneath his feet. Some sprinkled beyond the covering of the rushes to land upon the tile. "I shall not be long."

Bess made no move to invite him farther into the house. "Have you come with some news about the inventory of my brother-in-law's goods?"

"It has concluded. But I am not here in that regard," he said. "You were seen leaving Langham Hall yesterday. What was your business there?"

She and Bennett had warned Margery to stay away from the Langhams. Bess had not considered that she need heed the advice as well. "I was called to tend to a kitchen servant who had cut her hand."

"No other reason?"

"None. I tended the girl's wound and left immediately thereafter."

Master Enderby cocked his head. "It is my understanding that the son courts the daughter of your sister. A young woman who stays with you at this time."

She lifted her chin. He overstepped the limits of his authority; he was but the man who collected fines and fees for the church, ensured that the churchyard was maintained and the prayer books kept in supply. He might fine her for not attending services and transfer possession of all of Dorothie's goods to Wat Howe, but he was not quite so powerful as he imagined.

However, he was powerful enough.

"My family does not welcome Bennett Langham's suit," Bess said. "Neither does Mistress Langham approve, I suspect. My niece's friendliness toward him is merely the fruitless pursuit of a silly, young woman."

"They are seen together often."

"He will be returning to Bristol soon. Once he has finished the Michaelmas accounts."

His eyebrow twitched the faintest amount. She had revealed too much knowledge of Bennett Langham's business. *Guard your tongue better, Bess.*

"I have another, more vexatious concern." His stare burrowed into her head. "You missed a church service last Sunday. You know the punishment for recusancy."

Fines. Banishment and loss of property, or jail and death, if the quantity of her misdeeds grew great enough.

"I do, but I am no recusant. I have allowed the needs of my patients to draw me away from my duties to God. Needs that do not respect day or time," she replied.

Her excuse failed to sway him. "The fine is twenty pounds per month, Mistress."

"I've not the money, and I cannot ask my brother to suffer such a penalty for my sake." Bess rolled her lips between her teeth and swallowed her pride. "I shall attend tomorrow. You have my vow upon it."

"I pray so, Widow Ellyott. I do not wish you ill. I simply desire you to comply," he said. "For I know not if your loyalty lies with the Crown or with those who would continue to rebel against it. Master Topcliffe has turned his attention to us, madam, in this humble corner of the realm."

The name of Richard Topcliffe froze her blood. He was the queen's hound and torturer, and she had heard stories of the cruelties he had carried out upon captured priests in his attempts to unearth their treason. Mayhap the rumors about the vagrant being a Jesuit were not rumors, after all.

"Indeed. Topcliffe," repeated the churchwarden. "I cannot protect any within this parish who might cause trouble for our good queen. 'Twould be too dangerous for all of us."

"You have no need to doubt my loyalty to Queen Elizabeth." But Bess now saw that her family's cordial treatment of the Langhams had cast suspicion upon them. Despite Fulke's prior actions, which had once secured their allegiance as certainly as a wax seal upon parchment.

Fulke was gone now though, and there would be no more benevolence from the man who presently swept through the doorway and out onto the street, leaving a cold wind in his wake.

★  ★  ★

"Have you food in this house, Kit?" asked Gibb, the rumble of his stomach clear across the span of the first-floor hall where they both stood. "I am missing dinner."

"There might be cheese in the buttery." Kit stared out the window of the narrow house he rented, out across the square upon which it stood. The churchwarden, his dark robe swinging, strode across the cobbles and passed the market cross. He must be freshly returned from the Croftons' property. Kit wondered if Wat would reward the churchwarden with any of the goods his men were taking pains to tally.

The butcher gave the churchwarden a wide berth as they crossed paths.

"Only cheese?" complained Gibb.

"A bit of stale bread perhaps."

His cousin sighed loudly.

From the window, Kit could also see the Stamfords' shop, bustling with customers inspecting a new supply of kersey. How had a piece of violet ribbon, which Bess Ellyott had seen inside the Stamfords' shop and Kit had noticed as well, come to be in Rodge Anwicke's possession? By means fair or foul?

"When are you to engage a proper servant, Kit? 'Tis not as though you cannot afford one. Or two. You cannot live here respectably by begging to use the neighbor's servant girl when you finally realize that your bedding needs to be aired or your clothes laundered." Kit looked over his shoulder as his cousin ran a finger across the wainscot at his back and held up the blackened tip of his glove. "Or the dust needs to be removed."

"Ask your father to send me one of your servants, if you are so worried about my respectability."

"I think I shall. I would like to see you have to thank him." Gibb searched for somewhere to wipe his glove. "Can we not at least venture over to the Cross Keys for a meal and some beer?"

Kit resumed observing the square, the shadows deepening in the alleys as the sun set. "Marcye has her eye on me again. A visit so soon after the one I made yesterday might encourage her."

"So I am to starve." He groaned.

Gibb must have decided to sit, for the room's stool creaked as it took on weight. Next came the twang of Gibb picking the strings of Kit's gittern. "You should teach me how to play this one day."

Kit turned and plucked the instrument from his cousin's hands. "I've not the time and you've not the talent."

"Unfair, Kit. Most unfair."

Gently, Kit laid the gittern within its leather case. The lacquer finish protecting its pine and maple wood reflected the light in shades of gold and ivory. It had been the only gift his father had ever given him; he loved it nonetheless.

Kit closed the lid upon the instrument and his thoughts. "You are not here to complain, Gibb."

"No. I came to tell you there is no fresh news of the vagrant. Mayhap he has fled."

"Godspeed to the fellow, if he has," said Kit. "I have fresh news for you though, Gibb. I have found Master Crofton's hat."

He explained about the find and about Rodge Anwicke.

"Do you want me to take the boy to the jail?" asked Gibb.

"No, and hear out my reason." Kit leaned against the ledge formed by the deep inset of the window. "Besides the hat, he'd hidden a sixpence as well. More coin than an unskilled boy like him would see for a full day's work."

"Unless that work was criminal. Perhaps he aided Crofton's killer."

"Just so," said Kit. "I would know who paid Rodge. Keep a watch on him, Gibb. See who he speaks with, where he goes. Rodge Anwicke is now aware that I suspect him of involvement in Crofton's death."

"And he might run to the man who gave him that money to warn him." Gibb nodded. "I follow your thoughts."

"I would know *everyone* Rodge interacts with, Gibb. Even if he meets with Wat."

"Wat?"

"He squabbled with Crofton over some property the fellow had owned and that our cousin coveted. He may now be able to obtain it, as Crofton is conveniently out of the way."

Gibb's brows lowered. "He would never . . ."

"Would he not?"

"That was long ago, Kit. An accident," said Gibb. "You were there. We both were. You know it was an accident. We were all like that then."

"Not you, Gibb. Besides, you were a child then. What do you recall clearly?" Kit asked. "But I *was* there. 'Tis the problem. I was there, and I remember quite well."

★ ★ ★

"What mean you to set the constable on my husband to ask about some foolish argument he had with Fulke Crofton?" asked Amice Stamford, standing at Bess's door.

"Come in out of the rain, Mistress Stamford," said Bess.

The woman stubbornly proceeded no farther than the passageway. "Well? Have you a response?"

"The constable came to question him?"

"Yesterday," said Mistress Stamford. "Do you not deny sending him?"

"I simply told Constable Harwoode your husband and my brother-in-law argued the night before Fulke died," said Bess.

"So you did encourage this. I knew it." She wagged a finger at Bess. "I should see you pilloried for slander."

"What I told the constable is not slander. It is the truth. A truth that is widely known, Mistress Stamford."

"It is what you implied with such a comment that is slanderous, Mistress Ellyott. I am not fooled by your prevarication," she replied. "Fulke Crofton sinned by taking his own life because of guilt. Guilt over his false claims that Arthur was lying about the poor quality of your brother-in-law's wool. We all know what a cheat was Master Crofton."

Bess's cheeks warmed. "I did not mean to cause you distress."

"Did you not? You are all alike, Marshalls and Croftons. You enjoy causing trouble." Amice Stamford lifted her chin to peer down the length of her nose. "Do not seek to buy cloth from our shop again, Mistress Ellyott. You are not welcome."

"I—"

"And if you truly sought to identify the cause of your brother-in-law's upset, you would have the constable speak to his cousin. But I suppose he would not dare do so."

"Do you mean Sir Walter Howe?"

"Know you not about their great quarrel? You, who seem to possess knowledge of every spat in town?" Amice Stamford's mouth set in smug lines. "Arthur witnessed a fearsome argument between Master Crofton and Sir Walter. He told me your brother-in-law shouted that he would be dead before he would allow Sir Walter to get his hands on his land. Clearly, his mind was disordered to be so bold as to say such words to the lord of Highcombe."

Bess blinked at her like a mindless fool.

"What say you now, Mistress Ellyott?"

*Jesu.*

★   ★   ★

Dorothie's servant, Lucy, showed Bess into the hall. The room's contents had been stacked in ordered piles, ready for removal, carpets taken up and wound into rolls, tables moved, and tapestries stripped from the walls. The house felt already lifeless, as lifeless as Bess's London home the day Joan and she had departed, when she had made her tour of every room to bid them and all her happy memories farewell.

Her sister sat by the hall windows, staring at the garden beyond through the leaded panes. How miserable she looked, her hair untidy beneath her coif, her gown missing the farthingale required to keep its proper shape and dragging upon the floor.

She had heard Bess enter but did not look over. "I pray that each day will bring me more strength, Elizabeth, but each morn comes with all the same weariness of the last."

Bess brought over a stool to sit beside her. The view would not improve her sister's spirits. The drizzle had become rain, snaking down the glass, distorting the sunless world outside.

"I wish I could claim the loss shall become less of a burden, Dorothie." Martin's death had carved free a portion of her heart that would never grow back or be repaired, no matter how she prayed otherwise. "However, over time you may learn to bear the weight more easily."

Dorothie trembled as though cold. Bess needed to ask Lucy to bring a hand warmer for her mistress. If the churchwarden's men had not forbidden the girl from touching it.

"The churchwarden's men only add to my distress. I am convinced those thieves have pocketed some of Fulke's coins," said Dorothie. "They have also stolen items of mine. Mean they to reward their wives with bits of finery? At this moment, a pair of them pick through my chests in my chamber. Which another two have already done. Think they that my boxes have secret compartments hiding jewels?"

As if in response, Bess heard an object thud to the floor above their heads.

"It shall all be restored to you soon enough. Once the constable has resolved this matter, and the true cause of Fulke's death is known to one and all."

"How it contents me that you have faith in his abilities to do so," she said scornfully. She glanced toward the entrance to the hall. "Did you not bring Margery with you? Does she not care to visit me?"

"I asked her to braid a new girdle for me, to calm her mind. I thought you did not want her here, with strange men in the house."

"Nevertheless . . ."

"Dorothie, why did you not tell me that there were others besides Arthur Stamford whom Fulke had quarreled with of late?"

"What do I care about any others?" She glared at Bess. "You vex me, you do."

"Why would Fulke not sell Sir Walter his land?"

"You have come to ask about that?" Dorothie asked. "Of what import is their dispute now? Your message was that the cottager's boy had Fulke's hat. He is involved in my husband's death. The constable must arrest him, but Roland tells me it has not happened. Why can this not be ended?"

"The constable believes the boy did not act alone and means to use him to find any others involved." Bess clasped her sister's hands to warm them. "Why would Fulke not sell Sir Walter his land, Dorothie?"

"He offered an insulting price."

"And Sir Walter would not raise it when Fulke refused?"

"He did, but by then Fulke would have none of it," said Dorothie. "They are both stubborn men, you know. Easily angered. I fretted that Fulke would bring trouble upon himself by going to Devizes. My dream . . ." She sighed. "And so he did bring trouble upon himself."

"If the coroner is not convinced to overturn his ruling, shall *you* sell the land to Sir Walter?"

Dorothie scowled. "I will not hear such irksome talk. Begone, Elizabeth. Leave me in peace."

Bess pressed a kiss upon her sister's head and went in search of Lucy. She found the girl seated in the corner of the kitchen, crying into her apron.

When she heard Bess's footfalls upon the flags, she sat bolt upright and scrubbed at her eyes. "Roland, if you've come to ask again how I am, I shall scream!"

"Lucy," said Bess, to make her identity known.

She peeked over the edge of the apron. "Oh, 'tis you, Mistress Ellyott." She jumped to her feet. "My apologies. I did not hear you at the door."

"It was unlocked. Do not fret. I understand," she said. "I came to tell you that your mistress requires a hand warmer. She is chilled, sitting by that window."

"I would bring her one, if I could but find it. The churchwarden and his men have moved everything, and I know not where to find my brass kitchen pan let alone the mistress's hand warmer." She moaned. "Oh, Mistress, where am I to go after we are forced from this house?"

Bess had no answer. Lucy would not find a position in this town; so long as Fulke's death was ruled a suicide, a shadow was cast upon all those closest to him, including his servants.

"Might I come work for you?" she asked, her tone pleading.

"We already have Joan and Humphrey at my brother's house, Lucy. My sister and Mistress Margery shall likely be living with us, but I am not free to offer you a place."

Shoulders sagging, Lucy crushed her holland apron in her fists.

Bess regarded the girl. "Lucy, what do you recall of the

days before your master died? Had he any visitors who may have angered him?"

"You mean who upset him so he . . ." She chewed her lower lip. "Do you believe what they say, Mistress? That the uneasy souls of those who've killed themselves walk the earth at night?"

Bess did not, but others did, and Fulke had been staked to the ground as a result of the old superstition. "Had there been visitors?"

"Bennett Langham had come."

Bess had hoped not to hear his name. "When?"

"I do not recall the exact day, Mistress, but he was fiercely angry, he was. About his father's death in that prison." She blushed at the admission she had overheard their fight. "I could hear him shouting all the way in the kitchen."

"Did it come to blows?"

"No. Master Langham stalked off," said Lucy. "But the master had some tart words about the fellow after."

"Anyone else? A stranger perhaps?" Bess asked. "Or mayhap Sir Walter Howe or Arthur Stamford? Did either of them visit Master Crofton of late?"

"Is Master Stamford the draper who has a shop on the market square? The tall one?" Bess nodded, and she continued. "Well, he came the day Master Crofton died, wanting to be admitted to the master's warehouse where he stores the wool."

Bess knew of the building, which stood at the far end of the yard beyond the garden.

"I had heard, though, that Master Stamford was aware

your master was bound for Devizes that day," said Bess. "Why might he have come here looking for Master Crofton?"

"Oh, he knew well enough, madam. 'Twas why he was here, for Master Crofton would never let Master Stamford see the warehouse after their great argument out in the yard a few days earlier! What a fight that was. After, the master told me to never let Master Stamford into the house again," she said. "I tried to turn Master Stamford away, but he'd not listen. He was to prove that the master's wool was inferior—that was what he said, 'inferior,' spitting the word out like he'd taken a bite of moldy cheese. He asked for Roland, who has the second key to the padlock upon the warehouse door, but I said he was busy. And he was. He was in the yard nearly all morning and into the afternoon mending the thatch on the calf-cote, for Master Crofton was to go to the fair next week and buy us a calf."

"At what time of day was Master Stamford here?" asked Bess, recalling that Goodwife Anwicke had seen Fulke alive during the afternoon.

Lucy pinched her brows together as she tried to remember. "Around midday, I think. Right after I had served the mistress dinner and she had gone to visit the vicar's wife," she replied. "'Tis fortunate for him the mistress was away, else he'd have suffered a scolding."

"Did Roland let him into the warehouse to show him the wool?"

"Oh, no. And Master Stamford made terrible threats, wishing harm to the master. He claimed he had to see the wool before some meeting Master Crofton had set with him for the next day, but Roland would not budge. So Master Stamford stomped off. I had a bit of a laugh about him not getting his way." She sobered. "But then the master did not return from his travels, and Mistress Crofton got so scared. It helped not that Mistress Margery was away at Master Crofton's sister's. The mistress will accept no comfort from me."

Dorothie had been scared for good reason, it turned out. And Bess had been so dismissive of her sister's fears. Fears that remained relevant.

For a killer had yet to be found.

# CHAPTER 12

Bess prodded the kindling in the base of the low brick oven in her still room, then retrieved the pan that would hold the ingredients to be distilled.

*Arthur Stamford. Sir Walter Howe. The Langhams. A vagrant.*

If she stirred those names together into the pan, which one would condense out and form the answer she sought to the question of who had murdered Fulke?

Would that it could be so simple. The problem was that Fulke had too many enemies. Certes, those who had gathered upon the road to watch his body being cut down from the tree had not mourned his passing. Perhaps she should stand outside the door of church that Sunday and ask all who exited to declare their love or their hatred for him.

*Most amusing, Bess.*

She collected the bottles and paper envelopes of her ingredients: chamomile and dried gillyflowers, pepper grains and the powder of sage and rue. Spikenard, nutmeg, and fennel seed. Thinking she heard her niece's voice in the kitchen, Bess paused. She hoped Margery was coming to join her. But the voice belonged to Joan, who took up humming, as was her wont, and Margery did not appear.

With a sigh, Bess weighed each ingredient upon the brass pans of her scale, not more than a dram each. Such a tiny amount but such a significant impact when all were brought together as a whole.

Not unlike the minor hurts and annoyances that occurred between people and which built until the sum total was more than each part, becoming an explosive mixture.

Joan entered with a lantern, for the room grew dark.

"I thought I heard Margery's voice," said Bess. "But it was you humming."

"Your niece has gone to the church, Mistress. She said she wishes to pray, so unhappy is she."

"Did she, now." Bess glanced out the room's narrow unglazed window to the damp scene beyond. "'Tis not like her. Especially in such weather."

"These are not ordinary times. She is affrighted."

"As are we all."

Joan knitted her brows. "Think you we shall have another visit by whatever it was that alarmed Quail last night, Mistress?"

"I pray not, but tell Humphrey to ensure that all the exterior doors and gates are securely bolted."

"You can be certain I shall."

Quail, perhaps hearing his name, came in search of human companions, his nails tapping across the flags. He settled nearby. Joan ruffled the dog's ears.

"Marcye at the Cross Keys stopped me in the square this

morning," she said, fetching a pot of red wine that Bess had prepared the day before.

"Oh?"

"She told me Master Crofton confronted Master Langham as he sat drinking in the tavern a few days ago. He demanded to know if the Langhams were hiding another Jesuit."

*Jesu.* Worse news and worse. "Lucy has told me Bennett shouted at Fulke because of his father's death. Should the constable learn of these fights, Bennett will surely be arrested, if any are," said Bess, tipping the mixture of herbs and spices into the wine.

"Will not the constable arrest the Anwicke boy?" asked Joan. "He ought, for he is a troublesome lad, that one. He vexes the girls on market day when he's come into town. It is said he steals apples and the like as well."

"You know Rodge Anwicke?"

"A lad like that who is soon to be a full-grown man? Aye, Mistress, every unmarried woman in this town knows to keep a weather eye on such as him."

"The constable does not arrest Rodge because he wishes to use the boy as a lure." Turning back to the still, Bess spread the burning kindling to quiet the flames. She set the deep pan atop the fire, its three long feet holding it well above the embers, and poured into it the wine infused with herbs and spices. "In hopes of drawing out the man who may have paid him to assist in the crime. If that was Rodge's role."

"It sounds a dangerous game."

"Aye, and likely futile." Traps had not caught those who had schemed with Laurence.

Joan placed the cone-shaped alembic atop the still,

and Bess pressed a paste made from rye around the joint to seal it.

Finished, she wiped her fingers upon a scrap of cloth lying on her worktable. She looked over at her servant. "How did all this come to pass, Joan? Here we are once more, a murderer in our midst."

An unknown one this time.

Joan had no comforting response. "Mayhap I should have accompanied Mistress Margery to church to pray for our protection."

She picked up the used plate of paste and retreated to the kitchen.

Bess settled upon a stool. The aqua vitae dripped into the glass flask she had set beneath the downturned spout of the alembic, the sight as bewitching as watching sand flow through the neck of an hourglass. However, the gentle crackle of the burning wood, the steady drip of the water had not their usual power to calm her. What, though, was there to be calm about?

The flow of water slowed, then halted. Selecting two of her ceramic jars, Bess carefully poured out the aqua vitae.

"So, this is where you spend your time. When not creeping about at night."

His voice startled her. As intent as she had been upon her task, she'd not heard footsteps in the service rooms' lobby.

Quail, tail wagging, jumped up to greet him.

"When I am not needed to tend to my patients, Constable Harwoode, this is where I can be found." She paused to glance over her shoulder, the lantern lighting the somber look upon his face as he observed her actions.

Blushing beneath his scrutiny, she almost spilled aqua vitae onto the plank that served as her worktable. "I am unhappy with you, Constable. I have learned of a dispute between your cousin Sir Walter and Fulke. A most serious dispute that you did not inform me of." She would not tell him about the argument with Bennett that Lucy had overheard.

"I learned of it only recently myself," he said. "But Wat has sworn he had no wish to harm your brother-in-law."

"Does his vow mean he has come to believe that Fulke was murdered?"

"Even if he did believe so, Wat's opinion would not change the fact that I must convince the coroner. And he will not be convinced until I name the murderer."

"So we get nowhere," she said crossly, forcing wooden bungs into the jars. "And I do not understand why you are here."

Her crossness made a muscle in his left cheek twitch. "I encountered one of my cousin's servants upon the road. Wat's wife is in need of physic," he said. "I came seeking a recommendation from you for a midwife."

"Lady Howe must have the services of one."

"Wat blames the woman for the loss of his wife's other infants," he said. "I told my cousin's servant I'd ask if you know of a competent one. But if you would rather not help—"

"I can attend Lady Howe."

His brows rose.

"Do not look so, Constable Harwoode. I have midwifery skills and have tended to other women with child.

I have even delivered babies before. Successfully," she added, as much to reassure herself as him.

"Are you certain?" he asked. "As you said, your brother-in-law and my cousin were not exactly on good terms."

The iron poker resting against the wall clanged as Bess picked it up. "Their relationship does not dissuade me from wanting to help Lady Howe. She would be a patient, and I would be concerned only with her health."

Bess jabbed at the embers within the base of the still, spreading the unburned wood. This opportunity to meet Sir Walter Howe, the man whom Fulke had refused to sell land to, had come as though a gift from heaven. A gift she would not pass by.

"My thanks, then," he said.

"There is no need for thanks." Stripping off her apron, she looked at the constable. "Let us go to her."

★ ★ ★

"A tiny amount of blood. There has been no pain, however," said Cecily Lady Howe. The ease with which she relayed the details Bess required revealed that she'd often had to speak of miscarriage.

Poor creature.

Upon their arrival at the house, Kit Harwoode had handed Bess off to a servant. The girl had guided her up the staircase and through a series of lavish rooms to the bedchamber where Lady Howe rested.

"What you describe tells me that you need not fear, Lady Howe." Bess soaked a scrap of linen in the cool mixture of water and muscatel she had poured into a tin bowl. "So long as there is no pain, you should recover with rest."

"No pain. So far," she said, her face taut with fear despite Bess's reassurance.

Careful to prevent any drips falling upon the bedding, she laid the soaked linen across the young woman's bared navel and smiled reassuringly. The cool to draw the heat. The calm to temper the passion.

She returned Bess's smile. With eyes as warm as polished walnut wood, a pert nose, and fine-boned face, she was astonishingly lovely. And so very young, much younger than her husband, who Bess had once heard—from Robert, she thought—was more than forty years of age. Lady Howe had to be around Joan's age, just past twenty. That Sir Walter had married a woman many years his junior was not out of the ordinary, but Bess had expected—irrationally, she now saw—that he would have chosen someone older. A widow, perchance, with experience of the world, and who'd be best equipped to help him manage his estate and the duties of the town. Lady Howe, were she not sweating upon the plush feather mattresses of her bed, looked more suited to giggling over her needlework or weaving daisy chains to adorn her lush, near-black hair.

And her, had she married him because he came with a house bedecked with finery most could only imagine? Robert lived comfortably, with beautiful furnishings and servants. The Howes lived extravagantly. Bess suspected that if she searched their buttery, she would find only the best silver and clearest glass. Lady Howe's tester was hung with fringed velvet curtains, the bed linens of the finest weave, and set with more pillows and bolsters and arras cloths than were contained within all the chambers of Robert's house. The air was scented with perfume, and in a neighboring room, a talented servant strummed a lute to soothe his mistress.

Or perhaps, perhaps Lady Howe truly loved her husband. The man who may have killed a stubborn Fulke in order to obtain a strip of land from his widow.

"I will also leave you tansy syrup," Bess said to Lady Howe. "A few drops, twice a day for the next few days."

An old recipe to hold the child in the womb, but one she'd seldom had opportunity to use. In London, women were more likely to request physic that would hasten the birth of a child than attempt to hold on to one.

"You must tell my husband. I will forget."

Bess refreshed the linen, squeezing out the excess liquid into the bowl, then returned it to Lady Howe's belly. What she ventured to say next brought Bess nearer the reason she had leaped at the chance to visit Highcombe Manor. "I should make a note upon a scrap of paper. For I expect Sir Walter has many tasks to occupy his mind."

"Indeed so." Lady Howe's eyes sparkled with pride. "But he never complains about his duties. He attends to them with great seriousness."

"The past few days have likely been difficult ones for him."

"I know not of what you speak, Mistress."

"The incident of which I am thinking involved my brother-in-law. However, if Sir Walter did not tell you, then he meant for you to not be concerned."

"Who is your brother-in-law?"

If Sir Walter came upon them as they discussed Fulke, he would be outraged. "Fulke Crofton. Have you ever heard of him? Your husband sought to purchase land from him."

"I cannot say that I have, but then my husband rarely burdens me with such concerns." If she lied, she was expert at falseness, for her body, her countenance did not betray her. "I am sorry if there have been troubles for Master Crofton though."

"You are most kind." And she was. Sweet and pure as fresh cream.

There was a knock upon the door, and Sir Walter entered. Bess stood to offer a curtsy, her heart hammering in fear he might have overheard.

"Sit, Mistress Ellyott. Sit." A crisp wave of his hand accompanied his words, exhibiting no lack of confidence that he would be obeyed. Nothing in his manner, though, suggested he had heard their conversation. "There is no need for formality here."

"Sir," she said, retaking her spot upon the stool.

"Are you well, dear heart?" he asked his wife. Lady Howe nodded, and he turned to Bess. "I have heard there are stones from Cyprus that are to be worn about the neck to preserve the child in the womb. Do you have any of those?"

"I do not. But I have a syrup for her to take that should work as well."

"I sent my servant for the apothecary, but I am told the man is ill. And you have come instead upon my cousin's recommendation." He examined her. "He has vouched for your skills, and you have my thanks for offering to help.

Others have failed before, and I would not have Cecily suffer again."

"See how good he is to me, Mistress Ellyott? He fusses and frets like the old nurse I had as a child. And he stays with me often, neglecting his duties to his manor and town." She smiled at her husband, her face as radiant as an angel's.

"While you are here, Mistress, I would extend my sympathy for your brother-in-law's passing."

His manner was kindly. He did not look evil. More importantly, he did not look guilty.

"I am grateful for your kind words, Sir Walter," she said.

A wry smile flickered. "And no doubt unexpected, coming from someone who had once argued with Master Crofton."

Bess inclined her head.

"Wat, who is this fellow—" Lady Howe gasped. Grimacing, she pressed fingers to her belly. "There is a pain! I shall lose the child!"

"Shh," Bess said to the young woman, running hands over her abdomen and feeling no contractions. The pain was likely a passing cramp. If there were more though . . . "Breathe slowly and deeply, madam. Do not become alarmed."

"I should have been with you earlier," said Sir Walter. "You needed me."

The deep breaths had given Lady Howe ease. "Nay. You are good to me always." She pressed the hand he rested upon the counterpane. "And I mind not your afternoon walks. They bring you peace."

With care, Bess assessed Sir Walter's reaction to his wife's revelation that he regularly left the house in the afternoon. His countenance remained unchanged, and he appeared as innocent as any lamb.

"I also find a lengthy walk calming, Lady Howe," said Bess.

"He has taken to strolling even in the rain, Mistress Ellyott," she continued. "Except for the other day when it rained so very hard. He went out at midday; otherwise he'd have returned drenched." Her laughter over her husband's foolishness bubbled up from her throat.

"Do you mean that dreadful rain of this past Tuesday, Lady Howe? I was caught out in it myself, returning from tending a child who had burned her hand."

"Aye," she replied. "And 'twas most clever of him to avoid such foul weather. To stroll in the rain invites sickness, does it not?"

"Indeed." If Sir Walter had gone out at midday, he could not be accused of causing Fulke's death. He had been here, at his wife's side during the afternoon, when Fulke had come to harm.

Bess searched about for a sense of relief but still remained uneasy.

"Are you unwell, Mistress Ellyott?" Sir Walter asked.

"Forgive me. I was allowing myself a moment of weakness by envying your daily strolls, Sir Walter," Bess said hastily, removing the damp linen from Lady Howe's navel and rolling it into a ball to carry home.

She collected the tincture of tansy syrup and handed it over to him along with the instructions on its use. He appeared so grateful that a pang of guilt struck. *I had wished him responsible.* Still wished him responsible, and could not shake the sense that she was hunting in the dark for a truth just out of reach.

A manservant came to the chamber door, and Sir Walter went to speak with him.

"My cousin was called away by Gibb, Mistress Ellyott," he said. "A vagrant has been spotted near the mill and must be removed."

"Is it that fellow Cook saw near the woods?" asked Lady Howe, her fingers curling upon her blanket. "The thin-bellied one in brown robes? Cook claims he is a Jesuit."

Bess inhaled sharply, but neither of them appeared to notice her sudden disquiet. He had to be the man she'd seen at Langham Hall. He *had* to be.

"You must not become alarmed, dear heart." Sir Walter bent over his wife and kissed her upon the forehead. "I would go with Kit to help run down this fellow. He has been causing mischief. Will you be well while I am gone?"

"I shall be well. See to your duty, husband. But take care."

He nodded and departed.

"He is a silly man to fret so," said Lady Howe. "You should return home, Mistress, before night falls and catches you out upon the road. If you desire an escort—"

"I shall be fine, madam," she said. "But you do not wish me to remain with you?"

Just then, a young servant girl stepped into the room.

"I feel so much better, and she will stay with me," said Lady Howe, indicating the girl.

"Fare thee well, then, madam," Bess said, gathering up her belongings and tying her cloak about her shoulders. She was eager to be gone so she could think over what she'd learned.

A servant showed her out, and she hurried from the house, her thoughts tumbling like loose stones rolled in a rushing stream. Vagrant. Jesuit. Brown robes. Langham Hall. Links in a chain. A chain that could see the Langhams hanged.

★ ★ ★

Bess did not slow as she rushed along the road, putting distance between herself and Highcombe Manor. What would she say to Margery when she reached home? What should she tell the constable? She no longer knew if she could preserve the Langhams and Margery from harm, or if she should even try.

*Your desire to save the world will bring you harm one day, dearest Bess.*

Martin would chastise her thus. He had done so when she had tried to nurse a mud-soaked kitten abandoned by its mother, clutching the tiny animal to her body to warm it, only to lose the creature within hours. When she had brought home Joan, shivering and filthy, more rags and bones than a female of flesh, who had, she thought thankfully, been far stronger than a poor grimalkin.

And when she had brought home Laurence, not so thin as Joan but as ready to shy from contact or a kind word as a whipped dog. He had proved strongest of all.

All about her, the gloom deepened with approaching nightfall. The damp of the day's rain was causing a fog to lift from the fields, concealing the contours of trees and hedges. The vagrant had been seen near the mill, a good half mile from the roadway, but the distance did not ensure that she was safe. She should not have refused Lady Howe's offer of an escort.

Bess increased her pace. A rabbit darted across the road, and a sparrow lifted on beating wings into the dark of the cloud-covered sky. Not far away, she heard boys calling to each other, one crying out with laughter. On the horizon, smoke rose from countless chimneys. A dog barked, and the church bell tolled. She could see the flare of a torch as a watchman began his rounds. Everyday sights. Everyday sounds. This close to town, this close to all that was regular and normal, she could not be in danger.

Ahead, the burned remains of the plague house and the tumbled stones of the priory stood bleak and lonely. Bess hugged the edge of the lane. In the misty gloom of oncoming evening, the ghosts rumored to haunt the rubble seemed all too real.

*And my imagination has grown fevered.*

She was almost upon the ruins when an unearthly, low wail echoed off the priory walls. The sound was followed by a thump and a rustling. An animal, a loose stone had surely caused the noise.

Heart pounding, she slowed. "Is someone there?"

Would stones answer?

Clutching the strap of her satchel, she rushed along. From behind her came the sound of running feet. *No. No!* She sped up, tripping over the hem of her petticoat. She dared look back. The person was upon her, his arm raised into the air, a rock in his hand.

As he swung it, she screamed.

# CHAPTER 13

She raised her hand to fend off his attack. His arm collided with hers, sending a jolt through her body. The stone he swung crashed hard upon her shoulder. She stumbled, her leg twisting beneath her, and fell, the grit of the road digging into her palms.

Pain seared her ankle, shot up her leg. She scrabbled to her knees, trying to get away. Expecting another blow. Which did not come. Breathing hard, she cast a glance around her. Where had he gone? The light was fading fast. If he waited nearby, she could not see among the shadows.

"Come!" she shouted. Stupidly. She had no weapon besides a satchel filled with jars of physic that were likely now broken.

Her attacker did not appear though. He had to have fled.

She tried to stand, but her ankle would not hold. Taking slow, deep breaths, which turned to mist before her face, she reached up to feel her shoulder. A lump swelled the size of a Seville orange, and her fingers came away sticky. She did not need illumination to know it was blood.

She closed her eyes and wondered how long it would be

before someone found her. Joan would grow concerned and send the watch out. Surely, she would. The cool evening air chilled the sweat that dotted her forehead, and the cold ground beneath her made her shiver. Bess thought she heard the sound of horse's hooves. Or was it the ebb and flow of raised voices? She could not tell if the noises were real or a dream.

"Here!" a man shouted.

A horn-paned lantern bobbed nearby. The person carrying it thrust it before her face. The flare of light made her recoil.

"'Tis the herbalist!" he shouted. "Master Marshall's widowed sister."

Along the road, a knot of onlookers collected, a huddle of shadows in the gloaming. From among them, a man came and kneeled at her side. He wrapped an arm around her to provide support. "Mistress Ellyott."

She peered at him, his face limned by the lantern. "Constable."

"Have I not warned you of the dangers of wandering about at night alone, Mistress?"

"I fear I do not listen."

"Are you badly hurt?" he asked.

"He struck my shoulder with a stone," she said, wincing as pain lanced down her arm. "And I have twisted my ankle badly. But otherwise, I am unharmed."

He looked down and noticed the blood upon her fingers. His eyes when they met hers were filled with concern. "Did you see the fellow? Can you provide any description at all?"

"I saw just an arm," she said, her attempt to recall nauseating her. "He was about your size. I can say no more."

"Can you stand, Mistress?"

"Without retching the day's meals onto the ground?" she asked. "Not yet."

"Then we wait until you are able."

"Constable, come here. Quick," a man called from the depths of the ruins.

"You. Help Mistress Ellyott."

The constable gestured to one of the fellows who'd gathered to stare. The fellow separated from the others, hurrying over. It was the town's barber, a jovial fellow, and he winked as he took the weight of her body, which the constable had yielded.

"I have you, Mistress," he said.

With a deep inhalation, she turned her head to see where the constable had gone. "What is going on?"

"I cannot say," answered the man. "Do you want to try to stand now?"

"Aye."

With a great deal of gentleness, he lifted her to her feet. She swayed unsteadily on her one good leg.

"This man," she croaked, addressing the crowd. "The man who came from the ruins and hit me. Did any of you see him flee?"

Her question was met by murmurs and shrugs.

"A man," she repeated, more insistently. "You must have seen him run off."

"It has grown too dark to see, Mistress," said the barber.

She looked to where the constable bent over an

indistinct shape, a black outline against the ground. "Take me there," she said to the barber. When he hesitated, she repeated her demand.

He helped her limp over. The man with the lantern had moved off to search among the stones, but he returned to cast its light over the form. The yellow glow showed legs, a threadbare coat tangled about a torso, a body facedown in the muck and mud, and a shock of red that was not all blood.

She gasped.

The constable turned at the sound and straightened. "Mistress."

"Rodge Anwicke." She could not tear her gaze from the boy's body. "He is dead?"

"Aye," the constable answered. "Murdered."

Bess crumpled, the barber struggling to hold her.

"I will take her from here," said the constable to the barber. "The rest of you, search for the vagrant."

The fellow with the lantern thrust it forward to show the way.

Kit Harwoode wrapped an arm tightly around her. "Lean against me, Mistress."

Without hesitation, she did.

* * *

The journey back to Robert's house was slow. Every time Bess winced in pain, the constable stopped and would not proceed until she assured him she was able to go on. A group of inquisitive boys followed them, caught up in Bess and Kit's progress like fish entangled by a trailing seine.

Through the streets of town came the call of the hue and cry. Doors were thrown open, and folk spilled into the roads, torches and lamps in hand. The person who had killed Rodge Anwicke must be found.

A lantern, no doubt lit by Joan when Bess had not returned before nightfall, glowed at the gate to Robert's courtyard. She was home at last.

Joan met them at the door.

"Mistress?" She stared at Bess's shoulder, her eyes widening in alarm. Blood must have seeped through the wool of Bess's cloak. "Bring her into the hall, Constable. A fire already burns there."

Margery stood up from the settle. "What has happened?"

"Mistress Ellyott has been wandering about at night again," said the constable, easing Bess onto Robert's chair.

She set down her satchel, hearing the clink of broken jars within it. "Rodge Anwicke is dead, Margery. His killer sought to quiet me."

Margery went as pale as Joan. She should not have been so blunt, but niceties no longer served.

In the entry passage, Quail barked at several boys attempting to crowd into the house. Joan shouted at them to get out and join the hue and cry. She slammed the door and rushed across the hall, bound for the still room and Bess's supply of salves.

Margery bent to undo the ties of Bess's cloak. A knot of concern wrinkled her forehead. "When I returned from church and you had not come back from Highcombe Manor . . . I was right to be alarmed."

"Aye, Margery," said Bess.

The constable stood aside. "You are in capable hands now, Mistress. I must attend the coroner. This time, I do not doubt what his conclusion will be."

"Rodge was killed for what he knew about Fulke's death. Tell him that," said Bess. Joan came back with an earthenware jar, a pitcher of water, and a stack of cloths with which to clean the wound. "Tell him he must now believe that Fulke was murdered."

"I will tell him, but I make no promise he'll listen." He turned to Joan and Margery. "Take good care of her. I'd not have it otherwise."

He offered a bow, so unlike him it took Bess aback, and marched out of the room. Joan hurried ahead to open the door.

When she returned, it was with a lifted eyebrow and a quirk of her mouth. "Well."

"Read not too much into his concern, Joan," said Bess, wincing as Margery undid the laces binding her sleeve to her gown. The sleeve stuck to the shift beneath, which tugged upon her shoulder wound, causing it to bleed afresh.

"Oh, Aunt Bess, how terrible!" said Margery. "This is simply terrible!"

"Mistress Margery," said Joan, "we shall require more cloths and your aunt's stitching quill."

She undid the bung sealing the jar. From the aroma that rose, Bess could tell it was her defensative of flour, honey, and turpentine. "Who was it, Mistress?" she asked once Margery was gone.

"I did not see who attacked me," said Bess. "It could have been anyone."

Joan finished removing Bess's sleeve. The shift beneath was ruined, and after an unnecessary apology, Joan tore the linen away from the wound.

"Mistress Margery is right. This is terrible." She pressed a pad upon the gash to stanch the bleeding. "Only a vile creature would do this to you."

"I wish I had seen his face," said Bess, trying not to flinch as Joan dabbed at the blood. "And now we shall not learn who gave Rodge that coin, or how he obtained Fulke's hat." A trap had again failed. This time, a boy was dead. "The murderer shall escape, will he not?"

As Laurence had, drifting like dust among the darkened passageways of London? "If no one else with knowledge of the crimes comes forward . . . he might."

"He must be found," said Joan. "You were near killed. I could not bear that."

"The wound is none so bad as all that, Joan."

"But Rodge Anwicke *is* dead, and you were attacked," she said, replacing the blood-soaked pad with a fresh one dipped into cool water. "By a man whose face you did not see and cannot identify. If you do not know who this fellow is, Mistress, how can you protect yourself should he seek to attack you again?"

Bess's gaze met Joan's fretful one. How could she answer that? "The constable has set the hue and cry upon the vagrant."

"Why does he think the vagrant is responsible?"

"The fellow is easiest to blame," said Bess. "None of those who came running saw my attacker, Joan. None of them. 'Twas as if he had vanished into the air."

Joan's hands ceased their work. "Deal we with a living being, or a specter?"

"God save us if the ghosts have risen to strike us down."

★ ★ ★

*A specter.*

Bess gripped the edge of her chamber's curtain.

As a child, she had heard the tales. A ghost could not appear outside the hours of midnight and cockcrow. Bess's attacker had struck as twilight had faded into night. Furthermore, the figure that had raised its arm to wield a stone was no specter. He had been as solid as the form of her niece, who watched Bess as she stared out her bedchamber's window into the gloom of night.

Margery crossed the room to join her. "You should rest, Aunt Bess. There is no more news to learn."

Humphrey had heard that the coroner had correctly ruled Rodge's death a homicide, but despite the efforts of every able-bodied citizen in town, the hue and cry had not found the culprit.

"My shoulder and my ankle ache too much for me to sleep," Bess said, wrapping her arms about her night rail, insufficient warmth against her deep chill. Below them, the watchman's pole struck the roadway as he passed, his bell tinkling. Across the way, the neighbors snuffed out the candle placed near their hall window, the light blinking out like a star hidden by a passing cloud. "But I would not have you lose sleep as well."

"I do not mind staying with you," said Margery. "Shall

I fetch some sweet violets to bind to your head to help you rest?"

"My thanks for your kindness, sweeting." A man rushed along the street, a lantern held aloft. The last of those gone out to attend the hue and cry, she supposed. Her gaze tracked the lantern light until it disappeared inside a house. "But neither sweet violets nor lavender will help me rest tonight. Not when another person has died, and I cannot say who is guilty and who is innocent."

She turned away from the window and drew the heavy curtains into place.

Margery set her jaw stubbornly. "The Langhams are innocent. And the constable has placed the blame upon the vagrant."

"Do you not understand, Margery? The constable has already attempted to connect the vagrant to the Langhams," she said. "If the fellow is sought as Rodge Anwicke's killer, it is not so great a leap to extend blame to Bennett and his family. After all, the vagrant is rumored to be a Jesuit, and it is well known that the Langhams are recusants."

"Bennett has no knowledge of this stranger's designs."

"Can you be so certain?" asked Bess. "Only a few days ago, your stepfather accused Bennett of hiding this fellow, of being a traitor once again."

"And they have paid for the error of their faith with Master Langham's life," Margery responded sharply. "But they do not hide Jesuits. And they do not wish to assassinate the queen."

"I have heard that this vagrant wears brown robes," Bess said, quietly. "When I went to the Langhams' to tend to their servant, I saw a man there, also in brown robes. I asked you about him."

"As if brown robes are so unusual. He could be anyone. A servant, as I said."

Her gaze was as flinty and cold as a winter stone. It broke Bess's heart, but she could not allow affection to pull her up short. "I will ask you again—have you seen such a man at Langham Hall?"

"If I had, would I betray Bennett and his family by claiming so?" she asked. "I know not who this vagrant is, Aunt Bess. And I am sorry if it was he who attacked you."

"I cannot say if he was my attacker. But until he is found, are any of us safe?" asked Bess. "That is my concern. Are *you* safe?"

She tried to take her niece's hand, but Margery evaded her, turning to storm from the chamber.

★ ★ ★

"Marry, Kit," said Gibb. "How could he have vanished without a trace?"

They had left town early, before Sunday services, as the morning sun struggled to break through fog and low-hanging clouds. The chill bit through Kit's padded doublet and the jerkin he had pulled on over it. Winter was approaching.

"If he is flesh and blood, he could not have," said Kit, stretching out his back as he walked. He'd had little sleep and less food. "But the muddy ground around the priory ruins was so trampled by the horde that had come to gawk that any footprints the fellow might have left were erased."

"I could have prevented this, had not my father insisted I finish reviewing the ledgers yesterday." His cousin scanned the fields that spread in rolling waves around them. "An hour's distraction and now Rodge Anwicke is dead."

"Do not reproach yourself, Gibb. I expect the man who killed him would have found another time to murder the boy, if not yesterday."

"But I would have witnessed the crime, and we would know whom we pursued."

"If we aim to assign blame, then assign it to me," said Kit. "If I had seen Rodge put in jail for stealing Fulke Crofton's hat, he would still be alive."

*And I might have slept last night, rather than twisted and turned upon my mattress, the sight of the boy's crushed skull refusing to leave my mind.* The remembered sight of blood upon Bess Ellyott's fingers torturing him, too, making him even angrier.

"At least Mistress Ellyott is not seriously injured," said Gibb, as if reading his thoughts.

"This time."

A plowman was out in the nearest field, tending to a pair of oxen that munched a pile of hay. He spied Kit and Gibb and signaled to them to stop.

He slogged across the field to the road and doffed his cap. "Have you found the fellow, Constable?"

"If you mean the murderer, no," said Kit.

The man nodded in the direction of the Anwickes' cottage. "'Twas their boy who died, was it not?"

"Aye. What do you know of him?" asked Kit.

"I will say I am glad he was not my son," he answered. "His father will not be sad though."

"Is his father a violent man?" asked Gibb.

The plowman's gaze narrowed. "I thought the vagrant was blamed for killing the boy."

"We must consider others," said Kit.

"Well, the lad's father would not bother to lure him to those ruins and strike him down there. What fear had he from the law if he punished his son too severely and the boy died because of it?" The plowman shrugged. "None."

"Another, then," said Kit. "For example, one who may have paid Rodge to complete a task that this person did not wish others to learn of."

"'Tis no secret that lad could be hired to do any sort of job. Even foul ones."

"Can you put names to those who hired him?"

The fellow began to list people, turning as he pointed out almost every house and cottage within eyesight. He and Gibb might need to question all the villagers about their actions yesterday at twilight. "I hear he has worked at Langham Hall, and the gardens at Highcombe Manor as well," the plowman added.

Kit did not care for the amused glint in the man's eyes as he relayed that piece of information. "Is this not Sir Walter's land you rent?"

The glint vanished, and the plowman slunk backward, his moment of rebellion quashed.

"What about the ruins where the Anwicke boy was found," said Kit. They sat in the distance, curling bands of fog creeping across the damp meadow to lick at their stones. "Have you ever seen the vagrant there?"

"The Jesuit, you mean," the fellow said. "Nay, sadly. For if I had ever seen the fellow, I'd have tracked him down and brought him to the burgesses. I've no love for his kind."

"If you hear news of him, tell us." Kit thanked him and continued on.

Gibb trotted alongside, his hand gripping the weapon at his waist to keep it from slapping against his hip. "Everyone thinks the vagrant is a Jesuit. Topcliffe or his fellows will come here for certain."

"'Tis trouble we have no need of."

"And to hear that the boy *had* done work at Highcombe," said Gibb. "You were right to wonder if Wat knew the boy."

"He did not recognize Rodge's name when I mentioned it."

"Mayhap Wat has no need for names."

"Mayhap so."

They arrived at the Anwickes' cottage, its windows shuttered and door closed.

"Are they gone to church already?" asked Gibb.

"We shall find out." Kit pushed open the gate hanging loosely from the wattle fence and strode up to the door to knock upon it. Several moments elapsed before Goodwife Anwicke answered.

Her eyes were red-rimmed, and the babe she bounced upon her hip sniffled and clung to its mother's sleeve.

"Have you found Rodge's murderer?" she asked. From within the cottage, the girl who'd been Mistress Ellyott's patient peered at them. The hazy light coming through the open door fell upon her bruised face, and her large dark eyes stared like those of a cornered animal.

"I've no such welcome news for you, Goodwife," he said.

She squeezed her lips together as fresh tears rolled down her cheeks. "Why?"

"Do you know of any who wished your boy harm?" asked Gibb, his voice sweet. He had a soft manner when it came to questioning women, a manner that could calm them.

"The lads in town were cruel to him. Called him a dullard and a wantwit. All because he could not read. Who has the time for such fine things as hornbooks when there are mouths to be fed, I ask you?"

"I do not believe he was killed by one of the town boys, Goodwife," said Kit.

Another girl, older than Maud and equally thin, came from the back room to join her sister. She sidled over to Maud and put her arm around her, but the younger girl threw it off.

"That coin and that hat were accursed," said Goodwife Anwicke.

"You mean that odd hat Rodge had? The tall one with the feather?" asked Maud's sister. Maud scowled and slapped the girl's arm. "Ouch. Stop that, Maud. What is the matter with you?"

"Fighting now?" cried their mother. "At such a time? Put on your blue kirtle for church, child."

Maud stomped into the rear room.

"Must we go to services today?" asked her sister. "After what happened to Rodge?"

" 'Tis the best time to go," said her mother.

"When did you see Rodge with the hat?" Kit asked the girl, before her comment was forgotten.

She scuttled over to the doorway, seemingly pleased to be asked a serious question, like an adult. "The other day, sir. When I went to fetch him to dinner. He had it then."

"Which day?" asked Gibb.

"Why, the day Maud got her bruise and the healer from town came to tend her burn," she answered. "The day that man hung himself."

"Tuesday at midday, then," said Kit. Hours before the lad had claimed he'd found the hat in a ditch. Hours before Fulke had supposedly been seen upon the road, returning from Devizes astride his horse and with his hat upon his head and his cloak about his shoulders.

"Aye, sir." The girl gave him a look as if he were daft to not have understood. "Afore dinner."

"Goodwife Anwicke, you told Mistress Ellyott that you saw Master Crofton riding along the Devizes road on Tuesday afternoon, did you not?"

"Aye, so I did." Her gaze darted between Kit and her daughter. "I do not understand."

"If Rodge already had Master Crofton's hat at midday, it was not Fulke Crofton you saw that afternoon," said Kit, his jaw setting. "It was either the murderer or his accomplice."

"But what has that to do with Rodge?" she asked.

"I am not happy to say this, Goodwife, but a coin in his possession suggests he may have been paid to help a killer," said Kit. "Perhaps to ride around wearing a dead man's cloak and hat."

# CHAPTER 14

"Mistress, we may leave now," whispered Joan. She had come from the church's rear seats, meant for servants, to take Bess's arm. "They have all gone from the porch and retired to their homes."

Bess lifted her eyes to the simple wooden altar. At one time, according to Robert, the arch above the chancel had been decorated with a great doom scene of Christ and his mother and the angels trumpeting the coming of the judgment. But that scene and the colorful images of heaven and hell that had once adorned the walls were buried beneath plain white plaster, all signs of its former life as a Catholic church obliterated. There were no images to gaze upon now, the worshippers to focus upon God, not symbols. Those in attendance had not been focused upon God, however; they had been focused upon Bess. They would gossip—not all of them unkindly—when they returned to their halls to dine that day.

Had she heard the vicar's sermon or joined in the prayers? She had prayed for peace for the Anwickes, that she recalled. She had prayed for Dorothie as well. Prayed for her sister's boys and for Margery and the Langhams . . . for all of them, for strength against the darkness that hung like heavy summer clouds presaging a storm.

"My head aches, Joan," she said, rising from the pew. "Has Margery gone back to our house?"

Her niece, hands gripped tightly in her lap, had sat alongside Bess with her head bowed. The congregation would gossip about her, too. The Stamfords had occupied a pew not far behind Bess and Margery. At least Bess had not had to look upon Sir Walter, who attended another church with his kinsmen, and wonder if he had, in truth, gone to the mill last night to chase down a vagrant. Or if he had instead lain in wait in the ruins of a priory to kill a boy he no longer trusted.

"Aye, she has done," said Joan, taking Bess's elbow. "With Humphrey."

They slowly made their way out of the church, Bess limping upon her tightly bandaged ankle. As it was Sunday, most shops were shuttered, and the structure that housed the market stalls stood empty. Three young boys splashed through pools of water that had collected from a spit of rain before sunrise, whirligigs spinning in their hands. Groups of people, strolling home from the morning service, chatted with one another. They paused to look her way as she and Joan crossed the square. It seemed the only living creature that did not halt upon spotting her was the pig that once again wandered free of its cote to snuffle in the rubbish of a nearby gutter.

In London, it was simple to be anonymous, a person's

actions known to but a few and commented upon by even less. Not so in a town of this size.

"Do not mind them, Mistress," said Joan. "In fact, the barber's eldest girl asked most kindly after your health."

"They mistrust me for being a stranger." Or for being a witch, if the constable's alarming comment had been any indication of some people's thoughts. "Mislike me for being related to Fulke. Mayhap they even believe I deserved last night's attack."

"Nay, do not think so, Mistress. They have come to respect you for having healed so many," she insisted.

They continued past the market cross, the building that housed the stalls, and the central well. Amice Stamford had already returned from church to stand in her shop's doorway, watching Bess's progress. Before the woman could hike the skirts of her gown to dash across the square to intercept them, Bess heard her name being called.

"Widow Ellyott," the man repeated.

It was the churchwarden in his usual all–black attire, swooping toward her like a raven intent upon a piece of carrion.

Bess extracted her arm from Joan's grip. "You may go on, Joan. I can hobble the rest of the way alone."

Joan frowned at the churchwarden as he drew nearer. "Are you certain?"

"I would keep you away from him," she said. "Go prepare the meal. I shall be home anon."

Bess shooed her away and greeted the churchwarden. "Master Enderby."

"I am pleased to have seen you at service this morning."

"I said I would attend."

"Even in your condition. Most commendable," he said. "I heard of your misadventure last evening."

"I am grateful to Constable Harwoode and the men who rushed to my aid for chasing off the man who attacked me," she said. "If they'd not, I might not be speaking with you now. Or able to attend services."

He tilted his head to one side to better inspect her. The pose reminded her of a bird watching for insects. "I have heard you did not see the man's face."

"I did not."

"So you cannot say for certain it was the vagrant?"

"As I said, I cannot identify my attacker, Master Enderby," she replied, holding his gaze. "All I know is that it was a man."

"Ah." He gathered his robe in his fist. "Lest I forget, I would have you know that Master Topcliffe does indeed intend to visit us. I am most glad I can be assured that I need not inform upon you."

"May I ask the reason for his visit?"

"It is not in my power to say," the churchwarden replied.

"Is he coming because of the vagrant?" If so, the Langhams were in great danger.

A tiny smile flitted across his broad face. "Good day to you, Widow Ellyott," he said and strolled off.

In not two breaths, Amice Stamford bolted from her shop doorway and charged across the square toward Bess, her farthingale making her skirts sway like a bell.

"Mistress Ellyott, I was surprised to see you at church.

After what happened yester-even," she said, her pale eyes scanning Bess from tip to toe. "I am glad you are not severely injured."

"My thanks for your concern," Bess answered, awaiting the true reason Mistress Stamford had stopped her.

"It is whispered about town that the boy's death is connected to that of your brother-in-law," she said. "And that the constable has decided Fulke Crofton was murdered. You have convinced him with your foolish ideas."

"He has seen the proof I have seen."

"Which is?"

Bess would not answer that question. "Were you aware your husband sought to examine Fulke's warehouse the day that my brother-in-law died? There is no need to deny his visit, Mistress Stamford," Bess said, forestalling her rebuttal. "My sister's servant recalls it quite clearly. He was angry and demanded access to the building where the shearings are stored. He made threats against Fulke."

Amice Stamford paled. "You yet seek to blame Arthur. I did not realize you hated us so to make such vile claims."

"Mistress Stamford, you are an honest woman. This I know."

"You wish to flatter me now?"

Bess reached for her hand. Her skin was soft, as soft as Margery's. Did she anoint it with the oil of almonds to keep it so? Bess's own fingers were rough, coarse from hours spent grinding spices and washing herbs, mixing salves and plasters.

"Tell me that your husband did not go out at twilight last night," said Bess.

"To do what? Murder that boy?" She twisted her fingers free from Bess's grip. "For what possible reason?"

"Fulke was murdered. Rodge Anwicke was murdered," said Bess. "Their killer must be found."

"And that person is not my husband!" she spat. "Arthur had returned from meeting his weavers in Chippenham to sup with me at that time. And, though I be but a female and the wife to my husband and can make no claim in the courts, I shall tell the constable and any justice of the peace who wishes to question me just the same. There will be others who will vouch for him as well. I vow that, Mistress. And you are a foul creature to think him responsible."

She spun so sharply on her heel that her gown flared about her ankles.

Bess turned as well and, pretending not to notice all the eyes, all the murmurs, hurried for Robert's house.

Joan had spotted her and flung open the door. "Mistress!"

"I have made an enemy of Amice Stamford, Joan." *Why can I not be more circumspect? Less unruly?*

"Ah, that one," Joan said, stepping aside as Bess entered. "What did Master Enderby want with you?"

"Master Topcliffe," said Bess. "He is coming."

"Humphrey did hear aright." The frown upon Joan's face was severe. "Mistress Margery has gone out. I fear she has gone to Langham Hall. Humphrey mentioned, in her hearing, that Master Topcliffe is headed our way. Mistress Margery fled soon after, and I have no power to stop her."

Margery *would* go to Langham Hall to warn Bennett about Master Topcliffe's impending arrival.

"Fetch my mules and my cloak," Bess ordered, unpinning her hat and handing it to Joan. "I go to the Langhams' as well. To fetch Margery home before she embroils herself too deeply in their treason."

★ ★ ★

The rain that had left puddles in the square returned, quickly turning the lane muddy. To avoid passing the priory ruins, Bess had taken the westernmost road to Langham Hall, but the route she'd chosen was longer. By the time she arrived, she was as mud-spattered and bedraggled as a dog left to wander in a storm.

The same servant who had opened the door before once again answered her knock. She surveyed Bess's appearance before allowing her into the screens passage. She was to go no farther.

"Have you come to see Anne, Mistress?" she asked.

Bess's cloak dripped grimy water onto the chevron-patterned reed matting that stretched the length of the passage. "Is that the name of the kitchen maid with the cut finger?"

"It is. But she is well and has no need of your services, so far as I know."

"I am pleased to hear it, but I have not come to see to Anne," said Bess. "I am looking for my niece, Margery. She is here, is she not?"

The servant's face went as pink as one of Robert's roses in summer. "I . . . your niece?"

"No doubt you know her." The girl's behavior made no sense. Bess peered at her, which made the servant even more uncomfortable. "Margery Crofton. She comes to visit Master Langham."

The pink shaded to red. Had this girl helped them secretly meet, charmed by the thrill of forbidden love?

"She is not here today, Mistress," she said.

"I do not believe you. Fetch my niece here now," Bess said sternly, "lest I tromp through Langham Hall in search of her myself."

To ensure she was taken seriously, Bess took a step toward the opening in the screens passage the led to the hall.

"Mistress, wait!" she squealed.

Bess strode through the opening just as Margery rushed across the hall toward her, Bennett close behind.

"Aunt Bess! I thought I heard your voice."

Bess extended her hand. "Come, Margery. It is best we leave, and quickly." Before they were seen by whoever had informed the churchwarden of Bess's prior visit. The rain should offer them cover.

"Do not be cross, Mistress Ellyott," said Bennett. "I sent a message bidding your niece to come here."

"After you had told her, in my presence, that it was unwise for you to meet?"

"Bennett, do not lie for me," said Margery. "My aunt knows why I am here."

Bess raised a hand to quiet her before she said too much. The servant who had shown her into the house likely stood nearby, her ears pricked.

"You were wise to suggest my niece not meet with you, Master Langham," she said. "I wish she had listened."

"I believe I have convinced her of the danger." Bennett

gestured for Margery to join Bess. She did not. "I must tell you also that I had naught to do with yester-even's events, Mistress Ellyott. Neither I nor any in this household."

"Does that include the brown-robed man I have seen here?" He had to be aware of the fellow's presence. At least one of the servants would have to tend to the man's needs, and Bennett would not be blind to the comings and goings of trays of food or the emptying of chamber pots.

"No one in this household caused that boy's death or meant any harm to your brother-in-law or you," he replied firmly.

"I'faith, I want to believe you, Master Langham. I do." For his eyes seemed to speak truth, and she did not care to recall how readily she could be duped.

Bess beckoned more sternly for Margery to join her. Her niece crossed the hall but refused Bess's hand.

"Fetch Mistress Margery's cloak," she instructed the servant, who had materialized in the screens passage with suspicious haste.

She returned with the cloak, and Margery shrugged it on.

"I bid you farewell, Mistress Margery," said Master Langham. "I leave for Bristol soon and will not see you before I go."

Margery's breath caught upon a sob and she stumbled from the house, running ahead of Bess and across the gravel courtyard. Out into the rain, where the water could mingle with the tears streaming down her cheeks.

★  ★  ★

Bess's head thrummed, pain radiating from the wound upon her shoulder, as she hobbled along the boggy road. Her sore ankle—and thick mules—prevented her from running to keep up with Margery. Her niece had sprinted so far ahead that Bess could no longer see her through the sheeting rain. So she set a more sedate pace. Her path would take her past the ruins though.

She tugged the hood of her cloak farther over her face. The priory was but a sad pile of stones, she told herself, their gray darkened by the rain. The man who had attacked her and killed Rodge was gone. There was naught to fear during the daytime. All was as it should be. Sheep in the fields. Cattle huddled near a large tree. A cart trundling in her direction, its driver hunched beneath an oiled cape.

Naught to fear . . . if she had not been staring at the old priory, she would not have noticed the shadow moving among the tumbled walls. Bess clutched the edges of her cloak. Was she seeing things? Or had the person who'd killed Rodge returned?

Up ahead, the road rose slightly and would offer a better vantage point. She crept forward. The rain had eased, but the improved viewpoint did not enable her to see through walls.

If she had any sense, she would hurry to town and alert the constable. Her departure, though, would give the concealed man—if he was a man and not just a wisp of fog—the opportunity to once again escape.

"Ho!" she called out from the safety of the road, hoping to flush him like a startled rabbit.

"And pray tell what, Bess," she muttered to herself, "hope you to do if he does run out?"

Attack him? Arrest him? Prove to herself he was a living being and not a ghost? No answering movement came. Cautiously, she started down the slope, making her way toward the priory. Her mules slipped on the damp grass, and pain shot through her injured ankle. She would keep her distance from the building. She was not so stupid as to step through the massive entryway and have him leap out from hiding.

"Ho!" she cried again as she rounded the nearest corner of the structure.

One of the window openings gave a better view of the inside. There seemed to be no place to hide though. Not among the grass growing where tiles, long since scavenged by a local householder, had once covered floors. Or behind the fluted blocks that formerly supported rows of columns.

*This is foolishness, Bess. Dangerous.*

"Is there anyone there?" Nothing moved, except for the drip of water off stone.

"You *are* foolish, Bess."

Just then, a figure in brown robes darted from behind one of the far walls. He dashed through the gaping entryway and scrambled up the incline of the road.

"Stop there!" she cried and hobbled after him, her ankle protesting. "Stop!" she repeated, losing sight of him as he disappeared down the opposite side of the elevated highway. He had to be headed for the plague house. Although she could not comprehend how he thought to hide there either.

Bess climbed to the roadway and down the other side.

He was nowhere to be seen, and she hesitated. How had the fellow managed to elude her so readily? He had to be inside the house, for all around were open meadow and harvested fields that offered no sanctuary, except among damp sheep and some miserable cattle.

The front door of the house was gone, leaving a gaping hole that let onto the main room. Back in London, Bess had witnessed a plague-stricken house being boarded up with its residents inside. By law, they had to remain there to cope with the horrible disease, to survive or die. Most likely to die. Their cries had been horrific and had left her shaken by her powerlessness to help. However, she had no cure for the plague. If she'd dared defy the law and broken the seals that had entombed the family, she could have done no more than ease their pains or give them sleep. At last, one day the cries ceased, freeing her from her helpless guilt. But not freeing her of the memory.

The cart was not far distant now, and the driver perked his head to stare at Bess in curiosity. Walking nearer to the house, she peered inside. During the fire, the upper floor had fallen. Burned timbers littered the flagstone-covered floor and leaned against the massive stone fireplace that separated this room from the one to her left. A section of the original central wall yet stood. A trestle table had not fared as well.

The cart had pulled even with the house, and the driver called down from the road, "Oy! What do you there, Mistress?"

"I may search for a ghost," Bess replied.

"What?" he asked, alarm sharpening his voice. He jumped down from his cart.

Bess ventured inside. She could see easily, for a roof that no longer existed cast no shadows. Rain dripped upon her head as she picked her way between the fallen beams and looked around. A noise to her left, rather like the sound of wood rubbing against stone, drew her attention. But the rooms were empty. The man was not in the house, unless he was as thin as a sliver or as flat as a pile of ashes. There was nothing to see. Nothing at all. It was as if he had vanished into the air.

Like the specter of a dead man.

# CHAPTER 15

"I am sorry to disturb you on a Sunday afternoon, Widow Ellyott," said the woman Joan had shown into the lesser parlor. "With you still recovering from your injuries. A boy killed, and you struck down. What will happen next?"

Bess tried to identify her. Was she the cordwainer's wife or mayhap married to the turner? She decided upon the cordwainer. Short in stature, the woman was dressed plainly but cleanly in a gray kirtle and had an attentive gaze. Which repeatedly shifted from Bess's face to her shoulder as if hoping to spy the wound that throbbed beneath her clothing.

Margery, who'd joined Bess in the parlor but had said not a word since returning from Langham Hall, rose from where she had been finger-loop braiding by the window. Bess set aside the purse she had been embroidering and stood also. As it was, her needlework had been proceeding slowly, for her mind kept wandering to the man at the ruins and how he had succeeded in disappearing again. The woman's arrival was no disturbance at all.

"Those who need my help are never intruding. Not even on a Sunday," said Bess. "What is it you require?"

"My husband's sciatica is most fierce today, and I have heard your salve is the best," she said. "Better than that from the widow who lives near the market cross. And I'll not take him to the leech for a bloodletting. The man nearly drained my poor husband dry the last time."

Bess turned to her niece. "Margery, you may have to make new. Mustard seeds, honey, bread crumbs, and vinegar. You remember the recipe."

Margery inclined her head and headed for the still room.

"Your girl is very fair. They are such a comfort, are they not?" the woman asked, unaware of the pain the question caused Bess, who no longer had daughters of her own.

"She is my sister's child," Bess replied. "But I give you my thanks for the kind words, and so would Mistress Crofton."

"Ah, Mistress Crofton. My sympathies to her in this terrible time."

The woman looked about the room, her gaze lingering on the rich reds and blues and greens of the carpet tossed over Robert's writing desk before moving back to Bess. "My husband tells me the villain who attacked you has not yet been captured. I hear the vagrant is suspected. But not yet been found."

She had come to the house seeking more than a salve for the pain in her husband's hip.

"You hear correctly," said Bess.

"'Tis also said the vagrant is a wraith," she whispered. "You did not see your attacker's face, did you, Widow Ellyott? Does he even have one, I ask?"

"I did not see my attacker's face, but he was very much human," she said. The man at the ruins, though . . .

"Oh, what a fright this all is! A devil creeping about. And yester-even, when my boy came running, saying there had been screams heard at the ruins, my first thought was the old ghosts had risen up," she exclaimed. "I rushed to my chamber window and saw the torches of the men as they ran to help you."

This was intriguing. Bess regarded her. "Mistress, from your house can you also see the fields that surround the ruins?"

"Aye."

"Did you see anyone fleeing across them?"

The woman paused to consider. "I think not. No. I am most certain not," she said. "I saw a man on horseback riding south, but not coming from near the ruins. At least, I do not believe so."

Her attacker *had* vanished. Like a vapor in the heat of the sun. Though it was more likely that Bess's visitor had simply come to her window too late to see the fellow making his escape.

"Unless . . ." The woman across from Bess narrowed her gaze. "Unless the fiend *was* human and was that man on horseback. I could not see his face to name him, as he was too distant and night was approaching. But such a distinctive cloak. Lined with red. It flickered like tongues of fire as he rode along."

"How interesting." However, she could not recall if she had ever seen anyone with a cloak like that.

"You are most fortunate to be alive, after Rodge Anwicke was struck down. My poor Davye is most sad.

Good friends, they were," the other woman was saying. "As it is, my girl has heard from the Anwicke girl—"

"Maud?"

"The one who does not speak? She could not have heard from her, could she have done? Nay, the other one," she said. "As I was saying, my girl has heard that Rodge Anwicke was seen by Goody Anwicke herself—not that the woman was aware it was her son—riding about in Master Crofton's hat and cloak the very afternoon of the day your poor brother-in-law . . ." Her gaze narrowed further, until her eyes were two thin slits. "Is it true he was murdered? 'Tis what they are saying."

"Where did you hear this news about Rodge?"

"I said. From my daughter, who heard it from the Anwicke girl," she answered. "The constable paid the Anwickes a visit this morn, and 'twas then they discovered the cruel trick Rodge had played. That boy. He has met the end, 'tis sad to say, that he deserved. I've warned Davye about keeping with that lad. Wait, where are you off to?" she shouted after Bess, who had bolted from the room.

★ ★ ★

"Am I welcome?" Gibb strolled into Kit's hall, his damp shoes leaving a trail of footprints across the oak floor. He dropped onto the settle by the cold hearth. "When you play upon your gittern, I never know."

Gibb had walked into the house without announcement, startling Kit, who'd been strumming a tuneless song, rapt in speculation.

"You are welcome," said Kit, setting down the instrument. "What have you learned?"

"That the plowman spoke true when he said near everyone in town hired Rodge Anwicke. Even Crofton. To help shear sheep, according to his servant." Gibb stripped off his gloves and rubbed his hands together to warm them. The damp and cold had seeped inside with the morning's rain, lingering long after it had stopped. "But to a man, all their reasons sounded honest and innocent."

"You went to speak with Wat after services."

"Aye, and he continues to profess he has never heard of Rodge Anwicke and was rather displeased I asked, after you had done so the other day." Gibb frowned. "He will complain to my father."

He would, to the effect that Gibb would spend more time helping with his father's accounts and less helping Kit.

"Wat's gardener was also at services this morning, and I asked him about Rodge." Gibb spied a fleck of mud on his plum-colored paned trunk hose and brushed it off. "The fellow did hire the boy, but said it was months ago. Further, he recalled what he'd paid the boy—a groat. Not a sixpence. All the others paid similarly, a few pence, no more. Crofton's servant, however, did not know how much Crofton had paid the boy."

Kit paced the room. "The trinkets, the coin may mean nothing at all. It is possible we follow a trail that leads nowhere."

"We must presume the vagrant is the killer," said Gibb.

"But where does he hide, and how did he escape without

detection?" If the miller had not been so positive that he had seen this vagrant, Kit would believe they were dealing with an apparition. The townspeople were beginning to claim that he was.

"The beast is clever," said Gibb.

*And I am not.*

Kit halted by the hall's window just as Stamford hurried across the square, dodging puddles. Headed for a round of archery, a clutch of boys, long bows in hand and quivers of arrows upon their backs, scattered out of the draper's way. Marcye from the Cross Keys, making her way to the tavern, paused to greet Stamford, only to be rebuffed.

"I wish I'd seen Stamford at the ruins. I care not for the fellow."

"You would have noticed Stamford if he had been at the priory ruins yester-even. As tall as he is," said Gibb.

"I suppose I would have." The truth of which did not improve Kit's mood.

Stamford arrived at the door to his business. At the adjacent shop, the cordwainer's son loitered in the doorway and smirked after him.

"If we but had other eyes to see . . ." said Gibb.

"We may." Kit tracked the tavern keeper's daughter as she wended her way to the Cross Keys. "Fetch Marcye Johnes here. The girl sees everything."

"Up here?" Gibb sounded aghast. "What will her father say about a visit to your rooms?"

"He might claim I need marry her. Bring her up nonetheless."

Gibb rushed off. He appeared upon the square beneath Kit's window and hailed the girl. Marcye did not hesitate to accompany him. Indeed, she appeared rather keen.

The girl fairly danced into Kit's hall. She dropped a curtsy as she gazed about her. Besides his gittern, the hall was bare of any decoration. A plain, useful room. In need of a cleaning. Mayhap she thought it could use womanly tending.

"Constable Harwoode," she said breathlessly. "How might I help you? Whatever you ask."

She shot a glance at Gibb, a tiny wrinkle upon her forehead, perhaps perplexed that he lounged against the doorway and had not left them.

"I have a question, Mistress Johnes," said Kit.

"Aye?"

"About Arthur Stamford."

Disappointment formed a different wrinkle on her forehead. "Oh."

"From the Cross Keys, you can see the door to his shop and residence," he said. "Have you spotted Rodge Anwicke there in recent weeks?"

She chewed her lower lip as she thought, the sight of the tips of her teeth drawing attention to her shapely mouth. "I have seen Rodge at the cordwainer's next door. He is Davye's mate. But at the Stamfords'? Nay. Not of late."

"Last night, did you see Master Stamford arrive back from a journey?"

"Ask you because you think I spy upon everyone?" She pouted. "I am not a gossip."

Gibb smirked behind his hand.

"No, you are merely very observant, Mistress Johnes," said Kit. "And a help to me, if you can answer."

The pout became a coy smile. "I did see him," she said. "He had rented a horse from the inn and clattered across the square in a huff. Not long before the sun had set. He jumped down and rushed inside. After a bit, his oldest came out to return the horse."

"Did he leave again?"

She shook her head. "My father complained he did not come to help with the hue and cry, defying the law. My father was most ireful about that, when he had gone and shut the tavern so we and the customers could assist. As is required. But not for Master Stamford, apparently. I hope he is fined severely."

"I will see to it. My thanks, Mistress Johnes."

She slunk off behind Gibb. Kit dropped onto the settle. Fulke Crofton and Rodge Anwicke had died, and he was no nearer to finding their murderer.

Footsteps sounded outside the hall doorway.

"Gibb, I agree that the vagrant must be responsible."

"Why did you not tell me?"

The irate voice did not belong to his cousin.

Kit jumped up to face the door. "Mistress Ellyott." He inclined his head. "I went to your house earlier to ask after your health, but your servant told me you were not at home. I see, though, you are recovering."

"Why did you not tell me?" she repeated. Gibb had accompanied her, and he leaned against the wall near the door, an amused look on his face.

"Forgive me, Mistress, if I do not follow," said Kit.

"About Rodge Anwicke's ruse that he was Fulke, riding about with my brother-in-law's hat. And upon his horse as well."

One day he would learn that gossip traveled swifter than a spark through dry straw. "According to the lad's sister, all that is certain is that Rodge had the hat before midday—"

"Is that *all* that is certain, Constable? For the Anwickes appear to think otherwise."

Kit felt positive he was blushing. *Bloody* . . . "I may have suggested more to Goodwife Anwicke when Gibb and I visited."

"I dare say you did." She let out a sharp breath. "You could have informed me as soon as you learned of it. Instead, I had to hear this news from the cordwainer's wife, whose children are friends with the Anwicke children and clearly know more than I do."

"You were not at home, Mistress, when I came by earlier," he reminded her.

"So you did mention," she said, pausing to regain her composure. "But this news means that any who have no account for where they were Tuesday morning must now be considered suspects. Such as your cousin. He walked his grounds earlier than usual, according to Lady Howe when I tended her yesterday."

"As I have told you, Wat has sworn he did not harm your brother-in-law." To be required to defend Wat was galling.

"What of last night?" she asked. "Did he meet you at the mill, as he claimed to me were his plans? Or did he lie in wait at the ruins?"

"He had not arrived at the mill by the time Gibb and I left," he admitted. "However, that does not mean he did *not* go there, Mistress."

"Sir Walter should be considered guilty."

Kit glanced at Gibb, whose face was drawn.

"The person most likely responsible is the vagrant, Mistress Ellyott," said Kit. "You should accept that this is the reality."

"The vagrant. Always the vagrant," she responded. "As far as I can tell, he is an apparition that slinks among the ruins south of town, Constable Harwoode."

Kit lifted an eyebrow. "You sound as though you have seen him there."

She hesitated. "I admit that I thought I did earlier today, but I was mistaken. 'Twas but a shadow."

"I did search them, Kit," Gibb reminded him.

"I've not forgotten," said Kit.

"The cordwainer's wife had more of interest to tell, Constable," said Mistress Ellyott. "She can see the ruins from the upper windows of her house. She saw no one flee across the fields, but she did observe some fellow on horseback upon the highway. He wore a red-lined cloak. I do not recall a horse near the ruins last night, but think you it is possible this man was the assailant?"

"Very possible."

"Does Sir Walter own a red-lined cloak?" she asked.

"I have not seen him with one." But what of Stamford? Marcye had seen him ride up to his shop in haste. But the time of his arrival was wrong, too early to have killed Rodge Anwicke and then ridden home.

"We will find the fellow, Mistress," said Gibb, solicitous as ever. "Do not fear for your safety."

She smiled graciously at Gibb, then looked straight at Kit. "Promise me, Constable, that all possible suspects will be pursued, not merely the vagrant."

"I will not protect my cousin, if he is guilty," said Kit. "The killer is frightened, which is why Rodge Anwicke had to die. Soon, he will stumble and make an error that reveals his identity."

"But who else will have to die before he makes that error?"

★　★　★

"They have come to interrogate the Langhams." Margery met Bess at the door, Quail jumping and barking around her legs, tangling in her skirts. "Mother has brought the news."

"What is this?" Bess asked Joan, standing behind Margery in the entry passage.

"Master Topcliffe has arrived, Mistress," she answered, kneeing aside the dog. "I saw him myself, while you were at the constable's. Did you not? The town waites, playing upon their hautbois and shawms, have been sent to greet him as though his arrival is to be cheered."

"I did not see him or hear the waites." Bess limped into the hall, Margery hurrying behind her. Dorothie sat upon Robert's chair, her back as straight as an iron post. "Dorothie, how are you this day?"

"I have lost a husband and may lose all I possess. How think you I might be?" she answered tartly. "Nonetheless, I roused myself from my own distress to see how you fared after last evening's misfortune. I was on my way here when I learned of Master Topcliffe's arrival."

"This is dreadful," said Margery.

"It would seem the queen's men have come at last for the Langhams," said Dorothie, looking at Bess, though her words were for her daughter. "As I have long suspected they would."

"Bennett will not let his mother be taken to London to die," said Margery, her voice taut. "He will insist on going in her place."

"We know not precisely why Master Topcliffe has come or what is intended for the Langhams," said Bess. She lowered herself onto the settle, her body one great ache from ankle to shoulder. "It profits us naught to speculate."

Margery dropped onto the settle beside her. "Is it true what they say about Richard Topcliffe?" she asked. "That he is evil and delights in using the cruelest torture?"

"Thankfully, I have not met him, so I do not know," said Bess.

"He is a foul-looking fellow." Joan tucked the settle's pillows and bolsters against Bess. "He rode into town on the south road, Mistress Ellyott, and the way he stared at everyone from atop his horse . . . as though he searched for traitors among those gathered."

"Hush!" commanded Dorothie. "Do not dare speak of one of the queen's men in such a fashion. You shall see us all in trouble with such words."

"Dorothie, 'tis only us to overhear her," Bess chided. "Joan, fetch us some wine. We have need of it."

"Mayhap we should flee," said Margery.

"Why might we flee? We are not guilty of any crime. I will not hear such nonsense from you, Margery," said Dorothie. "I do wish Robert would return from London. He would sort this out."

"Master Topcliffe's visit does not involve us, so Robert would have nothing to sort out," Bess said, holding on to whatever calm she could muster, which was sparse indeed. "Master Enderby told me he was pleased we all attended services this morning and has no need to mention us to Master Topcliffe. As your mother said, Margery, we have no reason to flee."

Margery chewed her lip. "He has come because of the vagrant, has he not?"

"That Jesuit creature," said Dorothie. "You can be sure he is to blame for much. He is the one who attacked your aunt and killed that boy. And probably your stepfather, too!"

Now her sister suspected the vagrant was the culprit? What of Master Stamford or Sir Walter? "Enough, Dorothie," Bess chided.

Margery had gone ashen. "No one knows for certain that this vagrant is a Jesuit. It is only a rumor. He could simply be a wandering Abraham-man. Or a gypsy."

"He is a Jesuit," insisted her mother. "And the Langhams shelter him."

"That is not true!" Margery retorted. "They do not! No matter what Aunt Bess thinks!"

"What is this, Elizabeth?"

"Prithee, peace, both of you," said Bess sternly.

Subdued, her sister and niece quieted. "We must not fight among ourselves, especially at such a trying time."

Dorothie was not finished though. "I know your heart is tender toward Bennett, Margery, but do not try to defend the Langhams. You are full aware of their past."

"But she could be right about the vagrant, Dorothie," said Bess. "We must allow that Margery could be right and all the rumors wrong."

"Fie. You do not honestly believe that, Elizabeth."

No, she did not.

And they would learn the Langhams' culpability soon enough. For Topcliffe, if he had come for the Langhams, would fall upon them like a ravenous dog and tear the truth from them.

# CHAPTER 16

"Answer me, Wat," said Kit, pacing after his cousin, who strode from his stables toward his house. "I would have the truth about Fulke Crofton."

"You yet think to tie me to Crofton's death?" Wat tugged off his heavy leather riding gloves as they crossed the courtyard behind Highcombe Manor's main building, its stone walls and oriel windows rising before them. The short cloak that snapped in the wind behind him was lined not in red but in silk the color of slate. "Take care, Kit. You are beholden to me. You and Gibb, who dared to question me in front of Cecily about that cottager's son. My wife had felt well enough to attend services but has taken to her bed again, thanks to him."

"I do not wish to harm Lady Howe," said Kit.

"I pray not," answered his cousin. "And think not to ask any further questions about Crofton, coz. You should be hunting down the vagrant, rather than annoying me."

"We do hunt the fellow." After Mistress Ellyott's comment about seeing a "shadow" among the ruins, Kit had searched them on his way to Highcombe. And had come up empty-handed, as Gibb had before.

"Not well enough," said Wat, his stride lengthening. "If you have time to annoy me at my home."

Kit grabbed Wat's arm and yanked him to a halt, his cousin's boots crunching in the gravel as he spun about. "You will speak to me about this matter."

Wat gazed down at Kit's hand. "And you will release me."

Kit slowly uncurled his fingers, and Wat jerked his arm away.

"You told Mistress Ellyott you were bound for the mill last night, to help find the vagrant, yet you did not arrive before I left. Nor did I see you along the way." Kit stepped up to Wat, close enough to feel his cousin's hot breath upon his face. "And the day Fulke Crofton died, you had gone for a stroll earlier than was usual for you. Close in time, perhaps, to when the fellow met his end."

"This is your reasoning for how I am guilty?"

"Tell me where you strolled, Wat," said Kit. "Where were you?"

"I walk. 'Tis no sin."

"With no one to witness where you go."

An angry flush reddened his cousin's throat above the edge of his ruff. "Fie on you, Kit Harwoode."

"If these walks are so innocent, then you'll not mind admitting where your feet take you."

"To the river," he spat.

*The river.*

The response so startled Kit that it had to be an honest

answer. He could name the precise spot. The last known place a young hothead had been seen in the company of an equally young and hotheaded Wat Howe.

"Does visiting the river ease your guilt?" asked Kit. "Or do you go there to serve penance for your crime?"

"You and Gibb. Two of a pair." Wat's tone was derisive. "You both think you know what happened that day."

Cocksure. Yet guarded. Kit could see the uncertainty in his cousin's eyes. *The tables have turned, coz.* "I do know what happened."

"The fellow was never found," answered his cousin, as coolly as he had ever done. "He disappeared. Left the county."

"So you have always said." Kit clasped his dagger, slung from his belt. "And I presume you want me to believe you walked to the river rather than join the search for the vagrant last night. An evening stroll."

"I did go to the mill, but my help was not required," he answered. "I left immediately. The uproar made me concerned for Cecily, so I returned to Highcombe and sent my servants to assist." He peered at Kit. "Do you believe me?"

"Do you care if I believe you?" For he never much had before.

Wat crushed his gloves in his fist. "Not really."

He marched off. Through a window, a servant spotted his approach. He rushed to fling open the rear door then slam it shut behind his master.

★　★　★

Bess limped across her bedchamber, removed the candlestick sitting upon her stool, and dropped onto the seat. At the foot of her bedstead, Quail opened an eye to look at her.

"Ah, Quail, another sleepless night for me."

The dog readjusted his head and closed his eye.

The pain in her shoulder throbbed in time with the pulsing ache in her ankle, sore from too much walking that day. From the adjacent chamber came the sound of Margery's weeping. Outside, the watchmen patrolled the streets with greater frequency than before. Somewhere in the village, the burgesses feasted and flattered Richard Topcliffe in their eagerness to prove their devotion to the queen. While Master Topcliffe likely schemed his worst for the morrow.

More importantly, a stranger in brown robes flitted among stones and up staircases. And Bess had not told the full truth to the constable of her encounter with the fellow. Out of a desire—were she honest with herself—to shield the Langhams and, by extension, Margery. In violation of the law.

Was he a killer, though?

"Jesu," she breathed aloud and grabbed the candle she had put upon the floor. Her head was beginning to ache along with everything else. A cloth soaked in her preparation of rue-steeped vinegar would help the pains.

"Stay, Quail," she ordered the dog and went downstairs, the candle lighting her way.

As she turned to enter her still room, she heard a faint noise in the kitchen. The dull glow of the hearth fire cast Joan, hunched upon a stool, in its light.

She heard Bess's approach and looked up from what she had been doing. "Can you not sleep, Mistress?" she asked, rising.

"Nay. Between Master Topcliffe's coming and my many pains, I cannot even recline upon my pillow." She nodded at the hornbook dangling from her servant's hand. An old piece of parchment, printed with the alphabet and the Lord's Prayer, was tacked to its oak surface and covered with a thin protective sheet of horn. "What do you there?"

"'Tis a means to calm myself. I practice my letters, but I have no paper upon which to write them." She held up the book and traced her fingers atop the letters. "I brought it with me from London. It may be a silly use of my time, but I want to learn to read and write. Mayhap I would be of more use to someone, with my . . ."

She need not motion to the scar upon her face for Bess to understand.

"Learning to read and write is not a silly use of your time, Joan," she said. "Martin had begun to teach you, had he not?"

"Aye, and Mistress Margery helps me now, when she is here and has time to do so." Joan's eyes searched Bess's face. "You must yet miss him greatly."

"Most deeply, Joan," she answered quietly. "And at a time like this, when I could use his wise counsel and the strength of his arm and of his heart . . . I feel his loss keenly."

"We will survive these dreadful events, Mistress. If we survived what happened in London, we can survive again."

With a smile, Bess clasped the hand her servant proffered

and felt the ache in her head slip away. The love of a friend a better cure than vinegar and rue.

★  ★  ★

Early the next morning, Kit made his way across the market square. The Stamford girl peered through the open window of their shop as he neared the row of buildings that housed both the draper's and the shop belonging to Davye's father, the town's cordwainer.

The man looked up from where he sat at a bench, stitching the sole of a shoe onto a delicately pinked upper. "Master Constable, good morrow to you."

Kit was met by the warm smell of leather, pieces of which hung upon the walls and were stacked on trestle boards. Wooden forms, modeled from customers' feet, sat in a neat row upon a shelf. The cordwainer's tools—blades and awls, pieces of chalk to mark a pattern, thick needles sticking up from a pincushion—were spread across his bench. Pairs of completed shoes waited near the window.

The fellow himself, a canvas apron tied over his shirtsleeves and breeches, rubbed his back as he straightened from his bent position and stood. Wrinkles crisscrossed his forehead, left there from squinting at his work. He glanced down at Kit's feet. "Need you new shoes?"

"I need to speak to your son, Davye."

Frowning, the man set his needle and unfinished shoe upon the bench. "What has he done now?"

"I do not know that he has done anything wrong, but he may have information I require."

Rather than bring him, the man turned and bellowed the boy's name. From the room behind the shop came the sound of running feet.

Davye burst into the shop. "Aye?" he asked, sneaking a wary glance at Kit.

"Speak to the constable, boy," his father said, shoving his son, who tripped over a pair of shoes on the floor.

"I've done nothing!" protested the boy, as wiry and sharp-eyed as Rodge Anwicke had been.

"Might we speak in private?" Kit asked the cordwainer.

Sighing, the fellow wagged a finger at Davye and disappeared into the rooms behind the shop.

"I have heard that you and Rodge Anwicke were mates," said Kit.

"Aye, we were," he said tentatively. "He is dead now."

"Sadly so." From where he'd hung it upon his belt, Kit untied Rodge Anwicke's pouch. He cleared a spot on the cordwainer's workbench and emptied the contents onto its surface. The silver sixpence glittered dully. "What can you tell me about these items? Have you ever seen them before?"

Davye's gaze danced from the articles strewn across the bench to Kit's face and then off into other parts of the shop. When it lingered on the street at Kit's back, he suspected they had drawn unwanted attention. Kit turned to face the window, and Stamford's daughter and another girl ducked out of view.

The boy's gaze returned to the bench, where it focused upon the silk ribbon as though, by sheer force of his gaze, he could will it out of existence. "Uh . . ."

"Let me make a suggestion. You have seen them in Rodge Anwicke's possession."

The boy's gaze flickered.

"Come now, Davye. Your friend is no longer with us to be angry if you tell me," said Kit. He should have brought Gibb, who could get a stone to speak. "And you shall not be in trouble for speaking the truth. This coin, for instance . . ." Kit tapped it. "Who gave it to him?"

"Never seen him with that."

"But mayhap you *have* seen the ribbon before?"

Davye eyed him. "I may have done."

"I would say you have, Davye," said Kit. "Tell me how he got it."

Davye shrugged. "Cannot say. And Rodge cannot either."

"Do you wish me to question you about a missing pig, boy?" The lad blanched. "I thought not. So, did your good friend steal the ribbon, or was it given to him?"

Davye chewed on his lower lip as he pondered his options. "I will not be in trouble?"

"No." Although, thought Kit, that did depend upon what the lad told him.

"Rodge got it for doing someone a favor," he said in a rush.

"Someone. A man or a woman? One of the Stamfords, mayhap?"

"He never said a name I remember. Just 'someone.'"

"When did he do this favor?" asked Kit. "And what was it Rodge did?"

"May have been a week past. Or two weeks," said

Davye. "Rodge wanted fine things like what the rich folk have. Said he was going to give the ribbon to his mother." The boy frowned. "Never did, though, did he? And cannot now."

What had happened a week to two ago? A pig had been stolen. A vagrant had arrived. Bennett Langham had come to town. "And the favor . . . what was it?"

"Rodge was to just watch. That was all, watch," said Davye, releasing what he knew piece by piece, as slowly as the drips from a leaky bucket.

Kit drew in a lengthy breath. He had no patience for this sort of work, which Wat had also known when he'd made the recommendation that Kit become constable. "Watch what or who, Davye?"

Davye blinked. "Them at Langham Hall. Them papists."

★ ★ ★

"I mislike this, Mistress," said Joan, handing Bess her hat. "You haring off to the mill to ask questions."

"I cannot idly sit and wonder if the Langhams will be accused of harboring a Jesuit," she said. "I would learn from the one person who has seen the fellow if he is a priest at all."

She had other questions as well, which he might have answers for.

"You are still injured," said Joan, frowning.

She smiled. "Do not fret, Joan."

The mill stood upon a bend in the river, where a race had been carved into the land to carry water to the wheel, then back out to the river again. Two stories high and built of stone, it was one of the most solid structures in the village besides the church. Inside revolved the heavy grinding stones, turning grain to flour. As Bess drew near, she could see through the windows a fine flume of dust clouding the lower level. Though it was a busy time of year for the miller, just after the harvest, it appeared she was in luck—no customers crowded the mill, and he was alone with his apprentice.

Bess stepped through the ground-floor entrance. "Master Miller," she called out. The sound of the millstones drowned out her voice, so she waved and called again.

His apprentice, a strong-shouldered lad, noticed her. He set down the bag from which he'd been pouring grain into the hopper above the millstones and signaled to his master.

With a frown, the miller looked over at the doorway where Bess stood. He craned his neck to see beyond her, perchance wondering if she had brought a wagon loaded with grain, and frowned more severely when he determined she had not. She was merely a pest interrupting his work.

Bowlegged, his clothing whitened by a thin coating of dust, he strode over. "What want you, Mistress?" He smelled of raw flour and sweat. He pointed a thumb at the interlocking gears behind him. "I've grinding to oversee."

"I require but a moment of your time."

He peered at her. "You are that healer woman who lives with Master Marshall. The one who was attacked at the ruins after that Anwicke boy was killed."

His comment had made her questioning a great deal easier. "I am." Bess shook her head mournfully. "After what happened to that lad, I suppose I am fortunate to be alive."

"That you are."

"And what a frustration that the fellow responsible has

not been caught," said Bess. "I expect Sir Walter is most concerned about the threat this man poses. He even joined the search that night, did he not?" Her first question.

"Sir Walter did not come here to help look for a vagrant," said the miller. "He sent his servants."

Sir Walter had lied, then, to Bess and to Lady Howe as to where he had intended to go.

"Now if I may return to my work, Mistress."

Bess stayed him with a hand. "Prithee, good sir, my servant is most fearful of this strange fellow," she said, creating a story in hopes he would be more willing to speak. "It is said he is a Jesuit, though I do not understand why any would think a Jesuit would come here. We do not favor them in Wiltshire."

"Do not some of us?" He cocked an eyebrow. "Your brother-in-law knew better."

And may have died because of that knowledge. "What do you know about the vagrant? What have you seen of him?" Her second question.

"I've told the constable all I know."

"Can you not tell me, though?" she asked pleadingly. "He may be the one who attacked me, and I need to be able to identify him should I encounter him again."

"As you will." The miller swept his hands before him, indicating she should go out into the yard. The apprentice slid them a curious glance as they left.

He walked over toward the wheel, which creaked and groaned as it turned in the flow of the race, the paddles gently striking the water. " 'Twas when I saw the fellow sitting near the sluice that I realized what he was. At first, I thought it might have been that Rodge Anwicke. Always loitering about, as he does, and causing trouble rather than minding what that father of his needs done."

"Was this the first time you saw the vagrant?"

"No. Saw him nine or ten days ago. At the time, I thought him a traveler passing through. Stopping to fish at the river."

Nine or ten days ago. Around the time Fulke confronted Bennett about harboring a Jesuit. "And the next time was the day I was attacked."

"Aye. I found him just outside the mill. I was done for the day and had gone home. But I'd come back to fetch a torn apron I'd left here, for my wife to mend. 'Twas then I saw him," he said. "I've heard about them Jesuits slipping into the country. As sure as I am standing here, he be one of them. And now Master Topcliffe has come, which means I am right to think so."

"How can you be so certain he is a priest?"

"The fellow had beads in his hand. Papist prayer beads. Just sad it is that he saw me and ran off. In truth, I would have throttled his skinny neck if I had been able to lay hands upon him."

"Skinny? I thought them all plump."

The miller gave a laugh, which turned into a rattling cough. She had a passing thought that she should provide him a drink of honey water stewed with raisins to help his throat.

"Not this one," he said, once his cough subsided. "Thin under his brown clothes, and with sharp bones on his clean-shaven face."

A man precisely like the one she had seen.

*Oh, Margery, the fellow is not a simple Abraham-man.*

"He did not wear a red-lined cloak?" she asked, her third question. "A villager told me they had seen a fellow so attired fleeing after Rodge was killed."

"Plain brown clothes. That is all, Mistress."

"Oh. I do wonder who it was with that cloak . . ."

"Never seen one," he said. "Those Langhams will pay for their treason though. Helping hide a Jesuit. Master Topcliffe will see to it," he said, lumbering off before Bess could ask any more questions.

★   ★   ★

"What did you learn?" Margery asked, looking up from the finger-loop braiding she had been working on near the hall window. "Joan told me you went to speak to the miller about the vagrant."

"I am glad you have kept yourself occupied this morning," said Bess, coming across to inspect her niece's handiwork. "Well done."

She untangled her fingers from the loops of silk thread. "Aunt Bess, I am no child in need of protection from the truth."

Bess considered Margery's lovely face, which had lost the soft contours of youth. In the year Bess had been in Wiltshire, her niece had indeed gone from child to woman. However, she was less certain that Margery no longer required protection from the truth.

"The miller has good reason to suspect the man is not a simple wanderer but is a priest, or at least a devout

Catholic," said Bess. "He is trouble in whichever package he comes."

A rapid knock sounded upon the front door, and Joan sprinted from the service rooms to answer it. Rising, Margery shot Bess an alarmed glance.

Mistress Langham's servant, the one Bess had tended, hurried into the hall. She had carelessly tied on a straw hat, and it sat askew atop her head.

"I am sorry to disturb you," said Anne, dropping a curtsy. "I have a message for Mistress Margery."

Anne held out the note. Her hand, with the cut finger Bess had bandaged mere days before, trembled.

Margery bolted from where she stood and snatched it from the girl. "'Tis from Bennett. This is his seal." She tore it open and read. "Master Topcliffe's men have come for Bennett and his mother. They are taking them to the churchwarden's house, where Master Topcliffe has been staying."

Joan gasped.

"When?" asked Bess.

"They are with him now, Mistress," said Anne. "Master Langham had but a short time to pen that message and give it to me before the men stormed into his bedchamber and took him and the mistress away. Once Master Topcliffe's men all left, I ran here as fast as I could."

"I must go to him," said Margery. "I must go to the churchwarden and demand Bennett and his mother be released. They have done nothing wrong."

Bess grabbed her arm before she could make good on

her idea. "You shall do no such thing. These are dangerous men, and offering yourself into their hands will not help Bennett."

"I would ask what they are charged with, that is all," she said.

"You shall not."

"Mistress Ellyott." The constable strode into the hall. He looked around at all of them, frozen in their places. "I trust you have heard the news."

"What are they charged with?" Bess asked.

"With aiding a Jesuit." His gaze was sober. "You have been summoned, Mistress Ellyott, as well. The churchwarden has tasked me with bringing you to his house, to be questioned by Master Topcliffe."

"No!" both Margery and Joan cried out.

Bess reached for Joan's steadying arm and returned the constable's gaze without flinching. "So be it."

# CHAPTER 17

They stared, all of those who noted Bess's procession through town. Every person who had ever called upon her to heal their ill child, tend to their sores, cure their aches, their rheums, their rashes. They had made a connection between Topcliffe's arrival and her march across the market square, and the connection was not to her credit. She could not hide in the shadow cast by Kit Harwoode, and she would not cast her eyes at the cobbles beneath her feet. She was guilty of no crime. She had not aided a Jesuit, sought to unthrone the queen or lessen her authority, prayed over a rosary or heard a Mass. Her father had been raised a Catholic, but he had lifted a finger to test the winds of change and had early realized they blew against him and his family. However, if Bess's sin was an unwillingness to inform upon people proved guilty of nothing more than supposition, then she was indeed at fault.

Bess held her chin high. Out of the corner of her eye, she noticed the unhappy frown on the baker's face. The wife of the cordwainer, who had required a salve for his sciatica, watched pityingly. Amice Stamford, standing in the doorway to her shop with her husband at her side, smiled with unconcealed gratification.

"We are nearly there," said the constable, his voice quiet and steady. "I will stay with you, if I am allowed."

"They will not permit you to stay," Bess said, deeply touched that he wished to protect her. "They will desire no witnesses."

Dearest God, but how her gorge rose. If they tortured her, she did not know how she would bear up, what she might confess. I'faith, she owed the Langhams nothing. She should inform any who would ask that she had seen a suspicious fellow in their house. A fellow who matched the miller's description of the vagrant, the suspected Jesuit.

Yet all she could think upon was Bennett's gentle affection for Margery and Mistress Langham's sincere protest that she was innocent of any plot to harm the queen. Bess could not live with her remorse if she were to profess to Master Topcliffe that the Langhams were guilty, merely to save her skin.

"They only wish to ask you questions, Mistress," he said. "Not subject you to the rack."

"How I do pray that is the case, Constable."

The churchwarden lived in a modest house located upon a narrow, crowded lane not far from the church. The upper level jettied above the lower, with a bank of casement windows and detailed timbering on the gable that faced the street. A broad-shouldered stranger in a simple dove-gray doublet with crimson knee breeches, the livery of the man he served, answered the constable's knock. The stiff way he carried himself, and the ferocity of his probing gaze, gave him the air of a former soldier. He showed them into the cross passage. The churchwarden awaited Bess in the hall to their left.

He was alone in the room, a space as austere and devoid of ornamentation as his attire usually was. Perhaps the absence of retainers was meant to reassure Bess that he was not a threat. She did not feel reassured.

"Constable, you are not required," he said, his voice echoing off the rafters and the bare tiled floors. A brief, forced smile crossed his face, then was gone.

"I will stay to hear the charges against Mistress Ellyott," the constable answered, resting his hand upon the dagger he carried at his side. He would stand firm by his promise if he could.

"There are no charges, Constable Harwoode. We merely wish to speak with her," said Master Enderby, whose tone was mild but whose gaze was cold.

"Concerning what?" asked the constable.

"If you insist, then I shall tell you." The churchwarden leaned back in his carved oak great chair, folding his fingertips atop his waist. The light angling in from the windows outlined the churchwarden's profile. She had never seen him look so cruel. "Concerning a bit of news freshly received that Widow Ellyott is aware of the presence of a priest in this area and has not reported what she knows about this traitor."

Bess's pulse leaped. Who had informed upon her? "I *did* tell the constable of a man I thought I saw hiding near the ruins, only to discover no one there."

"I did not inform you, Master Enderby, because I determined Mistress Ellyott did not see anyone at the ruins," said the constable, defending her. "If you do not believe me, though, mayhap you should question my loyalty to the Crown as well."

The churchwarden, who had been so carefully observing Bess, turned his attention to the man at her side.

"Widow Ellyott has befriended the Langhams, despite what her brother-in-law learned about their associations with Jesuits," he said. "They are recusants and dangerous acquaintances. I have already had to speak to her about her friendliness toward them as well as her own recent absence from church attendance, as is required by the queen's law."

The room encroached upon her, stiflingly close, as if the casements had never been opened to allow fresh air to thin the sharp aroma of the camphor that scented his clothes. Bess could scarce draw a breath.

"As I told you, Master Enderby," she said, finding her voice, "I went to Langham Hall to attend one of the servants, who had cut her hand. My visits have had naught to do with priests or plots."

"Is that so? I have also heard that you may have provided monetary support to the Langhams for this fellow."

"That is a lie. Who is your source that has made such a false claim?" Bess demanded.

"Come now, I shall not name the person," he replied.

"The person" did not reveal if the liar was male or female.

"In good earnest, Master Enderby, I vow I have not provided monetary support to the Langhams," she said, glancing over at the constable. She needed him to believe her. "I am but a poor widow, dependent upon my brother's charity. I have no funds to provide to anyone."

The churchwarden tapped his fingertips together. From somewhere in the house came a woman's cry, followed by loud voices.

"I cannot allow . . ." The constable reached for his dagger and charged toward the stairwell in the far corner of the room.

"Constable, I would not interfere with Master Topcliffe, were I you!" shouted Master Enderby.

Bess quaked at the possibility that the sound had come from Mistress Langham.

The house went quiet, and Constable Harwoode returned to Bess's side. He took her arm, his grip painfully tight.

"Permit Mistress Ellyott to leave, Enderby," he said. "She is not involved in whatever conspiracy you mistakenly believe you have uncovered. Furthermore, I have received no orders to arrest her."

He began to drag Bess toward the door, where they were met by the liveried servant. Bess could see now that he was taller and more muscular than the constable. He also carried a short sword, which she had not previously noticed.

"Ask your guard dog to move," ordered Constable Harwoode.

"He is not my guard dog, Constable. He is Master Topcliffe's," answered the churchwarden. "And I believe it is time for Widow Ellyott to meet him."

★ ★ ★

The constable was detained in the hall while Bess was shown up the stairs. The sound of his shouted complaints at the churchwarden as she was led away echoed through the house, followed by the slamming of the front door. The staircase let out onto an upper-floor great chamber, which fed onto other rooms, their doors shut. In this space, there were more comforts—a cloth painted with a banquet scene done in rich burgundies and gold, Spanish leather cushions and bolsters on furnishings, a lovely carved mantel over the fireplace. She would later marvel that she had made note of the furnishings, given the sinking dread that nauseated her and made her faint-headed.

The liveried retainer led her through an empty bed-chamber, similar in ornamentation to the great chamber. He knocked on a closed door set into the opposite wall.

"Come," said a man within the room beyond it.

The space was tiny—the churchwarden's privy study, Bess surmised—and hardly larger than a cupboard. The smell of fear, rank and stale, wafted out. The study was out-fitted with a narrow cabinet and a desk placed beneath a mullioned window, which lent insufficient light for any-one who might desire to work there. One of the panes was cracked; Bess did not know why she made note of such a detail. The desk's chair had been turned to face a stool. Upon the stool sat a man who smiled grimly at her.

"Widow Elizabeth Ellyott, is it?" he said. His accent was of the northern counties, which surprised her, as she had expected the voice of a Londoner. "I am Richard Topcliffe."

If she passed him in the market, she might make no note of him, not think to cower. He was plain enough, of average height and average weight, his stark black attire unadorned by pinking or elaborate embroidery, his graying beard long enough to hang over the front edge of his mod-est ruff. The only jewelry he wore was a thin gold ring on his right hand and a pendant, strung upon a heavy chain, that likely marked his office. His features did not bear a scar, nor did he possess a deformity that would, as many folk might claim, mark him out as touched by the Devil. The only outward sign of evil were his eyes, which carried a hollowness, an emptiness, as if his heart had never known compassion. Mayhap if she passed him in the market and looked into those eyes, she would cower. For he seemed a man, she decided, who would not permit affection to weaken his resolve, nor allow pity to stay his merciless judg-ment. A man to be feared.

"Do not quiver there so, Widow Ellyott. Sit, sit." He gestured at the chair opposite, then gave a signal to the ser-vant who had escorted her to depart.

The door shut behind the fellow, enclosing Bess with this most hateful of men. Soon her own sweat of fear would join the stench of the others', those who had been in this room before her. She dared not venture to ask after the Langhams.

Bess took the seat, clasping together her hands, which trembled like willow branches in the wind.

"Have I not heard the name of Ellyott before?" Master Topcliffe eyed her. "In London, I think, and associated with some treasonous plot."

Laurence's plot. He had entangled Martin in his schemes and continued to entangle her, like a spider casting its web far and wide.

"I cannot imagine that you have done, good sir, as

Ellyotts are not traitors." Her stays pressed against her ribs, and she longed for fresh, cool air. "Indeed, my husband provided money to the cause of defeating the Armada. He and his kin have always supported the Crown. And my family is loyal as well. My brother gave up one of his horses to be used by the armies in the Low Countries and has sent funds."

Master Topcliffe, whose hands rested atop the protrusion of his belly, tapped his fingertips together. "Ah." Her litany had not impressed him.

"Why am I called here, sir?"

"I appreciate your directness," he said, though the look in his soulless eyes suggested otherwise. "In my humble capacity as one of our great Majesty's pursuivants, I am rooting out decay, which threatens to topple the proud tree of our land."

His analogy appeared to please him, and he smiled.

"I am not decay, Master Topcliffe. I am a loyal subject," Bess said, though his smirk made plain he had heard such words many times before.

"I am informed you do not regularly attend church."

"I have missed but one service, which I regret most sincerely. Master Enderby will tell you that I and my family attended yesterday," she responded. "I have given my excuses to the churchwarden, good sir, as to why I have been remiss in the past. Such will not happen again."

It would not behoove her to beg for mercy. Richard Topcliffe was as likely immune to pleas as he was unimpressed by claims of loyalty.

"I am no Catholic," she added.

"Mayhap so. But there *are* hidden Catholics in this

town. Yes, even here in Wiltshire, where recusants are as scarce as black swans," he said. "And you know them. Support them."

"Whom do you mean?"

He shook his head over her vain attempt to feign ignorance. "You would do well to be honest, Widow Ellyott. I mean the Langhams, of course."

"I do not know if they remain Catholics, Master Topcliffe. I am not privy to their inner lives. We are not friends."

"They would be wise, I believe, to not view you as a friend." He consulted a scrap of paper, which had lain tucked upon his lap, hidden beneath the sleeves of his robe. Bands of wide black velvet trimmed the cuffs. "For is it not so that your brother-in-law, Master Fulke Crofton, received a reward some eighteen months ago for reporting the Langhams' support of the Jesuits? Hidden priest holes, I believe."

"I was unaware he had received compensation." Bess idly wondered what Fulke had spent the monies upon.

"You seem poorly informed," he said drolly.

To that, she did not reply.

"But now you consort with the Langhams." He squinted at her, the light from the window at her back glittering in his eyes. "Where lies your loyalty?"

"Most assuredly with the queen." Bess swallowed, her mouth gone dry, and she gripped the arms of the chair. "And I do not consort with the Langhams, nor do I provide them funds."

He leaned forward and placed his left hand upon her right. He pressed it onto the sharply carved wood of the chair's arm, which dug into the tender skin of her wrist.

"Tell me where the Langhams hide the Jesuit, Widow Ellyott," he said, leaning into her, the weight of his body pushing down. Tears rose in her eyes, and she fought to hold them back. "'Tis a simple enough request I make."

"I know naught of this." Every muscle in her body clenched. "You must believe me."

"The truth."

"Forsooth, you must believe me! I do not know where a Jesuit hides!"

The pressure of his hand increased as he shook his head. "I am most disappointed with you."

Before he could continue his interrogation, a knock sounded.

"What is it?" he barked.

The door squeaked open tentatively, and the liveried servant poked his head through the opening, nodding before he spoke. A wrinkle between his brows hinted he was troubled by the news he had brought. "I regret to tell you, Master Topcliffe, that they have found nothing of importance. And the servants have been questioned most acutely."

"They have not searched the house well enough."

"They vow they have."

Abruptly, Master Topcliffe released Bess's hand and stood. "I shall go there myself."

Bess did not move her hand. She would not rub at the ache that throbbed along her arm and disclose how greatly he had hurt her. 'Twas a pointless act of defiance, but she would not allow him the satisfaction of witnessing her pain.

"You shall remain here with Master Enderby, Widow Ellyott," he said. "Do not try to leave."

He swept from the study, and Bess clutched her wrist, allowing the tears to fall.

★　★　★

"You must see her released from that creature's grip, Enderby," said Kit.

The churchwarden had retired to his knot garden, to stroll among the faded flowers and quince trees as though it were any other autumn day and Topcliffe's men did not occupy his house at that moment.

"That creature, Constable, is the queen's creature and a dangerous man." He bent to pluck a leaf from a sage plant and lifted it to his face to inhale its aroma. "Not a man to be crossed."

"Mistress Ellyott is innocent of any offense," said Kit.

"He would not have questioned her if he believed that."

"She has done nothing wrong."

Enderby looked over. Beneath his black coif and cap, his face twisted into a frown. "She has been seen at Langham Hall. Her niece, who is often in her company and currently resides beneath her roof, keeps company with Bennett Langham. He is the son of a recusant who was jailed for his crimes, and neither Widow Ellyott nor the girl's mother forbid this acquaintance. You cannot hold that she has done nothing wrong, Constable, for those are crimes aplenty."

A servant exited the house and padded across the garden path. He bowed over the note he held out to Enderby. "A message has arrived."

The churchwarden read what was scrawled upon the paper.

"Well, Constable, you are saved from needing to further plead for the woman," he said, looking up from the note. "Master Topcliffe has finished at Langham Hall because he has been called to the Tower to attend to a priest discovered in Oxford. Widow Ellyott is to be released." He folded the paper and ran the crease between thumb and forefinger. "But think not that she is cleared of suspicion. I shall watch her most carefully." He tapped the note against Kit's chest. "And I advise you to do likewise."

# CHAPTER 18

Bess huddled in the corner of the churchwarden's privy closet, listening for Richard Topcliffe's return. The only noise came from her guard posted outside the door, who cleared his throat on occasion to make her aware of his presence. How long would she remain here? The church's bell had tolled, and her count of the chimes told her she'd been locked away at least an hour. Margery and Joan would be frantic. She wished she had some means to send them a message that she was well enough.

A loud voice interrupted the guard's throat clearing, and the door was flung open to reveal Kit Harwoode. Supporting her injured wrist, Bess scrambled to her feet.

"Are you hurt?" he asked, searching her from top to toe.

"Not terribly," she said. "Am I to be released?"

"Aye. And before any decide otherwise, let us get you away."

The constable took her elbow and guided her out of the room. Master Topcliffe's liveried servant was gone. When they descended the stairs to the ground floor, she saw they were alone, without evidence of Richard Topcliffe or his guard dog or the churchwarden. Or the Langhams, who might not be so fortunate as Bess and could yet remain barricaded within some room of the house.

Constable Harwoode ushered her outside. Once they were a few doors away, Bess stopped in the shadow of a nearby tailor's shop and pulled in a breath to quell her shaking.

The constable wrapped a fist around his dagger. "He did hurt you."

"In truth, it is not so bad." Though only her wrist was bruised, the throb had resumed and moved up her arm and into her already aching shoulder. The world around her took to dipping and spinning, and she leaned her head against the shop's timbered wall. "I fear for the Langhams though. That man is cruel."

"What did he want from you?"

"He demanded I tell him where the Langhams hide a priest," she said. "But I do not know. I do not—"

The world spun more rapidly, and she clutched at the wall behind her.

"Mistress!" The constable grabbed Bess to keep her from falling. "You should sit."

"Here? In the filth and muck of this passageway?" she asked, finding strength to jest. She looked into his concerned eyes. "I am better. 'Twas but a passing dizziness."

"You are safe from Topcliffe now. He has gone to London. A priest was found hiding in Oxford and has been brought to the Tower for Master Topcliffe's attention." Satisfied she'd not collapse, the constable leaned against the wall at Bess's side. "You will be pleased to learn that neither he nor his men uncovered anything treasonous at Langham Hall."

"No priest holes? No vagrant who might be a Jesuit?"

"No, Mistress," he answered simply.

Thanked be God. Perhaps the danger diminished. "With Master Topcliffe's departure, hopefully, the church-warden and everyone in town can be likewise convinced of their innocence."

"You have lived here long enough to guess how the townspeople might respond."

They might never be convinced. "But the Langhams shall be allowed to go free."

"Mistress Langham has already been released. Gibb takes her to her home as we speak," he said. He scanned the people who walked through the square. "We should not be resting here, where the town can gape at us, then gossip later. You need to tend your injury." He nodded at her wrist.

"Why cheat them of yet another opportunity to chatter about me?" For they did gape—the fellow cradling an ach-ing jaw who was heading for the barber's on the corner, the carpenter's ever-curious apprentices, the tavern keeper's daughter, who stared at Bess and Kit Harwoode with a frown marring her pretty face, to name a few. Even the cur that had paused to make water against the wall of the adja-cent glover's shop cast a glance in their direction before lop-ing off. "Besides, I need a few more moments to calm the tumbling in my head."

For the first time in days, the sun broke through the clouds. It slanted through the narrow gap between buildings to warm her face. The air, though carrying an unhealthy whiff of sourness from the gutter behind the butcher's, smelled far sweeter than the air within the churchwarden's study. She would never be able to look upon Master Enderby again without recoiling.

"I cannot fathom who told the churchwarden that I provide aid to the Langhams," she said.

"Someone who has decided you are an enemy," he said. "Perchance the same person who paid Rodge Anwicke in ribbon to spy upon them."

She looked over at him. "You have learned this?"

"From the cordwainer's son, who was once Rodge's mate," he said. "If you are recovered enough, we should get you home."

Constable Harwoode took her arm again and encouraged her to start walking. When Bess perceived that the wife of the tailor was leaning through an upper-floor window to eavesdrop upon them, she comprehended his reasons for getting her to move.

"Poor Rodge. Caught up in schemes we do not yet comprehend," she said, her ankle, her wrist, her shoulder . . . so many parts of her body throbbing. "Would the same person who gave him that ribbon have killed him though?"

"Mistress, I do not know," he said. "And I do not like that I do not know."

"I should tell you that your cousin misled us, Constable Harwoode. The miller says that Sir Walter never came to the mill the night Rodge died. Has he admitted as much to you?"

"You are questioning people?" he asked, his brows lowering. "Do you always court trouble?"

"Not always," she replied. "However, you did not answer."

"Wat claimed he went but turned back for home after determining his help was not needed," he said. "However, I did not meet him upon the road, and I should have . . ."

A man upon horseback spurred the animal through the square, weaving his way between the dairyman's wagon and a cart laden with supplies for the painter working on a house across the way. He nearly trampled a young child playing outside upon the cobbles, causing the girl's mother to shout at him, and reined in the animal before the constable's house.

"It appears you have a visitor at your house, Constable Harwoode."

"Indeed so," said the constable. " 'Tis Gibb."

The constable increased his pace, forcing Bess to hobble after him.

Gibb Harwoode tipped his cap at Bess. "Mistress Ellyott, 'tis good to see you well," he said. "I bring news of Mistress Langham, Kit. She collapsed when we arrived at her house."

"How poorly is she?" asked Bess.

"I am no physician, Mistress," he said apologetically. "But she is not well. I came looking for you, Kit, because her poor health concerned me, and I knew not what to do."

"Is Bennett Langham with her?" asked the constable.

"He has not yet been allowed to leave the church-warden's house."

"How does he fare? Do you know his condition?" Bess asked.

Master Harwoode shook his head. "Although his mother thinks Master Topcliffe spent most of his energies upon her."

Nausea rose. "I would go to her. Let me fetch my satchel from my home." She would need her mixture of black soap and honey for any bruising. If Mistress Langham required a plaster for broken bones—which Bess prayed would not be required—she would have to make a fresh supply.

"It is unwise to go to Langham Hall, Mistress," said the constable. "Even if it were safe, you are in no condition to travel there."

"Bring Mistress Langham to my house, then, if it is so unwise for me to go to her."

"Mistress Ellyott, you risk your standing in this town by tending to a woman interrogated by Topcliffe."

"My standing is already damaged by my own summons to that man," she said. "And, as you have so correctly pointed out, no one else shall be willing to tend to Mistress Langham after the interrogation she and her son have received. You know what I say is true."

He studied her. "I see you are determined."

"That I am."

"Then I shall bring her to your house," he said. "And I shall remain behind once she has been delivered. I do not want anyone claiming you and she met in secret to conspire against the queen."

"Many thanks, Constable Harwoode."

He inclined his head, his right eyebrow curving upward. "You do sore test me, Mistress."

"Being obstinate is a skill of mine. In addition to courting trouble," she said. "Ask my brother if you do not believe me."

The curve of his eyebrow was joined by a faint smile. "I have no need to ask your brother, Mistress Ellyott."

★ ★ ★

Margery and Bess stood at the lesser parlor's street-facing window, awaiting Mistress Langham's arrival. Margery gripped Bess's hand with a dangerous and alarming force. *She must love Bennett deeply.* A man she'd come to know well only at that summer's revels, when long days filled with laughter and the headiness of dancing and music warmed hearts. Robert had consoled Dorothie by claiming her daughter's affection was a passing fancy, one that would fade along with the summer sunshine. That Bennett would be forgotten when he returned to his uncle's merchant business in Bristol.

If only Robert had been right.

"Was it terrible, Aunt Bess, being with that man?" asked Margery.

"I shall not lie," said Bess. "Richard Topcliffe is a cruel creature. I pray he did not greatly hurt Mistress Langham, and that she fainted merely from weariness."

A tremor pulsed through Margery's fingers, and Bess pressed a kiss upon her niece's head.

"There!" cried Margery, pointing toward the road. "She has arrived."

An open cart pulled by a donkey trundled in their direction. The constable was driving, and Mistress Langham was tightly bundled in the back, her face obscured by the hood she had drawn close. She appeared to be awake, but she slumped against Gibb Harwoode, who encircled her shoulders with a protective arm.

Margery dashed from the house to greet them. Across the way, their neighbor—who seemed ever more occupied with peeking through her casement window than tending to the needs of her household—squinted to assess the identity of their cloaked visitor. The guessing would not be difficult.

Joan had come from the kitchen. "By God's mercy," she breathed. "Have they killed her?"

"No, Joan. She is yet alive," Bess said. "Place a thin mattress upon the settle before the fire. I would make our guest as comfortable as possible."

Bess went to the back of the cart to help Mistress Langham descend, and the constable hopped down to assist. The woman looked up at Bess. Her eyes, cast into shadow by her overhanging hood, were dark with pain and exhaustion. Dried blood caked her lips, and a bruise showed on her left cheek. Blood from her mouth had dripped upon her crumpled ruff, staining it brown. But resolve was etched upon her features. Topcliffe had not defeated her.

"Come, madam." Bess offered the woman her good hand.

"My thanks, Mistress," she said, her voice a strained whisper.

Gibb Harwoode helped her inch forward to the edge of the cart, and she pinched her eyes shut with the effort. She could not move her right leg without wincing. Beneath Mistress Langham's trailing skirts, Bess noticed hastily wrapped strips of cloth binding the lower part of her limb.

"How does Bennett fare?" asked Margery, leaning over the wobbly side of the cart as though she might find the news she sought hiding there.

"Gibb here tells me he remains under the churchwarden's care," said Constable Harwoode, gently taking Mistress Langham's arm to support her weight. "Lean upon me, madam."

"Is her leg broken?" Bess asked him, though Mistress Langham could answer her question well enough. 'Twas ever the habit of a healer to forget that the patient had ears and tongue.

"It would feel so, Mistress Ellyott," she said, groaning as the two men freed her from the cart and the shifting of her weight swung her injured limb. "But it is not. A bad strain I caused in my haste to depart good Master Enderby's house. I stumbled upon the stairs and twisted it."

"You do not seem a clumsy sort, Mistress Langham," observed Bess.

A taut smile was her response.

"Margery, I need you to make a plaster of flour and eggs to mend Mistress Langham's bones, if there is a chance she has sustained a break," said Bess. "And fetch the physic I use for bruises."

Margery looked longingly down the lane that would take her toward the center of town. "But—"

"I believe Bennett is well, Mistress Margery," assured Mistress Langham, caring for another despite her own miseries. "Fret not."

"Margery, prithee do as I ask," said Bess, sending her niece off.

"If I am not required here, Kit, I will go to Master Enderby's to inquire after Master Langham," said Gibb Harwoode.

The constable nodded and steadied Mistress Langham as she tried to walk. "I could carry you, madam."

"You would not wish to be seen offering such kindnesses to a Langham, Constable, so I shall walk as best I can," she replied, her gaze meeting Bess's. "Further, I would not have Mistress Ellyott's neighbor, who spies upon us, gossiping that I am at death's door."

Bess scowled at the neighbor in question, who hastily withdrew from her window. "Come, Mistress Langham, we will see what we can do to mend you."

Joan held the door open while they made their way inside the house. A limping Bess assisting a woman more severely hurt. What a piteous sight.

"Bring her in here if you will, Constable," said Bess as she ducked into the hall. She gestured toward the settle, over-draped with a thin mattress pulled from the truckle bed Robert stored in an unused bedchamber. "And Joan, fetch a cloth and water to wipe the blood from Mistress Langham's face."

With the constable's help, Mistress Langham lowered herself onto the settle, holding her breath to stop from crying out. The hood had fallen away, off her head, and Bess could better see the bruising upon her skin. What a cruel man. To beat a woman. Even if she was a secret Catholic.

Constable Harwoode stood aside. Gingerly, Bess helped Mistress Langham rest her legs upon the mattress.

Her eyes widened. "What has happened to you?" she asked, staring at Bess's wrist.

"I received some of Master Topcliffe's attentions myself. 'Tis naught more than a deep bruise. I will recover."

"He did this because of your association with us," Mistress Langham said.

Bess glanced over at the constable, who watched them both closely. "Do not fret for me."

Margery returned with the physic and fresh bandaging and set them upon the stool hard by the fireplace. "Might I help remove the old bandages, Aunt Bess?"

"You may. With care."

Bess stepped aside as her niece slowly undid the strips that had been clumsily wound around Mistress Langham's lower limb.

"You have suffered a great deal of late, Mistress Ellyott. To be tormented by Master Topliffe after having been attacked at the ruins along with that poor boy," said Mistress Langham, as Joan returned with a cloth and a bowl of water. The woman dismissed Joan's attempts to clean her face, taking the dampened square of linen to tend to her own bloodied mouth. "I confess I always pitied that lad and the rest of his family."

How bold of her to mention Rodge. Bess slid a glance in Kit Harwoode's direction to assess his reaction. Which she could not read.

"I pitied the lad even when my groom caught him creeping around the grounds," she continued.

Margery frowned over her comment and tugged too

hard on the final length of bandaging, jostling Mistress Langham's ankle and making the woman wince.

"When was this?" asked Bess.

Mistress Langham gave her a look that suggested Bess already knew the answer. "Before my husband was sent to the Fleet."

Margery flushed. "My stepfather—"

"Only did what countless others thought to do but did not act upon quickly enough," interrupted Mistress Langham, handing the wet cloth, stained with her dried blood, back to Bess.

"But it was wrong," said Margery.

"Margery, rather than debate the merits of your stepfather's actions, let us first attend to healing Mistress Langham," said Bess sternly.

Margery quieted.

Mistress Langham's injured limb appeared straight and true, if swollen. Bess probed her ankle and lower leg, feeling for the grinding of bone upon bone that would indicate a break. She felt none. "Can you move your ankle at all, madam?"

"Must I?" she asked, forcing a smile. Gamely, she turned her foot from side to side.

"Are you certain it was Fulke Crofton who paid Rodge Anwicke, Mistress Langham?" asked the constable, whom Bess could not chasten into silence. He buffed the backs of his fingers against his beard. His habit, Bess had come to realize, when he was troubled by his thoughts.

"The boy admitted he had come from the Croftons'."

Bess frowned. The link between Fulke and Rodge was now proved.

"Think you that my limb is broken?" asked Mistress Langham, misunderstanding the scowl upon Bess's face.

"Not at all." Bess drew the woman's skirts back down over her legs. "No break."

"I am relieved, then," she replied. She relaxed against the cushions propping her shoulders. "Of course, that was not the only time the Anwicke boy was discovered on our property. About a week ago, Bennett caught him again."

The payment of the purple ribbon, thought Bess. She glanced at the constable, who appeared to be thinking the same.

Margery reached for the woman's hand. "Prithee, forgive my family."

Mistress Langham smiled gently. "I do not blame you, Margery."

Bess straightened. "You will need to drink comfrey juice to mend, madam. Even though your leg is not broken, you are badly injured. Twice per day," she said. "Margery, spread some of the black soap mixture upon brown paper to wrap about her lower limb."

The girl grabbed up the physic and paper and rushed to Bess's side, allowing her aunt scant time to step away. Mistress Langham was in good care.

Bess went to join the constable, who had gone to stand across the room. "We have discovered the answer to a question."

"Aye." His gaze was upon Margery, murmuring

soothingly as she bound Mistress Langham's leg. "We have learned who paid Rodge."

"But not who killed him."

He looked down at Bess. "Have we not?"

Before she could reply, a knock sounded upon the door, and Joan went to answer it.

Margery finished wrapping Mistress Langham's leg in fresh bandaging just as Bennett strode into the hall. "Bennett, you are freed!" she cried.

"Are you hurt?" asked his mother.

Lowering the hood of his cloak, damp from the rain that had begun again, he offered Margery a smile. "My trials are nothing. I am well."

He strode to Mistress Langham's side, the cloak he wore fluttering as he moved.

His red-silk-lined cloak.

# CHAPTER 19

"Constable Harwoode," said Bess. "I beg you."

Though what did she beg him to do? Not question the man whom the cordwainer's wife had possibly seen riding along the highway in great haste the night Rodge was murdered? The man who had caught the lad spying upon his family again?

He ignored her pleas and strode over to confront Bennett.

"Master Langham, shortly after Rodge Anwicke was killed and this woman attacked," the constable pointed at Bess, "a man in a red-lined cloak was seen riding along the highway. Was it you?"

His mother elbowed herself upright. "What do you mean by this, Constable?"

Margery, ashen, stepped between Bennett and Kit Harwoode. "Leave him be. He would never harm my aunt, and he would never kill someone." She turned to Bess. "You know that is true. Tell the constable that Bennett is decent and honest."

"Margery, it is best you do not interfere," said Bess, indicating that her niece should join her. "Come, now."

"Do you accuse my son of killing that boy?" asked Mistress Langham of the constable, her voice rising in pitch. "Because of what I just told you? Bennett was not angry at finding Rodge Anwicke. We were all merely saddened that our family continues to be so despised. He would not revenge himself upon a child!"

"Your son may answer for himself, madam," he replied calmly. "Provide an explanation for what you were doing that evening, Master Langham. If it confirms your innocence, I shall leave you in peace."

Margery started to cry. Bess wrapped an arm around her and tugged her close. Joan watched them both with dread in her eyes.

Bennett lifted his chin. "I was that man your witness saw."

"No, Bennett," exclaimed his mother. "What do you mean by saying this?"

"Where did you ride from?" asked Constable Harwoode. "The ruins?"

Bennett, his body held stiffly, focused on the far wall. "No."

"Then from where?"

"I am not free to say."

Whom did he protect, wondered Bess, feeling Margery's quiet sobs shudder through her body.

"And the Tuesday last, the day that Fulke Crofton died—"

"He was at Langham Hall. With me," interrupted Mistress Langham. "As I have told Mistress Ellyott."

The constable gave Bess a displeased look. "Master

Langham, are there any others who can vouch for your presence at the hall that day?"

"A servant, mayhap, but would she be called upon to speak on my behalf at a trial?" he asked. "I doubt so. If you feel there is enough proof of my guilt, Constable, then I must submit."

"Do not say these things, Bennett!" cried Margery. She tried to tug free of Bess's grasp, but Bess held tight. "He will arrest you. Do not do this!"

The constable's sober gaze passed over those assembled. He did not appear to welcome the task before him.

"I must arrest you, Master Langham," he said, taking Bennett's arm. His mother sobbed loudly. "I accuse you of the murder of Rodge Anwicke and the suspicion that you had a hand in the death of Fulke Crofton."

★ ★ ★

"How can it be Master Langham, Mistress?" asked Joan, perched on a stool to tend Bess's bruised wrist. "I have always imagined him a good man, but it seems he conceals the truth."

"Lucy told me Bennett had a fierce argument with Fulke not long before he died," said Bess, seated in Robert's chair before the low fire in the hall hearth.

Shortly after a stony-faced Constable Harwoode had marched Bennett out of the house and down the road toward the town's jail, his cousin had arrived to take Mistress Langham back to her home. The woman, whom Bess had thought unvanquished by Master Topcliffe, had looked diminished, frail, and old as she had leaned against Master

Harwoode. She had insisted upon returning to Langham Hall well before Bess thought it wise. But to stay longer would bring more unwelcome attention and gossip upon the household, most likely in the form of the neighbor across the street. The first to speak good. The first to speak ill.

Margery had run upstairs to pace the chamber she borrowed and to cry. Bess could provide no comfort to her niece, and her own heart ached.

She held still as Joan finished winding brown paper coated with Bess's black soap mixture around her wrist. "I cannot believe, though, that he would have actually killed my brother-in-law."

Mistaken again, perhaps. *Martin, when shall I learn?*

"But he would not say where he had been," said Joan, tying a strip of linen around the paper to hold it in place. "If he is not guilty, why did he not give a full accounting, Mistress? He must have killed that boy and attacked you. And possibly also killed Master Crofton."

Bess met her gaze. "He protects someone. Unfortunately, I am forced to presume he protects the vagrant."

"Recusants, then. Loyal to their religion above all else." Joan rose. "Mayhap it is as well that Mistress Margery cannot hope to wed him any longer. The Langhams are dangerous to associate with." She nodded at Bess's injured wrist. "As you yourself have learned."

A noise came from the entry passage, and Dorothie pushed wide the hall door and charged into the room. Quail, who had been sleeping near the front entrance, barked at her arrival but did not follow her. The dog had never taken to Dorothie.

"Did you not hear my knock?" She brushed water from the sleeveless woolen robe she had pulled over her fern-green gown. "The news is everywhere. So it is Bennett Langham who is the guilty one. As I could have told Margery. She thinks too well of him. A Langham. I suppose she is distressed."

"She is. Joan, fetch wine for us," said Bess, sending her servant away.

Dorothie eyed Bess's bound wrist. "And this is what has happened to you because of them. Interrogated by Master Topcliffe." She dropped onto the settle, cleared of the mattress Mistress Langham had reclined upon. "What did he want with you? Were you badly injured?"

"Based upon a rumor murmured into Master Enderby's ear, Master Topcliffe wanted me to provide evidence that the Langhams continue to support the Catholic cause and harbor a priest. As for injuries . . ." Bess lifted her wrist. "This is the worst of it."

"A rumor? Master Topcliffe had no cause to single you out when everyone knows this about them." Dorothie eyed Bess. "Unless you *do* have particular evidence against the Langhams."

She had a great deal of evidence, if one wished to make chains from links. The sight of a brown-robed stranger upon a staircase. A glimpse of the fellow near the plague house. The miller's description, which matched that man—that vaporous spirit—and called him a priest.

However, uncertainty kept Bess from telling all she knew to Dorothie, who would happily forge the chain that would drag all the Langhams to prison to rot.

"It matters not what I think, Dorothie, as Master Topcliffe's men found no indication they are hiding a priest now," said Bess. "But it seems Fulke suspected they once again did. Mistress Langham has said that he hired Rodge Anwicke to spy upon them."

"What? After Fulke's death, she continues to defame him? Fulke never once mentioned hiring that cottager's boy. She lies," said Dorothie. "My poor, dead husband. Both he and that lad murdered. What manner of evil stalks this town? I thought it so peaceful here."

So had Bess.

Dorothie exhaled a shuddering breath. "Forsooth, Elizabeth, what shall we tell Robert when he returns?"

"As little as possible."

"That woman he hopes to wed will not wish to be associated with our family should she hear of this," said Dorothie. "At last, though, Fulke can be placed in the churchyard as is proper. And I might be able to mourn him without shame."

"I have not heard that the coroner has changed his ruling."

"He is away at an inquest, I am told. Once he returns, he shall. Now that Bennett has been arrested. The churchwarden believes so, for his men ceased removing my goods and left my house not a quarter hour ago. The thieves." She leaned toward Bess. "I told you I feared that they had pocketed coins. Well, I have indeed discovered that two pounds, three shillings are missing from Fulke's money coffer. Master Enderby's men have tallied how much it held, but the amount they claim does not match that recorded in Fulke's recent ledgers."

"Mayhap Fulke took the money with him to Devizes."

Joan returned with the malmsey, which she served before once again leaving.

Dorothie set her glass upon a nearby stool. "He would not take so great a sum. Not when he planned to be gone but a few hours and needed no more money than that required to buy a meal at an inn. Five or six pence at most, Elizabeth."

"You should show the ledgers to Master Enderby and demand a repayment," said Bess. Would he comply? Bess no longer trusted the man.

"They also eyed my silver spoons. This is how little we can trust those in authority over this town," she said, echoing Bess's unspoken opinion.

Bess's wrist took to throbbing. "Sir Walter lied about where he was the night I was attacked."

"That one as well. No better." Dorothie shook her head. "Oh, Fulke. Such enemies you made."

Bess contemplated her sister, who had taken up her wine and sipped it. "I do wish I knew who whispered that rumor to Master Enderby."

Dorothie cast a glance about the hall, empty now save for them. Visible through the rear-facing windows, the wavy form of Humphrey moved across the courtyard. In the service rooms, Joan was talking to Quail. "Eyes and ears and petty jealousies everywhere, Elizabeth. Even within our own households."

"I cannot mistrust my servants, Dorothie."

She arched an eyebrow. "Perhaps it would be wise to start."

★ ★ ★

Kit stood in the doorway of the town jail, a circular stone building no more than eight feet across situated north of the market square. Inside, Bennett Langham slumped upon the space's narrow wooden bench, his ankle chained to a thick bar affixed to the cold slab floor. The tiny room, which had no window apart from the barred one in the thick door, reeked of must and urine, the stench from those who'd been chained there before. Not even the rosemary that scented Langham's clothes could mask the stink.

"Why will you not better explain yourself, Master Langham?"

Langham looked up at Kit, squinting into the light that leaked around the constable's body. Not only did it smell inside the jail; it was dark. "All in this town think my family is guilty of some sort of crime. Why deprive them of the justice they seek?"

If Bennett Langham would not offer a story that Kit could make use of, the man's assize trial would be swift and certain. "Do not shield the vagrant, Master Langham, if he is the reason you will not speak. Tell me where I can find him, and I will see him accused of the boy's murder and you freed."

"I did not answer Richard Topcliffe. I shall not answer you."

Kit did admire the man's bravery. Mayhap, though, it was foolishness masquerading as courage.

"You risk being accused not only of murder but of treason as well for harboring a priest. I have seen a man drawn

and quartered, Master Langham. It is an unspeakably grue-
some way to die."

Langham blanched, but his gaze did not waver. "Topcliffe's men found no evidence that we have hidden such a
person. I cannot be accused based upon rumors."

"I shall not accuse you based upon rumors, but others
might." Kit exhaled. "Here are the particulars of the accusations against you. Your father was jailed for aiding Jesuits.
Upon your return home for Michaelmas, you learned that,
once again, Fulke Crofton had employed Rodge Anwicke to
spy upon your family. You sought vengeance upon the man
you deemed responsible for your father's death and who
promised trouble once more. Therefore, you killed him and
made the death appear a suicide."

"I was angry with him. Hated him because of what he
did to my father," said Langham. "But I did not kill him.
The man committed suicide."

"There are two lines upon Crofton's neck, one the mark
of the ligature that strangled him, the other that of the rope
he hung from."

Langham did not appear so brave now. "You have seen
this mark."

"I have," answered Kit. "You began to fear your plot was
coming undone when you learned—perhaps from Margery
Crofton—that Mistress Ellyott did not believe her brother-
in-law had killed himself."

He sat upright, the chains rattling as he shifted his legs.
"Do not assign any fault to Margery. She is innocent."

"It was then you decided to be rid of Rodge Anwicke,

calling him to the ruins to carry out the deed," said Kit, sup-position on his part. "What I cannot decide is if you murdered Rodge to silence him because he'd discovered where you hid the vagrant, or because he'd helped you kill Crofton and you became concerned he would expose you."

Langham said nothing, so Kit continued.

"Unluckily for you, Mistress Ellyott happened by at the moment you struck down Rodge, forcing you to attack her as well. You fled, and a woman of the village spotted you riding south toward home," he said. "What do you say, Master Langham?"

"I would say I sound guilty, Constable," he answered, the blood drained from his face. "God save me."

★ ★ ★

*They were walking, hand within hand, through an orchard not far from London's boundaries. When they were first wed, they had gone there often, to escape the crowding of the city. To see green and breathe air that did not smell of refuse and the smoke from kitchen fires. They would speak of home and speak of their future. The one they would build upon their love. They had many dreams, and she would cling to Martin's hand as if she could absorb through the touch of his skin his conviction that those dreams would all come to pass. He would not let her doubt. He would not let her whisper aloud her concerns. And she had believed him, believed in the rightness of their dreams.*

*But they were walking together again. She could feel his hand in hers. And Martin was speaking to her, though not about their dreams.*

*"Can you not see the flowers? The butterflies?" he asked.*

*She tried. She tried so hard, but however much she focused upon what he pointed to, she could not see. His features, too, blurred no matter how intently she stared. "I cannot see."*

*"Certes, you can, Bess." His hand clasped hers. "Do not doubt."*

She awoke with a start, the feel of Martin's touch lingering upon her hand. She pressed her palm to her lips, but none of his warmth remained upon it.

She knew, though, what she must do that day.

She must look again. And try to see.

★  ★  ★

Bess approached the ruins of the priory and the plague house warily, feeling the chill of the wind biting through her cloak, the layers of her gown and petticoat, and smock. The cure to her blindness resided within their walls.

The old priory was nearest, and she chose to search there first, though the brown-robed stranger had not disappeared from within its walls.

She hesitated. Off to her right was where she had fallen after her attacker had struck her. Through the portal, she could see the dark-stained patch of earth where Rodge had fallen, his skull crushed. She said a swift prayer in honor of a lad even more reckless than she was being right then.

Pulling in a breath, Bess passed through the old entry and scoured the lifeless and unwelcoming surroundings. A prior no longer lived to greet the vagrant, the Jesuit, and bid him warm himself by the fire or find consolation in shared prayer. The crumbling walls and vacant windows would offer meager comfort against the wind and the autumn fogs, or the chill rains.

Bending as much as her tightly bound pair of bodies

allowed, she examined packed earth that might be where a man had trod. Over there, a handful of stems wedged in a corner might have come from a berry bush and been picked clean of their fruit. Here, a white sliver could be a fragment of bone from a hasty meal of chicken. They were inadequate evidence of anyone's presence though.

Through a break in a wall, Bess peered at scattered stands of trees, including those where Fulke had died. Highcombe Manor peeked between the baring tree branches, and if she leaned through the break, Langham Hall would come into view. If her attacker had sought refuge at the hall, he would have had to dash across harvested farmland, or through sheep- and cattle-cropped meadows lined with hedges, or down an open road hemmed in by low growth. All of which would have left him exposed to observant eyes. But the cordwainer's wife had spied only Bennett upon horseback, his cloak streaming out behind him like a banner, no one else.

*I should accept his guilt.*

For Margery's sake, though, she would persist a while longer. Until she was freed of the nagging belief she had forgotten an important clue. Or until she found an earthly explanation for how the vagrant managed so often to elude detection.

Bess left the ruins. Unsheltered by its partial walls, she felt the wind snatch at her cloak. Nearby, a plowman coaxed his oxen across furrows without heed to what she was about. In the distance, a fellow walked along the highway. She would be quick in her examination of the plague house should he turn toward town, grow curious, and decide to intrude upon her attempt to discover the priest's secret.

A skittering of leaves, tossed by the winds that blew through the gaps and breaks in the roofless walls, greeted her.

Stepping across the threshold, Bess sought to remember precisely where she'd last seen the brown-robed stranger. She had chosen to first examine the parlor at her right but then had heard a noise that had drawn her toward the opening between the two main rooms. The room on her left had been the kitchen, the melted remains of pewter and charred earthenware pots indicating its past purpose. But he had not been there, once again slipping from sight.

She recalled Fulke's description of the priest hole at Langham Hall. Such a device was what she sought now. A hidden slot cut into a thick wall, like the one that abutted the brick hearth and chimney that still stood tall in the center of the building.

"Come out!" Bess shouted before she proceeded any deeper into the house.

There was no answering sound or movement.

Placing each step carefully, to not twist her ankle again, Bess made her way into the kitchen. If the fellow did leap at her from a hiding place, it would be difficult to escape the building, as it was littered with rubble. She consoled herself that the rubble meant it would also be difficult for him to give chase.

But a man who could vanish with the ease of mist turning to air might have other curious skills.

"Do not be dull-witted, Bess." *And do not turn this man into some fantastical creature.*

Gathering clouds threaded across the morning sun, dimming the light and making it difficult to see as clearly as she would like. With the toe of her shoe, she prodded at timbers that did not yield. Bess hiked her skirts and stepped around what appeared to be the remains of a narrow bed—a servant's, perhaps, or a child's—and wondered what had happened to the family who had once lived there. Had they died in the fire? Or had they already been dead and the fire set to consume their polluted bodies in order to safeguard the other villagers?

With a deep sigh, Bess stopped and looked around, the first drops of rain pelting her. A swirl of wind stirred ashes and resurrected the smoky scent of the burned wood. She squinted at the ashes, which had been disturbed by more than a breeze. A faint trail led toward the far side of the chimney and what had once been the back entrance. The rear of the house had suffered more damage than the front. Burned timbers rose above the stone half walls like the blackened teeth of a rake, the mud that had filled the space between the beams turned to dust. Her eyes traced the trail from its origin to where it appeared to fade and disappear. It led to nothing but a crosshatch of fallen timbers, the detritus of the table and stools that had once occupied this room, the bent remnants of a scorched brass kettle. If she dug around, she might find the nest of a family of mice, their tiny feet having worn the path over the months. However, she would not find a hiding place for a creature any larger than a mouse, let alone a man.

Mindful of the soot darkening the hem of her gown and ruining her shoes, Bess picked a path over to the chimney. Using her uninjured hand, she knocked against the bricks, but none sounded hollow. She pressed against the timber adjoining the chimney, which did not budge but did blacken her fingers. Wiping them against each other, Bess scanned the wall and the chimney one final time. The rain was coming down hard now, and she would be soaked and filthy.

"And frustrated," she muttered.

*Martin, I have failed. I do not see.*

Defeated and damp, Bess tucked the hood of her cloak closer about her face and retreated from the house.

"Mistress Ellyott?" called out a man's voice. Roland Fenn stood at the edge of the road, rainwater staining his deep-indigo jerkin and dripping from the brim of his hat. Doffing his cap, he gave a courteous bow. "What do you there, if I may be so bold as to ask?"

"Oh, nothing, Roland. I have always found these ruins rather sad and intriguing. I indulged my curiosity on a day equally sad," she said.

He extended a hand to help her climb the rise of the roadbed. From off his clothes, she caught a whiff of scent that was familiar, the smell of musk. The scent Fulke used to wear. Bess wondered if Dorothie knew that her servant had taken advantage of the confusion of recent events to help himself to her husband's perfume. She would not be pleased.

"How fares my sister this damp morn?" she asked.

"Mistress Crofton is hopeful that the coroner will change his ruling today, given the news about Master Langham. We have heard the coroner was conducting an inquest away from town but has returned."

"But even if the ruling is overturned, you shall not stay

on, shall you?" she asked, turning up the road toward town. "You have an inheritance, I understand. Life as a man of property is much better than a life in service."

A look she could not decipher—amusement at the obviousness of her comment, perhaps—flitted across his even features. "My term of service has been completed, Mistress, and I may now take advantage of my inheritance. However, service to the Croftons has been an honor I will forever be grateful for."

They passed the Anwickes' cottage, shutters in place but the door cracked slightly to admit some light. She needed to visit Maud again, to ensure the girl was properly healed. Mayhap she should stop now and also offer her condolences over Rodge's death.

"Walk on, Roland. I would visit a patient," she said.

She watched him hasten off, smiling to herself over his conceit of using Fulke's musk scent.

*That is it*, she thought, her hand upon the Anwickes' gate. Her attacker's scent, or lack thereof. For Bennett's clothing ever smelled of rosemary, as did his mother's. And her attacker had smelled of nothing more than damp wool.

# CHAPTER 20

"Why do you continue this needless discussion of Fulke Crofton's death, Constable?" The coroner, wearing a green cloak Kit had not seen on him before, stomped through his hall and into his privy office. Though the morning's rain had stopped, he tracked damp across the rush mats covering the floor. "I have been back in town but a few minutes and you cannot give me peace from this matter."

"Is that Master Crofton's cloak you wear, Crowner? I recall seeing it upon the man's body."

The man clutched at it jealously. "Sir Walter did not desire the man's clothing. Aside from Crofton's shirt and breeches, in which he was buried, I and the men who assisted in the burial split his goods between us."

"Then I comprehend why you do not wish to hear me out," said Kit, folding his arms as the fellow took a seat upon his cushioned chair. "You would have to return that cloak you wear to Mistress Crofton."

"I need do nothing of the sort."

"As you have only just returned from your short journey,

perhaps you've not heard that Master Langham is in our jail, awaiting transfer to the Fisherton jail tomorrow," said Kit.

"Enderby was here before you. He told me," said the coroner. "I congratulate you on identifying Rodge Anwicke's killer. The Langhams are a blot upon this good town. But this boy's murder has naught to do with Fulke Crofton's death."

"Hear me out. I told you about the two lines I saw around Crofton's throat," said Kit. "And Master Langham has reasons you well understand to wish Fulke Crofton dead."

The other man groaned. "God's truth, Constable, must you persist?"

"Further, a little more than a week ago, Langham caught Rodge Anwicke spying upon Langham Hall. At Crofton's behest," said Kit. "Trouble again from the man who'd caused the death of Bennett Langham's father. Trouble enough, perchance, to enrage him and to decide upon revenge."

"I see."

Kit took a step nearer the coroner. "Reconvene your jury and change your ruling, Crowner. Fulke Crofton did not commit felo-de-se."

The coroner pursed his lips. "Send the summons to my jurors, Constable. I expect your attendance so that all may hear your evidence."

Kit thanked him and strode from the room, back through the low-ceilinged hall and out the front door. Convincing the coroner was a minor triumph. Though if Bennett Langham were convicted and hanged, it would not be a triumph Kit would be proud of.

A sour taste in his mouth, Kit wove his way past the stalls

set up around the stone market cross. The square was alive with the tumult of market day. Thread and woven goods in that stall, cheese in this one, a gaggle of geese honking noisily over there. In the commotion, he almost missed Bess Ellyott pushing through the crowd, which had come out in goodly numbers after the rain.

"Mistress Ellyott!" he called out.

She hurried over to him, her cheeks flushed.

"The coroner has agreed to reconvene his jury," he said.

"He has?" she asked. Her gaze narrowed, and she scowled. "Because Bennett is imprisoned. That is why the coroner has changed his mind. But you must free Master Langham. He is not the man who attacked me and murdered Rodge."

He glanced around them; several of those in the square slanted looks their way. "Come away from here."

None too gently, he grabbed her arm and pulled her away from the bustle of the market.

"Constable, you may cease dragging me about," she said. "You have forgotten my ankle and my other hurts."

They stopped at the entrance to a nearby alley.

"You yourself told me of the fellow with the red-lined cloak," he said. "Has your niece convinced you to recant your story so that her beloved is freed?"

"My assertion has naught to do with my niece," she said sternly. "Constable Harwoode, this is what I know. The man who attacked me was about the same size as Master Langham, but his clothing did not smell of rosemary."

Kit arched an eyebrow. "Rosemary."

"Did you not notice its aroma upon Mistress Langham's

gown when you helped her into my house? They pack their clothing in the herb, she and her son, and the scent is always with them. Say you did, for I know you must have done."

"I have noticed."

She nodded, her point made. "My attacker smelled of damp wool. Mayhap a small amount of wormwood, but nothing more. And certainly not the distinctive aroma of rosemary."

"You were injured and in pain. Perhaps you do not recall properly."

"Constable, this is not a woman's fancy, and I know my herbs and my spices. You must release Master Langham."

"Mistress, even if I believed a remembered smell—or lack of smell—is proof he did not kill Rodge Anwicke, your recollection does not acquit him of killing your brother-in-law."

"To blame Bennett for Fulke's death, but not Rodge's, would have to mean there are two murderers, Constable."

He buffed his fingertips against his beard. "Just so, Mistress," he agreed. "Just so."

She peered at him. "Do you really think that situation is likely?"

"Until I know otherwise, I may have to."

★ ★ ★

"The constable will not release Bennett, Margery." Bess paced the hall, sidestepping a lounging Quail. The dog had sprawled across the floor beneath the windows as sunshine fought the clouds and warmed the spot he had chosen.

"I might be certain he did not attack me, but we have no proof, besides his mother's word, that he is not responsible for your stepfather's death. I am sorry."

Margery rose from the settle. Dorothie had permitted her daughter to remain at Robert's until all could be put to rights at their house. In truth, Bess wondered if her sister sought to distance herself from Margery so long as Bennett remained in the town prison cell. Her own daughter, set aside to protect her reputation. Shameful.

"I must go to Bennett," said Margery.

"You will do no such thing," said Bess. "We have drawn enough attention to this family, and for you to go there on a market day, with all and sundry to gawp, even folk from the countryside . . . Margery, you cannot."

Scowling, Margery retook her seat. "Then what are we to do?"

"There is naught else for us to do." Bess stopped by the window and stared through its diamond-shaped panes. Kit Harwoode had asked her to trust him and have faith he would continue to search for Fulke's killer. The prospects were grim, though, that Bennett would be found innocent of the crime. "Bennett's fate rests in the constable's hands."

"In the meantime, he suffers in that damp and cold cell," said Margery.

She looked over at her niece. "'Tis better there than at the jail in Fisherton. He is strong, and the constable will ensure he is treated well."

But Bennett would soon be transferred to the shire jail, too far away for them to tend to his care.

"I must confess something, Aunt Bess." Margery twisted her hands together. "About the brown-robed stranger. I *have* seen him at Langham Hall."

At last, the truth.

"I wish you had trusted me enough to have admitted that earlier, Margery."

"I was frightened for them." Margery's eyes searched Bess's face. "I am sorry. In truth, I am."

"I'faith, it no longer matters."

"I have more to tell you." She dropped her gaze and began picking at her fingernails. "The reason Bennett was riding upon the road the night Rodge died was because he had been with me."

*Jesu.* "You were not at church late that afternoon, then, as you told Joan."

Her niece shook her head.

Bess joined Margery upon the settle. "What have you done?"

Margery's face pinked. "Nothing like that! Nothing wrong. And no promises were made. I vow this, Aunt Bess," she said. "However, Bennett wished to protect my reputation, he is so kind and so good, and was willing to be accused of that boy's death. I should have told the constable when he was here yesterday, but I'd assured Bennett I would keep our secret."

She began to cry, and Bess drew her near. "Hush, now. We shall see justice done." *I pray.*

Joan, a jug of ale tucked beneath her arm, entered the hall, a draft of cool outside air chasing her. "Mistress, Goodwife Anwicke is here to see you. I met her upon the street as I returned from the alehouse. She wishes to speak with you most urgently." She glanced at Margery.

"Dry your eyes," Bess whispered to her niece. "It is Maud? Has her wound festered?" she asked Joan, and stood.

"She did not say."

"Send her in, Joan."

"She will not come inside," said Joan. "She protests that her shoes are too filthy, and she would not dirty our matting."

"Pish." Bess gathered her skirts and strode across the room and out the open front door.

Goodwife Anwicke stood at the side of the lane. She joggled her infant upon her hip. Margery came outside to join them upon the road.

"Has Maud come here, Widow Ellyott?" the woman asked. "Have you seen her?"

"No. Why?"

"She has run off. 'Tis not like her."

"She shall return soon," said Bess. "She may be at your house now, while you speak to us here."

The woman shook her head fiercely. "She has gone. She was all skittish this morning, and now she is gone." The child she clasped squirmed, its face pinching as it readied a wail. "I sent her sister to search for her, but she has not found the girl. First Rodge and now . . . Maud is lost. She is ne'er lost. I am afeared for her."

*Jesu.*

"Joan, go to the constable. Tell him we must alert the town to search for the girl before . . ." She glanced at Goodwife Anwicke and held her tongue. The woman already fretted for her daughter's safety; she did not need her opinion confirmed. "Tell him all who can must search for Maud. Goodwife, you should return home to wait for her."

"I will continue to look for my daughter. I cannot sit and wait."

The woman hurried off, the skirts of her faded gray-wool gown swinging and her infant bouncing upon her hip.

"I would help the search," said Margery.

"I prefer that you stay here," said Bess. "Joan, after you have spoken with the constable, you may help, should you so desire. And tell Humphrey I require him to assist. But if Maud is not found before the sun sets, return home. I trust not what has occurred. It is an ill wind that blows nobody good."

★ ★ ★

Townsfolk had spread out across the fields, their sturdy tunics and jerkins of brown-blue or faded red moving spots of color among the tawny harvested fields.

"Maud!" Bess cried out, scanning her surroundings.

Her call was echoed by those who trudged through adjacent fields, muddy from the rains. Others searched the meadows, scattering wary sheep. Startled birds lifted into the sky, a rabbit dashed across the road, and dogs barked and chased.

But no one signaled that they had found the girl. Though Maud was mute, they all hoped she would make some type of noise in response. Any noise. Any sound.

Bess noticed a man riding along the east-west road, the setting sun flashing off the spangles sewn onto his jerkin.

He paused to shout an order. It was Sir Walter, attending to his duty as the lord of the manor. Was it duty or guilt that spurred him to help find a lowly cottager's child, the sister of a murdered boy? Or had he a more devious motive?

He glanced in Bess's direction, then looked away and rode off.

"Maud!" she shouted again. The calls of fellow searchers sounded as frustrated as Bess felt. The only reasons for Maud to have vanished were bad ones.

A man who looked like the baker ran toward the trees lining the stream to the east of where she walked. The water probably surged high within its banks, with today's rain adding to the swell of recent days. Would they find Maud there, her body drifting on the water, her oft-mended dress snagged upon a fallen branch, the loose sole of her shoe flapping as the current tugged it? Her skin blue and cold, her soul gone to a better place. The person who'd killed her brother may have silenced her also, a mute child but not a blind one.

The baker reached the shrubs and plunged into the shadows. Bess did not have the courage to follow him; she was too afraid of the water.

*I can be such a coward.*

"Maud!"

Bess strode through the field, stumbling across the ridges made in the freshly turned earth, the mules she wore heavy with mud. Her sprained ankle ached with each laboring step.

She crested the small ridge, her gaze settling upon the priory ruins and those of the plague house. Two fellows picked and prodded among the stones of the priory. Another man warily poked his head through the plague house's doorway. After a hasty inspection, he decided against entering the building and skittered back to the road to rejoin his mates. They conferred for a few moments, then hurried off as though ghosts snapped at their heels.

Ghosts. Vapors. A disappearing man. A disappearing girl. *Maud, where are you?*

The baker reemerged from the trees empty-handed and headed toward town. He was not alone in his decision to return home. Others tramped back toward the village as well. Bess did not blame any for quitting; twilight approached, and the evening's meal awaited.

The breeze chilled her skin, and Bess retied her kerchief around her neck. She should go home also, resume her search in the morning when the light would be better.

But would Maud still be alive then?

Sighing, she limped across the field, choosing a path wide of the priory ruins. She paused on the road, looking back at the mournful remains of the plague house. She narrowed her eyes. Something was out of place, but she could not tell what.

She forded the water-filled ditch at the base of the road and cautiously approached the house.

"Maud?" she called, pausing to listen. The response was the whisper of the wind. Distant voices, sheep bleating. No sound that the girl had heard and tried to beckon to her.

"God save me," Bess murmured and stepped through the opening.

The day's rain had tamped down the ashes and turned

the narrow paths between fallen beams from gray to black. She tucked her gown and red petticoat into the girdle she wore, raising their hems off the ground.

"Maud!" she shouted.

In response, a noise. She could swear that she'd heard a noise in the room to her left, the old kitchen. Slowly, she moved forward. All looked as it had before though. The same jumble of destruction. The same yawning sky over her head. The same . . . No. Not the same. A new track wended through the rubbish and led to the pile of what had been the narrow bed set near the far wall. Which appeared to have shifted its position, from what Bess could recollect.

She crossed the room, each step trod with care, and squatted near the bed. And saw what she had not seen before.

"Ah, Bess. You were blind." She had searched for a hiding spot within the walls. Not beneath the floor.

As quickly as she could, she moved the rubble aside. Her efforts revealed the outline of a door cut into the floor, which at one time had been a solid expanse of limestone tiles. Not any longer, though. A square section had been removed and replaced with planks plastered over to blend in with the filthy limestone all around. She could not tell when the change had been made, but the origin of the door did not matter. All that mattered was that this portal explained how the brown-robed stranger had succeeded in vanishing from sight.

"Not a specter or a demon, then, are you?"

She felt around the edge for a handle or such and found a notch large enough to grip with her fingers. Firmly planting her one good foot, she tugged. The door swung upward easily, the concealed hinges recently oiled. Without a lantern, she could not explore what lay below, though. Leaning over the opening, she discovered she would not need one, for a faint light glimmered from the depths. A short flight of steps, hewn of stone and affixed to the clay soil, led to a shallow cellar. The space was lined with more stone to hold back the damp earth that surrounded it.

"Maud? Are you down there?" she called, gripping the edge of the opening. "It is Widow Ellyott. Come, you are safe with me, child."

She heard what sounded like a cascade of pebbles, faint and distant. Next, she would be greeted by a scurrying of rats, no doubt. But a rat had not lit a lantern.

"Maud! Come, your mother frets for you. I know you are down there." She knew no such thing. "Maud, I will help you."

*Come now, girl. Please.*

She held her breath as she strained to hear any noise at all.

Suddenly, there came a rustling, and a girl raced to the bottom of the steps. Maud looked up at Bess, her eyes wide. Right behind her stood a man.

A tall, thin man in brown robes.

# CHAPTER 21

*Jesu.*

"Do not hurt her. Prithee, I beg you," pleaded Bess. The ceiling was so low that the man had to stoop. "Hurt her?" he asked, resting a thin hand upon Maud's shoulder.

*He will not let her go.* A breath caught in Bess's chest. She had no means of fetching help without leaving the girl alone with this man. Who now realized that his hiding place had been discovered.

"Come, Maud." Bess held out her hand to the girl, who clung to the wall of the cellar and did not move.

The man brought the lantern he carried forward, the light illuminating them both. Clean-shaven, as the miller had described, he was of young age. Beneath his long, loose brown robe, though, his fading black tunic and breeches hung upon the bones of a fellow as gaunt as an old hag upon her deathbed. He was pale, and his eyes were rheumy from a recent illness. If he were the murderer, this fellow who could disappear without a trace, he did not appear capable of overwhelming Bess let alone wrestling a healthy man like Fulke to the ground and strangling him. But perhaps he was stronger than he appeared or had made use of Rodge's assistance. She would keep her guard until Maud was safe.

"I will not harm the child." His voice was deep and warm, assured, with only a hint of weakness from the malady he had suffered. His was a good voice for speaking. A good voice for preaching.

"Maud, prithee come." Bess wiggled her fingers to encourage the girl.

"I mean you no harm, do I, child?" Lowering the lantern, he crouched alongside Maud. As he did, the circle of dark-wood rosary beads tucked into the belt that cinched his gown swung free.

"You *are* a Catholic," Bess whispered. The miller had seen correctly. "A Jesuit."

The man looked up at her. His hand had not left Maud's shoulder. Oddly, the girl did not seem frightened of him.

He answered Bess's question with one of his own. "What mean you to do?"

"I saw you at Langham Hall," she said.

His gaze flickered. "Ah. Then I know what you mean to do."

He could not know, for *she* did not know what she meant to do.

"Did the Langhams tell you of this cellar?" she asked. "Someone had to have done, for its entrance is well hidden."

"I shall not answer that question. You understand why."

Bess tightened her grip on the edge of the opening. "Is the existence of this cellar the reason you murdered Fulke

Crofton? Because he had discovered your hiding place, just like he had learned of the Langhams' priest hole," she said. "Did someone help you kill him? Rodge Anwicke, perhaps? And then you had to be rid of him as well."

"I am not acquainted with either of the men you speak of, Mistress."

"Rodge was but a boy. Struck down in the priory ruins across the way."

"Ah. The night of the hue and cry. That was the cause of the commotion." He removed his hand from Maud's shoulder. Bess stiffened, preparing for that hand to reach for a blade, hidden among his robes. But he did not reach for a blade, and his hand rested at his side. "I have murdered no one, Mistress. To take a life violates God's commandment."

"You intend to murder the queen," Bess accused.

"I have not come to harm *any* living soul but merely to provide succor to those who remain faithful to Rome."

"Why should I believe you?"

His gaze was steady. "You have my word as a man of God."

"Prithee, let Maud go," she said. "I shall scream if you do not. There are people everywhere searching for her. They will hear."

"I . . . I will not go," Maud stuttered, her voice creaking from lack of use. "He is good. I will stay."

Bess gaped at her. "You can speak?"

"She is afraid of some man," said the priest. "I encountered her near the river. She was so frightened that I offered her refuge down here, until such time as the danger passes. If she had but known that the danger that accompanies my travels was near as treacherous, she might have chosen otherwise."

Dare she believe him? "Come, Maud. Your mother is most concerned," said Bess. "You should return home. I can take you."

Maud fiercely shook her head, the ties of her biggin flapping beneath her chin, and took a step backward.

"She is afraid," the man said, sounding exasperated with Bess's slow wits.

"Let her go."

"I am not keeping her here." He turned the girl to face him. "It is best that you go with this gentlewoman, child. She will see no harm comes to you."

"Not home." Maud shook her head again. "Not home. That man."

"Has he forced you to say this?" Bess nodded toward the priest. "Has he threatened you so that you accuse another to protect him?"

She clasped a small, dirty hand around the priest's fingers. "He is good!"

Bess reached for the child. "Your mother is frantic. You cannot stay here."

Maud clutched the priest's fingers more tightly. She curled her other hand into a fist and pounded it against her side. "But that man! That evil man with Rodge!" She was growing hoarse. Likely she had not spoken so many words in a very long time, if ever. "He find me there. He saw me. This morn. I ran."

An evil man with Rodge. Mayhap this child *had* seen a

murderer. If so, she had every reason to fear. Bess needed to get Maud to safety and inform the constable.

"Maud, if I promise to take you to my house where you will be safe, will you come with me?"

The girl looked at the man at her side. In the span of a few hours, she had come to trust him. *He is good.*

The priest disentangled his fingers from Maud's grip. "Go with her, child. You cannot stay here. You will come to grief with me."

He gave her a gentle push toward the steps. Reluctantly, Maud climbed them. Bess moved aside to allow her to pass through the opening. The girl huddled into a ball at her side.

"There. You have the child safely with you. What do you next, Mistress?" the priest asked.

"I will say nothing about your presence, unless you do not leave before dawn tomorrow." *This is wrong, Bess. This is horribly, horribly wrong. And one day you shall be forced to pay the price for your error.* "I have been made to suffer for you, a man whose cause I do not support. But one dear to me loves a Langham, who I suspect *does* support you. She would die of heartbreak if more harm came to him."

" 'Tis treason to protect me."

"I would say, should any discover my treachery, that you threatened to kill this helpless child if I did not cooperate. Do not force me to tell such a lie," she answered. "By dawn. I will inform the constable of your whereabouts if I have not learned that you are gone."

"My welcome here is long past." He reached for his beads. "God bless you, child. God bless you both."

"By dawn," repeated Bess, leaning back to rest upon her haunches. She restored the cover over the opening. Maud helped her place bits of timber and scattered ashes atop it to conceal its presence. Their efforts were feeble, and anyone who might look could find it. She hoped none would look.

"We shall take the path to the west of town." Bess took the girl's hand, the one that had been burned but was no longer covered in bandaging. The scald had crusted over and scratched roughly against Bess's palm. "That way you need not go near your home."

Maud nodded, but her eyes scanned the darkening road, her forehead creased with unease. She sought the man who had frightened her. But then, so did Bess.

★ ★ ★

They skirted town, but there were few entry points into the village, and their arrival was noticed. Bess rushed the girl past the curious, shouting out only that Maud had been found and to let her mother and the remaining searchers know. By the time they reached Robert's house, twilight had descended. Bess ushered the girl inside, where Joan rushed to greet them, Quail bounding behind her.

Maud, the thin kirtle that covered her shift wet and filthy, was shivering. Quail padded over to inspect her, but the girl cringed and drew back from the dog.

"You need not fear Quail, sweeting. He is harmless." Bess rubbed the dog's head as proof, then handed the child over to Joan. "Warm her by the kitchen fire. Also, fetch Humphrey and tell him to bring the flock bed from the hall chamber. It is to be placed in the kitchen. The child will be staying with us tonight."

"Her mother will want her home, Mistress."

"The child will not go. She is too afraid of some man she saw near her house this morning. A fellow connected to Rodge." She need not say more, for the look upon Joan's face revealed she understood who the fellow might be.

"Ah." Joan smiled warmly at the girl. "Come into my very fine kitchen, Mistress Maud. I have potage on the fire."

She led Maud away. Quail sauntered after them, a safe distance behind. Through the open door to the hall, Bess noticed Margery hurrying across the room.

"You have found her?" she asked. "When Joan returned, she said all had given over searching. Save for the constable and his cousin. Where was the girl?"

Bess hesitated. If Margery had honestly been unaware of where the priest was hiding, the less she knew now, the better.

"I found her among the ruins of the plague house. None were willing to search there carefully," said Bess. A small mistruth but a believable one. The child's clothes were filthy enough to imagine her huddled among the cinders.

"That dreadful place," said Margery, following Bess to the kitchen.

Maud perched upon a stool near the hearth. She was staring at the brass pot Joan had hung above the flames, the smell of the cooking food mingling with the fire smoke.

"You must be hungry," said Margery. Before the girl

could answer her, she collected a bowl and began scooping the mutton and onion potage into it.

Bess took a seat at the trestle table. Besides a meal, the girl was also in need of a thorough washing.

Joan returned with Humphrey, a mattress under his arm. With a sideways glance at the girl, he set the bed near the hearth and departed with a grunt. No doubt he would report to Robert when he returned home that Bess had been collecting grimy urchins in his absence.

"Here now, Mistress," said Joan, taking the bowl from Margery. "Let me tend to the child."

Margery joined Bess at the table. "Why will she not return home?"

"When Maud is ready, I am sure she will tell us about the man she fears."

"Tell us?" asked Margery.

"It appears she is not a mute, after all."

Joan finished filling the bowl and handed it to Maud. The girl nodded politely before swiftly scooping potage into her mouth.

"He is evil," said Maud. She paused to slurp more food, a trickle of broth running down her chin. She wiped it away with the back of her hand. "I saw him with Rodge. And then Rodge hit me."

Joan, standing in the corner of the kitchen, touched the spot of her coif that covered her scar. In the world she once inhabited, the world Bess had saved her from, men often hit or cut women.

"Your brother hit you because you saw him with this man?" Bess's gaze moved to Maud's cheek, where the bruise upon it had gone a pale yellow. "Did that happen the day I came to treat your old burn?" The day that Fulke had died.

"Aye," she squeaked.

Which was why the bruise upon her cheek had been fresh.

"Poor child," said Joan. She stepped forward to ladle more potage into Maud's bowl, which the girl had already emptied.

"The man gave Rodge things," she said. Bess had to strain to hear her, the girl's voice was so soft and raspy. "Stolen things. A hat. Green cloak. Purple ribbon, too. Said man would kill me. If I told Mother." She rubbed tears from her face, leaving behind a streak of clean skin among the grime.

"Oh," murmured Margery. "Aunt Bess, could he be—"

Bess hushed her with a wave of her hand. "Can you describe him, Maud?"

"He talks like a rich lord." She puffed out her chest and lifted her chin as though haughty. "Has dark clothes. Dark, devil's eyes."

Dark clothing described the attire of more than half the men in the village. However, Arthur Stamford was pompous enough to sound like a rich lord. Sir Walter as well, although Bess could not summon to mind the color of his eyes.

"And you saw him again this morning," said Bess.

Maud nodded, which meant the evil man was definitely not Bennett, locked away in a cell since yesterday.

"I have another question, Maud. Had Rodge gone to the ruins the day he died to meet this fellow?" asked Bess.

Maud shrugged her skinny shoulders. "He went out.

After supper. Father did not see. I did, but I was too afeared to follow."

"That was wise, child," said Joan.

Bess looked at the women assembled in the kitchen, who watched her closely. She signaled to them to move away from Maud, and they huddled together near the entrance to the buttery.

"So what do we know?" asked Joan.

"Not as much as I would like," said Bess. "However, if this fellow sounds like a rich lord, there are but two men to suspect—Sir Walter and Arthur Stamford. We can be assured, Margery, that she does not mean Bennett, as he remains in his cell and could not have been seen by her this morning. That, in addition to my recollection that the man who attacked me did not smell of rosemary—"

"As Bennett always does," interrupted Margery.

"Seems proof enough of his innocence in every regard." They dealt with one murderer, not two. That realization was not much relief, however, when that murderer had yet to be identified.

"But what of the vagrant, Mistress?" asked Joan. "I thought he was the person you most suspected."

Bess shot a look at Maud, who had clambered down from her stool and was focused upon dipping the wooden spoon she'd been given into the pot over the fire. "I have come to decide I was mistaken."

Joan lifted a brow but did not question how Bess had arrived at such a decision. "Then which is it—Sir Walter or Master Stamford?"

"Mayhap she means the churchwarden," said Margery.

"He wears dark clothes and can be quite fearful looking. He sounds like a lord."

"He is not the fellow who attacked me," said Bess. "I would have smelled the scent of camphor and pennyroyal that he ever reeks of, and I did not."

"When, though, does Sir Walter wear dark clothes?" her niece asked. "Aside from the occasions when he appears in some official capacity."

"So, if not the vagrant, it must be Master Stamford," said Joan. "He wears dark clothes. In fact, on Sunday last he was attired all in black at services. We should tell the constable, Mistress."

Rapping sounded upon the door, and Quail leaped up to bark.

"Who could that be at such an hour?" asked Joan. "Not good news, I dare say. Mayhap 'tis the person who lurked outside the other day."

"Would he knock?" asked Bess.

Joan smirked and ordered Quail to follow. She returned with a scrappy boy in a rough tunic.

He doffed his cap and held out a note, his fingernails grimed with Wiltshire dirt. "Brought you this. From Mistress Crofton."

"Joan, fetch a penny for the lad."

Grinning, he scampered after Joan.

"Does my mother beg my return after all?" asked Margery.

"Nay. She wishes me to attend to her. She is distraught. The coroner canceled his inquest today, because of the search for Maud," said Bess. "Your mother has developed a pain in her head and frets that she will not be able to sleep tonight."

"Lucy knows naught of physic and cannot help her."

"What is this, Mistress?" asked Joan, stepping into the kitchen.

"My sister has need of me, and I must tend to her," said Bess.

"Must you go now?" asked Joan. "It grows late."

"I cannot ignore her summons," said Bess. "I shall not be long. If Dorothie will not be calmed, I shall stay the night. Do not fret."

Joan frowned. "I mislike this. The fellow who killed Maud's brother and nearly killed *you* is yet out there, some-where. It is not safe for you to leave the village with dark-ness falling."

"I shall allay your concerns and take Quail."

"Scant comfort, Mistress."

Bess ran a hand down her servant's arm and smiled into her unhappy eyes. "Go to the constable and tell him what we have learned this night," she said. "Come, Quail."

★ ★ ★

"At least the girl is safe," said Gibb, raising his voice to be heard over the lively crowd inside the Cross Keys.

The place was well crammed with relieved searchers, and Kit and his cousin had to jostle through the men—and some women—to take the last two open seats.

"Alive. Which I'd not expected," said Kit, settling onto the bench against the tavern's far wall. Marcye had noted their arrival and was elbowing her way toward them with flagons of beer.

"I wonder what gave the child cause to hide," said Gibb, taking his flagon from Marcye, who lingered as she awaited a greeting from Kit.

He nodded at her, and she strolled off, grinning.

"My guess is the girl suspects who murdered her brother and became frightened," said Kit, scanning the room. One fellow, deep in his cups, caught Kit's eye and sloshed beer as he raised his tankard in a salute. They were a merry group. Soon, someone would take up singing, and ten would follow. "But since she cannot speak, her knowledge does us no good."

"More's the pity," said his cousin. "When do you mean to release Bennett Langham? If Mistress Ellyott is certain he is not the man who attacked her and killed Rodge Anwicke, we should let him out."

Kit took a drink of his beer just as the baker's son started to sing. "Her observation does not prove Master Langham did not kill Fulke Crofton." As he'd also told her.

"Marry, Kit, what a wretched business this is." Gibb frowned. "I think I shall resign from it."

"Go to, Gibb. You said that when we could not find the apothecary's stolen pewter dish," said Kit as three men joined the baker's son's wailing. "And the time we accused the innkeeper along the highway of coin clipping, only to later discover the fellow's sister was guilty."

"Aye. But this time I mean my words."

*Damn.*

A commotion sounded near the door, and Mistress Ellyott's servant girl burst into the tavern. She searched the crowd until she located Kit and Gibb. She rushed over, eyes and murmurs following her. Including the eyes of Marcye, who stared after the young woman.

"I was told I could find you here." Glancing at Gibb, she reached for the strings of her coif and tugged, pulling the flaps closer around her cheeks. "My mistress has gone to her sister's, and I fear for her safety."

Standing, Gibb offered her his place on the bench.

"Are you afraid for her because it is almost nighttime?" asked Kit.

"Not only that, Constable." She sat and looked around. "But I shall be overheard if I explain."

"Gibb, create a distraction that will allow us to speak."

His cousin sputtered on his beer then began to cough. Suitable.

"You can speak freely now," said Kit, casting an eye over Gibb to ensure he was not truly drowning on his drink.

"Mistress Crofton sent for her, and there is no denying Mistress Ellyott's sister when she makes a demand," said Joan. "I tried to warn her of the danger of leaving the safety of the village to go to the Croftons' house, with the man who nearly killed her still wandering among us. As we know her attacker was not Bennett Langham," she added pointedly.

Kit sighed. "I realize your mistress believes—"

"Nay, Constable, we are *certain* he is not responsible. You are aware that the Anwicke girl is with us. She can speak— aye, she is not a mute—and she saw the man who gave her brother Master Crofton's hat and cloak. And other items," she said, whispering beneath Gibb's continued coughing. A fellow standing nearby moved away for fear of contagion. "Her brother had warned her the man was dangerous. She saw him again this morning—so he could not have been Master Langham—and hid herself away. Her only description of him, though, is that he speaks like a lord and wears dark clothing. We have concluded she means Master Stamford."

*But not Wat Howe?* Gibb forgot to keep coughing; he was likely wondering the same as Kit.

"Did your mistress go to the Croftons' alone?" Kit asked, getting to his feet.

"She took Quail."

An exceedingly friendly dog. *Damn and damn* . . . "Gibb, see this young woman safely back to her house. I go after Mistress Ellyott."

# CHAPTER 22

"Mistress Ellyott, you are good to have come at such a late hour." Lucy dipped into a curtsy.

"I do not mind the hour."

Lucy showed Bess through the passage and into the hall, Quail on their heels. The room was a mournful sight. Everything that Sir Walter was permitting to be auctioned off lay in piles about the space—a stack of mattresses, bolsters, pillows, and a bed frame against the wall; the few carpets of lesser value rolled against one another; kitchen goods, jointed stools, and benches had been set in the center of the room, the hall settle apparently taken away along with a tapestry and the Turkey carpet Fulke had purchased. Items of his clothing had been stacked as well, alongside Dorothie's gowns and petticoats. The churchwarden's men may have stopped removing her goods, but the delay in the coroner's new inquest had also delayed her ability to restore her home to order.

A tidy bundle waited near the doorway to the passage. A glint of silver indicated that it was Dorothie's plate, waiting for her to claim it. Quail sniffed at the package and, deciding it contained nothing of interest, sat upon his haunches to wait.

Lucy noticed Bess looking at the bundle. "Mistress Crofton claims a piece is missing."

"Her head pains do not keep her from counting her plate, apparently."

"You know your good sister, Mistress."

Indeed she did.

"She has gone to speak to Roland about the missing piece, out in Master Crofton's warehouse," said Lucy. "The men have already removed the wool from the building, but Roland felt obliged to tidy the space. In the chance any is returned. Should I fetch her now?"

"I will wait until she is finished speaking to Roland," said Bess, setting down her satchel.

"I do not envy her dealing with Roland this night though. He is in one of his ill humors," said Lucy. "As he has been ever since . . . well, I need not mention the reason, need I?"

"The horrible manner of Master Crofton's death has distressed us all."

"Aye, but I believe Roland *awoke* out of temper that day. Snapped at me, he did, when I chided him for tracking mud through the passageway that morning," she said. "He was not the one who'd need to clean the passageway before the mistress arose and saw."

*Mud.* Disquiet roiled Bess's stomach. "Was this after he had returned from seeing off Master Crofton on his journey?"

"'Twas later. From repairing the calf-cote, I think," she

replied. "Which he spent all day at, though he was needed to take the sheep into the far meadow that afternoon. The work would have gone faster if he'd used that boy who is ever around."

Who, thought Bess, would that boy be? 'Twas simple to guess. "What boy?"

"Why, the wiry one with the red hair."

"Rodge Anwicke, you mean."

"Is that his name?" Lucy asked. "Is he not the boy who was . . . oh."

"You should have mentioned him before."

Lucy chewed her lower lip. "Should I have done?"

Rodge. Roland. Curious. *Worse than curious, Bess.*

Maud had said the man with Rodge, the one she feared, wore dark clothing and sounded like a rich lord. Roland's excellent manners and refined speech had always marked him as superior to most manservants. And his livery consisted of a jerkin and breeches in an indigo color that was almost black. Further, until this morning upon the road, Bess had never known him to wear scent. Smelling only, perhaps, of damp wool and some wormwood. Just like her attacker.

*I have been utterly witless.*

Outside the hall windows, which gave a view of the garden and the warehouse beyond, darkness had descended. She could see no more than the pale shape of the building. Dorothie was out there with Roland.

"Lucy, stay here. But listen for me should I call for help."

Her eyes widened. "Why might you do that?"

Bess hurried across the room, Quail jumping to his feet.

From among the pile of kitchen implements arrayed upon the bare floor, she selected a small but sharp knife.

"Mistress Ellyott!" Lucy cried.

Bess handed Lucy a knife as well. "I pray I am mistaken, but you might have need of it." She glanced over her shoulder at Robert's dog and headed for the rear door. "Quail, come."

Knife clutched to her chest, Bess exited the house and crept across the garden, Quail padding behind her. A faint light shone through the open door of the warehouse, the shutters of its two windows closed and barred. Behind her, Lucy peered through the hall windows.

*Prithee God, have Joan reach the constable quickly and have him come to help me.*

Bess gestured for the dog to stay behind her as she edged toward the door, listening for the sound of voices. When she reached the opening, she heard Dorothie speaking. She stopped and huddled just out of sight of the two within, uncertain of how to proceed.

"What mean you that you know not where the piece of plate has gone? My charger, Roland. Too large for those men to slip beneath a tunic. I tasked you to watch them."

Roland's response was muffled, but Dorothie's reply suggested it did not please her. "You are keen to accuse Master Enderby's thieves, but now I must ask if it is *you* who are to blame. For the loss of my charger and the monies in Fulke's coffer."

"Have I ever cheated you, Mistress?" Roland's practiced, educated voice was a soft counterpoint to Dorothie's shrill one. Sounding like a rich lord.

"In good earnest, tell me the truth of it," she challenged. "Have you deceived me?"

"I am but your humble servant, Mistress."

"Pish. You have never been humble, Roland," she said. "You have served us for many years and faithfully. Return the coin and my charger, and I shall be lenient."

"I am most grateful."

"Why do you look at me with such insolence?" she asked.

Dorothie retreated from her servant, and Bess could now see the trailing edge of her sister's gown, dragging across the dirt floor. *Do not vex him so, Dorothie.*

Bess tightened her fist around the puny knife she clutched. Roland might carry a weapon as well. He had need of a blade in his daily tasks. If only she knew if he carried it now.

"Do you mean to suggest you resent the years you have spent in our service?" Dorothie asked. "Have we not treated you well?"

"Treat me well?" he sneered. "*Well*?"

Dorothie took another step backward, and Roland moved with her, coming into Bess's view. The source of light rested somewhere behind him and cast his face in its shadow. "Your husband never treated anyone well, and neither have you, Mistress."

"You dare say such a thing, now that you are on the cusp of leaving my household." She raised herself to her greatest height. "Where is my charger? Where is the coin you have taken from Fulke's coffer?"

From Bess's left came the crackle of leaves as a creature skittered through the garden. Quail let out a low gruff bark.

"Hush," Bess hissed, her heart pounding, and pressed her body against the whitewashed mud wall of the warehouse.

"What dog is that?" asked Roland, the stomp of his footsteps drawing near.

*I cannot flee and leave Dorothie. I cannot stay . . .*

Roland charged through the entrance. "Mistress Ellyott."

Dorothie followed him out of the wool warehouse. "Elizabeth? Why are you lurking out here?"

"Dorothie. I . . ."

Roland's gaze went to the knife in Bess's hand. "What have you there, Mistress?"

"Dorothie, move away. Now."

"What?" Dorothie glanced between Roland and Bess. "What mean you by this?"

Roland's eyes narrowed. He lunged for Dorothie, grabbing her arm and dragging her to him. Quail jumped and barked. Roland kicked at the dog, which leaped aside to evade his foot.

"Release me!" Dorothie screamed.

"Quail, away!" Bess shouted. "Quail, quiet!"

Suddenly, a blade appeared in Roland's free hand. He pointed it at Dorothie's chest, where the top edge of her gown met the white linen of her partlet. "What now, Mistress Ellyott?"

Quail snuffled and fretted at Bess's side, eager to be given the order to act.

"Let her go. Let her go and run off. Run as far as you can. I vow I will not follow. I vow I will tell no one. No one else suspects. No one else knows. Rodge's sister is gone," Bess said, hoping he'd not learned that Maud had been found.

"Bess," Dorothie pleaded, her breath coming in shallow gasps.

She could not remember when her sister had last called her "Bess." It was pitiful and frightening to hear. "Prithee, Roland. Do not harm her also."

Dorothie's eyes went wide. "It was you, Roland?"

The light cast by the lantern was faint, but the hatred upon his face showed clearly enough. "I am not responsible for Master Crofton's suicide. He was distraught."

"You sought to hurt your mistress, too," said Bess, coming to understand. "That is why Fulke's death had to be deemed a suicide. So that she would lose most everything she owned."

The knifepoint inched nearer Dorothie's throat. She wore no ruff to fend off its tip. "Roland, forgive me for however I have offended you. Have mercy!"

Her wail prodded Quail to bark and snap at Roland.

"Quail, stop!" shouted Bess.

Angered, Roland swiped at the dog with his knife. Bess lunged for Dorothie, trying to pull her away, but Roland wheeled on her. The knife sliced through the air, barely missing Bess's arm. She stumbled backward, her weak ankle buckling. Dorothie screamed. Then there came shouts from the direction of the house. A woman's upraised voice and a man's. Roland's blade arced backward, catching Dorothie on the chin, and then he sped off. Quail gave chase.

A spray of blood spewed red across Dorothie's partlet, and she collapsed. Bess dropped to her knees beside her as Lucy ran across the yard.

"Mistress!" the servant cried.

"Bring linens. Clear water." Bess undid the kerchief tied about her neck and pressed it to Dorothie's wound. "Without delay, Lucy."

"Mistress?" a man asked.

Bess looked up into his face, the dim lantern light from inside the wool warehouse illuminating the concern etched in its every angle. "Constable, Roland Fenn is the murderer."

"Are you well?"

"I am unhurt. Do not fear for me. Take the lantern from the warehouse and go after him."

He collected the lantern and ran, following the fading sound of Quail's barks. The light bobbed and became but a pinprick in the distance.

"Oh, Elizabeth." Tears gathered in Dorothie's eyes. That she had reverted to her habit of referring to Bess as "Elizabeth" was a sign her equilibrium was returning, however. "I harbored a killer beneath my roof."

"The constable will catch him and bring him to justice," said Bess, helping her sister sit upright. The kerchief was turning red from her sister's blood.

Stones clattered beneath Lucy's hurrying feet. "Here, Mistress," she said, handing over a linen cloth and a pitcher of water. "Your kerchief is ruined."

"It is of no concern, Lucy." Bess tossed it aside. She doused a corner of the linen cloth with the water and gently daubed her sister's cut to better see its depth. "The wound is not so deep. It should cease bleeding soon."

From out in the dark night came a pained yelp. Bess straightened to face the direction of the sound. *Quail.* Silence fell hard and heavy, the absence of barking alarming.

"Were there others with the constable, Lucy?" Bess had seen none, but mayhap they had waited upon the lane.

"Nay, he was alone."

"Here. Press your hand here." She motioned for Lucy to take control of the linen stanching Dorothie's bleeding. "Take my sister inside and make her comfortable."

"Do not leave me," pleaded Dorothie.

"I must." Bess picked up the knife she had set upon the ground and stood. "If the constable is alone and Quail has been injured and is unable to help corner Roland, Constable Harwoode will need help."

"Elizabeth, no!"

Despite the freshly throbbing pain in her ankle, Bess dashed into the night. Into the danger she could not ignore.

★ ★ ★

Whimpering, the dog struggled to get to its feet, but its hurt leg prevented it.

"Stay." Gently, Kit pushed the dog back to lie flat upon the dirt. Fenn had kicked the creature, knocking it to the ground. "Stay."

Raising the lantern, he squinted at the shadowed band of trees that stood ahead of him. A mist arose to shroud them in fog. Fenn was bound for the promise of cover, hoping to escape Kit's pursuit.

"God's bones, if I could but better see!"

As if in response, the thin clouds that rode overhead drifted clear of the crescent moon, and it shed its pale light. The trees followed the curve of the stream. Soon Fenn would be across the water, putting a greater distance between himself and Kit.

"Stay, Quail. I shall return for you."

Kit set the lantern on the ground near the dog. Without its light, he would be making chase in darkness. With its light, Fenn could easily track Kit's location.

He ran for the trees, pausing as he reached the edge of the field they bordered. Breath held, he heard splashing off to his right. Fenn was still in the stream and had chosen not to cut across directly but to angle away in better hopes of escaping.

Kit scuttled along the tree line, peering through gaps to search for any sign of movement. The space beyond was black as pitch. As if to further thwart him, clouds returned to overspread the sliver of moon.

Cursing beneath his breath, he halted. He could no longer hear the splashing of water. Had Fenn forded the stream, or did he lie in wait? The man had a weapon; the cut upon Mistress Crofton's chin was evidence. The clouds once again scattered. Kit was now limned in faint light, and despite the mist, easy enough to see for a man hidden among the shrubs and looking out toward the field.

*Where are you, Fenn? Damn, where are you?*

He could have made good use of Bess Ellyott's dog. Without the animal's nose and sharp eyes, Kit was almost blind.

He searched the ground for a sizable stone and found one. A stone hitting water would not make the same noise as that of a man plunging into the stream, but it might flush his prey anyway. Kit tossed the rock far to his right, where it crashed through the underbrush and struck the water. Nearly in front of him, sticks broke and pebbles scattered, the noise moving rapidly to Kit's right. Fenn, his feet churning the water, was making for the sound of the rock Kit had thrown.

Cautiously, Kit entered the line of trees. Here, the stream was deep because of the nearby millpond. And steeply banked, as his left foot found the edge of the water more quickly than he'd expected, plunging him to the ankle in icy water. He paused, expecting Fenn to turn and rush him. But he did not. A break in the foliage allowed a silvery gleam of light to dance off of Fenn, headed away from Kit. Bent over, he strode along the stream bank and scanned the undergrowth.

Kit pulled his dagger from its sheath. *God help me.* "Stand! I arrest you!"

Fenn spun about and charged toward him. He swiped his knife wildly, once, twice, at Kit's midsection. Kit leaped backward and out of the weapon's reach, his boots slipping on the loose rocks beneath them. Fenn pressed his advantage, lunging for Kit. He stumbled, and Fenn's knife connected with the sleeve of Kit's doublet, slicing through the padded material to the linen shirt and flesh beneath. Kit thrust upward with his dagger. The other man was quick and limber, evading the thrust by dancing to his right and into the water swirling near them. Kit regained his balance and thrust again, aiming for anything. The man fended off the blow and their wrists collided, sending a spasm through Kit's arm. Fenn's knife flew from his grip.

"Stand!" Kit shouted again as he shook feeling back into his hand.

Fenn kicked out, the thick squared toe of his leather shoe connecting with Kit's knee. His leg gave way beneath him. Fenn was upon him, the full weight of his body crashing into Kit, plunging them both into the stream. Water pushed up Kit's nose, down his throat, into his lungs. Fenn grappled for Kit's knife, his hands strong. *God save me*, thought Kit as his head spun. *God save me*.

★　★　★

"Oh, Quail. Poor Quail." Bess ran hands over the dog's leg. He quivered beneath her touch. A heavy bruise, perhaps, but no broken bones. Nonetheless, he was in clear pain. "I should not have brought you along. Robert will never forgive me."

Shouts drew her attention away. Reaching for the lantern the constable had left behind, the knife she'd taken from Dorothie's house firmly gripped in her other hand, she rose to her feet. She set out for the sound, which came from the area of the river. Quail whined and yelped, but she could not turn back.

She tugged at her skirts, trying to hold them aloft.

"Constable!" she cried, uncertain if it was wise to alert Roland to her approach.

As she ran, the lantern's pool of light jigged across the stubbled field. A narrow path cut across the damp ground, and mist, carrying the dank earthy smell of the matter decaying along the riverbank, swirled. Memories of a spring day in her childhood, the pond water closing over her head, then Robert dragging her free to safety, to life, froze the blood in her veins. Her legs refused to move any longer.

Her pulse thrummed. Men's bellows and the noise of churning water echoed.

*Jesu, Bess. You cannot let him die.*

"Constable!" she shouted and pushed forward.

She broke through the brush and held the lantern before her.

Roland had set his knee upon the constable's shoulders, forcing Kit's head under the water.

"No!" Bess tossed down the lantern and charged into the stream. The water dragged at her skirts, slowing her progress, and her feet threatened to slip from beneath her. "Stop!" She grabbed Roland's shoulder and pulled it hard. "Stop!"

He lurched upright, elbowing her off him. She fell into the chill water and struggled to keep her head above it. Roland turned toward her, his hands reaching.

"No!" The knife. She remembered the knife she held.

She arced the blade through the air. It bit into his nearest hand, spraying warm blood across her face. His yell was piercing, but he did not stop coming for her. She swiped at him again, screaming. He grabbed her hand and stripped the knife from her grasp.

"No!" she shouted.

Suddenly, he was tossed aside and away. The constable struck him with a fist, dazing him with a blow to his head. He collapsed into the water.

"Jesu," Bess breathed. She stumbled out of the stream.

The constable pulled Roland behind him and threw him down onto the bank.

"Is he dead?" she asked, alarmed by the fact she did not much care.

"Nay, Mistress. He breathes," he answered, shoving hair from his eyes. "Are you injured?"

"I am not, but you are. Your arm bleeds terribly."

He slapped a hand over the wound. "So it does."

A shout sounded, and a man hurtled through the brush. "Coz! Mistress!" Gibb Harwoode slid down the embankment to join them. The lantern, tilted on its side, had remained lit and showed the fear upon his face.

"'Od's blood, Gibb, do not look so frightened," said the constable. "But I am glad you've come."

"After I left Mistress Ellyott's home, I went to speak to the watch," said his cousin. "'Twas then we heard the dog barking out in the field, and I came running. Are you hurt, Mistress?"

Bess rose. Sodden to the skin, she shivered. "Unhurt, Master Harwoode, but I am most cold."

Roland stirred, and the constable hoisted the man to his feet.

"Hie you back to your sister's house, Mistress," said the constable. "We shall not be far behind you with this wretched creature."

# CHAPTER 23

The next day, in the crisp sunshine after the morning's fog had lifted, Bess knelt in the garden and snipped chamomile. How calm it was compared to last evening, when the constable had been in the hall with a gash to his arm, Dorothie bleeding upon her gown, and Margery in hysterics over the danger that had come so near. Through it all, Maud had managed to sleep by the kitchen fire, not rousing until her mother had come at daybreak to fetch her home.

Bess rocked back on her heels and considered the chamomile. She intended to trim the herb into a path through Robert's garden, upon which they could stroll to reach the bench against the wall. The scent released by their footfalls would be pleasing, mingled with the aroma of the peonies and gillyflowers and lavender when they bloomed. Robert and his new wife—if his journey to London had met with success—were certain to enjoy the fragrances. As for herself . . . where would she go? The house had more than enough room for her, but she questioned if Robert's wife would want Bess to live with them when there might be need of those chambers for children.

*You always rush ahead to the worst conclusion, Bess.*

*Ah, Martin, 'tis a skill of mine.*

"Mistress?" asked Humphrey, who was piling together rotted hay near their straw hive. He would set the hay alight to drive off the bees, for it was time to collect the honey within.

"Aye, Humphrey? What is it?" She tossed a handful of clippings into the wicker basket at her side. The clippings would be added to oil to make a curative for the phlegm and other such cold diseases, as the chamomile had properties of heat.

"The stable lantern has never been found," he said. "You must dismiss Joan, for it is certain she has broken it and will not confess."

"Ah, that," she said, looking over at him. "I have been remiss in offering an apology to you, Humphrey."

He lifted an eyebrow. "Mistress?"

"I am the one who took the lantern and mislaid it."

His countenance darkened for the briefest moment.

"I *am* most sorry," she said. "I should have admitted so earlier."

"Aye." He scowled and resumed his work.

She wondered, though, how long it would be before he forgave her.

Joan, returned from the baker, hurried through the back doorway, a basket of bread swinging from her arm.

"Mistress! You will not ever believe what I have learned from that Marcye at the Cross Keys!"

She was so disturbed by her news that she neglected to curtsy.

Setting down her shears, Bess got to her feet. "Humphrey, leave us."

He slunk off for the stables.

"What is it?" asked Bess, once Humphrey was gone.

"I was returning from the baker's when I spotted Marcye tidying around the front of the tavern. As we never learned who had told the churchwarden you were supposedly helping the Langhams, I thought to ask her," she whispered urgently. "Marcye makes it her business to mind who comes and who goes at the houses of those who run this town, and Master Enderby's house is no exception. I thought she might have seen who'd visited him to tattle on you."

"Did she?"

"No."

"Joan, you confuse me."

"I mean to say, Mistress, she did not see the person because it was *her* who had done the tattling." The basket swung as she gestured wildly. "When I pressed her for the names of those who'd visited the churchwarden that day, her guilt overcame her and the truth came out like a gush of ale through an unloosed bung."

The tavern keeper's daughter? "Whyever would Marcye wish to cause me such trouble?"

"She is a jealous, petty creature," said Joan. "Jealous of you and the constable."

Bess's cheeks warmed. "She has no cause."

"She has seen you together and noted his attentiveness," said Joan. "And she saw you leave his house the other day as well."

"I was helping him find Master Crofton's killer, and he has been grateful. That is all," she said. "And think not that there is more to his actions, Joan."

Joan bit back a grin. "I do wonder, though," she said, sobering, "if she was the one slinking around our house the other night and who upset Quail so much."

"What a dreadful thought."

Inside the house, Quail started barking, and the constable strode through the open rear door.

"Constable!" said Bess. Joan's grin returned, causing heat to rise on Bess's face again. "There you are."

"No one answered my knock upon the front door . . ." His glance moved between them. "Forgive me, but I interrupt."

"Nay. Not at all." Bess collected her basket of chamomile and shoved it at Joan. "Take this to my still room, Joan."

"Aye, Mistress," she replied with a sly smile and a curtsy before sauntering off.

"Joan was just telling me that it was Marcye at the Cross Keys who spread the tale that I was aiding the Langhams," said Bess. "Do you know the girl well?"

He looked somewhat abashed. "I visit her father's tavern."

*Ah, then.*

"I will speak to her about spreading dangerous gossip, Mistress."

"Just speak, Constable. I do not desire her punished in the stocks," said Bess. "Come and sit, if you will."

She walked over to the garden bench. The neighbor's

servant girl took to singing in the adjacent yard as she worked. She sang a tune about love; Bess rather wished the girl had chosen a different song.

The constable sat and cast an admiring glance about him. In the house, Margery had come to the upstairs parlor windows to peer at them. She was set to return home that day but had tarried over her packing.

"A fine garden your brother has. I envy him it," said Kit Harwoode.

"Constable, have you come to admire his roses?" asked Bess. "I think not. What is the news?"

"Roland Fenn has confessed all, and Master Langham has been released."

"Thanked be God. Dorothie will be relieved." *And Margery, also.* "Shall Fulke be buried in the churchyard now?"

"Aye. The vicar has arranged for your brother-in-law's reburial. Also, Wat has returned the items he had selected for his personal use, and I shall see that the churchwarden returns Master Crofton's cloak," he said, appearing as though he looked forward to doing so.

"My thanks to you, Constable," she said. "And now I would have you tell me all that Roland has said. I know he killed Fulke because he felt mistreated, but has he revealed how he managed the crime?"

"Aye, and once Fenn began to speak, he did not want to stop," he said, rubbing the bandage that last evening she had wrapped around his cut arm. She should examine the wound again today to look for infection. First, though, she would hear the story. "However, his reason was not solely because of mistreatment, Mistress. I believe he is a practiced thief."

"Oh?"

"Fenn bragged to me of having once served in a lord's household—"

"Which explains his refined speech and manners."

"Just so. Fenn implied that he stole from the man but fled before his crime was detected," he said. "He was also stealing from your brother-in-law."

"Dorothie accused him of taking money and a silver charger . . . But why?" she asked. "He has an inheritance in Suffolk that will see him well set."

"There is no inheritance, Mistress Ellyott," he said. "He concocted the story to explain how he could so readily leave town without concern for his future. A future he intended to support with the money and items he'd been taking from the Croftons. He had also hoped he might receive a reward from the Crown for reporting on the Langhams. He'd employed Rodge to spy on them—as Fulke Crofton had done before—with the inducement of a bit of ribbon taken from your sister."

"Rodge had told Bennett he'd come from the Croftons'. But he had been sent not by Fulke, as we had assumed, but by Roland," she said.

The constable inclined his head.

"But then Fenn learned that Master Crofton was bound for Devizes last Tuesday morn. He concluded, incorrectly, that your brother-in-law went there to report Fenn's thieving to the justices of the peace," said the constable. "If his plans to collect his reward and calmly leave town were to succeed, he had to prevent Crofton from ever arriving."

"And he hated my sister so much that he sought to punish her also by making Fulke's death look like suicide. He knew the ruling would cause Dorothie to lose nearly everything."

"Just so."

Constable Harwoode stretched his legs before him and folded his arms. Out in the courtyard, Humphrey exited the stable with a saddle to oil. He sat with it upon his stool and went to work. Robert was expected back any day now, and all must be in readiness for the master's return. Jesu, but how to tell her brother all that had occurred in his absence?

"As to the how . . . Fenn left the house immediately after Master Crofton did, making for the intersection of the eastern road and the road to Devizes," explained the constable. "Aware that his master rode slowly and had appeared distracted by his impending meeting, Fenn raced to intercept him. Fenn chose a spot not far from a ditch, thick with grasses and hedges and close by a quiet grove of trees. Perfect for committing a crime unseen."

A chill raced over Bess's skin. "And where we found Fulke."

"Fenn signaled to your brother-in-law, under the pretense that he'd left an important item at the house," he continued. "When he reined in his horse, Fenn convinced him to dismount, then strangled him with a length of twine he had concealed beneath his jerkin. Because of the morning's heavy fog, no one noticed as he hid Master

Crofton's body in the ditch, briefly covering him with fallen leaves."

"Roland is very strong. And to think I ever suspected Arthur Stamford."

"However, Fenn could not suspend Master Crofton's body from the tree—pardon me, Mistress, for my blunt words—without assistance," he said. "So he went to seek out Rodge and paid the lad with coin. The one we found."

"Then, during the afternoon, he had Rodge dress as Fulke to deceive one and all about the time of Fulke's death," she said.

"He did not think to do so until several hours after he'd killed your brother-in-law. His actions were prompted by Stamford's arrival to search the warehouse, when he also mentioned that Master Crofton wanted to meet with him the next day. Such a meeting was not the act of a man intending to kill himself, and Fenn began to fear that his plan to portray his master's death as a suicide might unravel. Therefore, he needed to provide himself an alibi, in case the coroner ruled the death a homicide once the body was found. If Master Crofton was believed still alive in the afternoon, Fenn had nothing to fear, because he made certain your sister's servant girl saw him mending the calf-cote at that time."

"Which she did tell me about," said Bess. "Lucy also mentioned that planned meeting with Master Stamford."

"Fenn took alarm, and thence began the ploy to have Rodge ride about on Master Crofton's horse," he said. "Fenn had tied the animal to a tree to prevent it from heading home, wanting to delay a search as long as possible."

At the house, the upstairs curtains twitched into place, Margery having grown bored with watching two people simply talk.

"If not for the fortunate discovery of Fulke's hat, which Rodge had kept, and Maud's watchful eyes, we would know none of this," said Bess. And Bennett Langham would still be accused and on his way to the Fisherton jail until a trial at the next quarter sessions. "I must apologize for wondering if Sir Walter was responsible, Constable."

"He stood to gain from your brother-in-law's death. Your belief was well reasoned," he said. "And it is your keen mind that came to comprehend the truth about Roland Fenn."

She was blushing again and had to look away. The neighbor's servant girl ceased singing her love song. In the courtyard, the chickens clucked and pecked while the cockerel strutted, and Joan came through the rear door to toss out a bucket of dirty water. Quail limped through the door behind her and barked at the chickens. Joan attempted to shoo him back into the house.

"Unfortunately, I did not comprehend in time to save Rodge," she said.

That morning, Goodwife Anwicke had gathered Maud into her arms with desperate eagerness. She may have cuffed and cursed Rodge, but the death of a child, no matter how difficult he'd been, was a pain most deep. As Bess so well understood.

"Do not blame yourself. You could not know that Fenn had learned we suspected Master Crofton had been killed."

"I should have known, because he likely learned of our

suspicion from me. 'Tis possible Roland overheard me speaking with Dorothie about the matter. I was uncareful," she said. "But after he murdered Rodge out of fear the boy would betray him, how did he get away from the ruins without being seen?" Had he been aware of the cellar hidden beneath the plague house?

"He hid among the men who'd come in response to your cries, Mistress," he said. "In all of the confusion, he managed to appear to be just another townsman participating in the hue and cry. He was among the first to depart in search of the killer, slinking off with a group of other searchers."

"I was too distraught and weak after the attack to notice all who stood around," she said. How Roland must have laughed at the irony of joining the search.

"However, he then grew concerned that Rodge was not the only Anwicke to fear," said the constable. "Despite the common belief that Maud was a mute, he wanted to ensure she was frightened and would never identify him."

"So he went to their cottage, and Maud went into hiding." Bess exhaled. "How thankful I am he did not kill her, too."

The constable had been watching Quail's antics. Joan, at last, succeeded in her efforts to control the dog and return him to the house. "With Fenn's confession, I rest assured that our vagrant was not a murderer."

"'Was'? Has he withdrawn from the area?"

He was studying her. Did he notice the tensing of her muscles? "Tell me you do not already know the answer to your question."

Her heart fluttered. But she could answer true. "I do not know the answer, sir."

His gaze, shaded by the brim of his hat yet still piercing in its intensity, swept over her face. "I am glad to hear so."

Out of the corner of her eye, Bess noticed Joan approaching.

"Constable Harwoode," she said, curtsying. "A messenger has come to say the stewards require your attendance."

He stood. "It seems I must bid you farewell, Mistress Ellyott."

Bess rose as well. "But your arm. I must see to your wound."

"Alas, my duty calls. Yet I feel confident we shall encounter each other again. Hopefully in more pleasing circumstances."

Taking her fingers in his, he bowed over her hand far longer than mere politeness required. Then he turned to leave. Joan lifted an eyebrow and followed to see him out.

Within moments, Margery dashed into the courtyard, startling Humphrey.

She raced across the gravel and flung herself down upon the bench. "I thought he would never leave."

Bess retook her seat. "The constable had much to tell."

"As do I." She eyed Humphrey and contented herself that he could not overhear. "I have just now received a message from Bennett. Their visitor has departed and goes north. His accommodations will be sealed shut."

Bess was glad her niece had thought to whisper. "Good news."

She could not fathom how the Langhams might block the entrance to the plague house cellar without being detected. A problem for them to manage though.

"But Bennett leaves in a few short hours. He returns to Bristol."

"I am sorry, Margery," said Bess. "However, it is best he do so. He is not safe here. You are not safe with him here. For now, at least."

"I fear I cannot live without him," she sobbed.

Bess gathered her niece in her arms. "Most certainly you can. If I can eat and sleep and breathe every day without Martin, you can live without Bennett."

"I am sorry. I did not mean to discredit your loss."

"I understand. I do," she said. "Trust me, though, that the pain of separation shall lessen with time."

"What if he never returns? There may be many pretty women in Bristol, women more interesting and clever than I. What if he finds another?"

"Then you shall find another as well," said Bess softly, the feel of Kit Harwoode's fingers rising unbidden in her mind. "And you will be ready to live again."

★ ★ ★

"Forsooth, Bess, how good it is to see you," said Robert, smiling down at her from the saddle. "The roads were foul from the rains. I meant to be here yesterday instead of near sunset this night."

"You have arrived safe and sound. 'Tis all I care about," Bess replied, happy to see him. Three days had passed since

Fulke's murder had been resolved, a period of time for much needed routine to resume in their household. "How fares Mistress Tanner? Are there plans for you to wed?"

"None yet, but I hope soon."

Humphrey, the strength of his frown deepening the wrinkles of his face, held his master's horse steady while Robert dismounted. "Humphrey, why so dour? Are you not pleased to see me as my good sister is?"

He slid Bess a sideways glance. "I am *most* glad you are returned, Master," he said, and set to removing the leather sumpters tied behind the horse's saddle.

Bess hastened to hug her brother close, her various scrapes and strains aching but a trifle. He smelled of the road and long miles but was solid and warm and unharmed. Unlike Constable Harwoode and Dorothie. Or Margery's heart.

"God's truth, sister! I did not know I would be missed so," he replied, laughing. He freed himself from her embrace. "But where is Quail? My own dog does not come to greet me? And Dorothie and Margery? I have gifts for you all."

He strode across the courtyard to retrieve one of the sumpters as Humphrey led the horse into the stable.

"Quail has a slight injury. Do not fret! 'Tis minor, and he recovers apace," answered Bess. "As for Dorothie and Margery, they are at their house. Once Humphrey is finished with your horse, I will have him fetch them here to greet you."

"How is it they remain at their house?" he asked, bringing over the bulging leather pack.

"That will require some explanation," Bess answered

with a smile. "Your sumpter looks fit to burst. Did you bring tobacco for our neighbor, as you promised him?"

"I did indeed. And I have brought the third book of *The Faerie Queene* for Margery, as also promised."

"She will be most pleased to see you. She always welcomes your gifts."

"Faint comfort for the loss of her stepfather."

"You know they were not ever close." Bess took his elbow and led him toward the house. "So she is well, aside from the damage caused by a broken heart. Bennett Langham left for Bristol today."

"Ah. For the best, though, I would wager," he said. "I also have a length of lace for Dorothie. And I have brought nutmeg and ginger for you, Bess, for your physic."

"I will have to fight Joan for those!"

He sobered. "I delivered the letter you helped Joan write to her friend, but I did not receive an answer before I left. However, I did receive a note for you. From that fellow you once mentioned. That Laurence."

The mention of his name set a chill upon her skin. So he had found a way to contact her. Bess took the note and folded it into her pocket.

"You do not read it now?"

"Any message from him can wait." The time was coming when she'd need to return to London. She could not run forever from what must be done. Later, though, to think upon that. Later. "It is time to hear of your travels."

He patted the hand she had placed upon his arm. Together, they crossed the threshold and turned into the hall, where Joan had lit a fire, which blazed upon the hearth.

Quail, tail wagging, waited just inside the doorway. Robert crouched to ruffle the dog's ears, receiving a lick upon the face as reward.

"It is most pleasant to be home," Robert said, as she helped him remove his cloak. With Quail following him, Robert took his usual chair by the fireplace, a relieved groan escaping from his lips. "But, Bess, what have you been about while I was gone? Has your young patient recovered from her burn? And you must explain how it can be that Dorothie and Margery have not been forced to leave their home yet."

Bess lowered herself onto the settle and smiled at him. Where to begin?

"Ah, Robin, I have quite a tale to tell."

# AUTHOR'S NOTE

In 1580, the first Jesuits arrived in England to preach to the few remaining Catholic faithful and rebuild the church. Elizabeth, already surrounded by numerous threats to her rule, had reason to question their intentions. Ten years earlier, the pope had called for his followers to repudiate the Protestant queen's claim to the throne. Furthermore, Elizabeth's most likely heir—Mary, Queen of Scots—was Catholic. A few power-hungry Catholics, emboldened by the Jesuits' arrival, tried to carry out the first of several failed assassination attempts. Increasingly punitive measures were put in place to suppress Catholicism in England, though the vast majority of Catholics wished only to practice their faith, not overthrow the queen. By 1593, the year of *Searcher of the Dead*, if nonconforming recusants missed church services, they could be heavily fined and lose their estates. Recusants were not allowed to travel five miles beyond their homes. And to help a Jesuit was to be convicted of treason. Despite this, people hid priests in secret rooms and aided their travels. A network of spies and the use of torture, however, eventually uncovered many of the priests and their supporters. During Elizabeth's reign, nearly two hundred of them were put to death.

In *Searcher of the Dead*, Kit Harwoode is the reluctant local constable serving a system very unlike modern law enforcement. In sixteenth-century England, there was no organized police force, and the role of constable was often considered a burden by the prominent citizens who were expected to take turns filling the unpaid position. When it came to catching criminals, townspeople had almost as much responsibility as the constables did. Townsfolk were expected to name suspects and help apprehend them (fines could be levied against them if suspects managed to evade capture) as well as serve as jurors. Once suspects were apprehended, trials often took place without lawyers, and defense witnesses were rarely called, as it was presumed they could not be trusted to be honest. Guilt or innocence might be decided by a person's reputation rather than the strength of any evidence. If the accused was found guilty, punishments were intentionally severe in an attempt to deter crime. Even trivial offenses carried stiff penalties. Gossips could be put in the stocks. Minor thieves lost their ears. Many offenses were punished by hanging. It was a world that could be harsh, indeed.

A note on the town waites or waits. From the Middle Ages until 1835, most British towns employed a group of musicians. Initially the waits accompanied the town's watchmen on their patrols, but eventually their job grew to include providing music for ceremonial events. Some were so talented that they were in demand for weddings and official dinners. A government order in 1835 abolished the town waits, but many groups live on, to entertain and educate.

Lastly, the town and characters are fictional. Except for Richard Topcliffe. He was very real.